FOUR SEASONS OF SUMMER

I0692003

Dana L. Brown

Published by:
Southern Yellow Pine (SYP) Publishing
4351 Natural Bridge Rd.
Tallahassee, FL 32305

www.syppublishing.com

This is a work of fiction. Names, characters, places, and events that occur either are the products of the author's imagination or are used fictitiously. Any resemblance to actual persons, places, or events is purely coincidental.

The contents and opinions expressed in this book do not necessarily reflect the views and opinions of Southern Yellow Pine Publishing, nor does the mention of brands or trade names constitute endorsement.

ISBN-13: 978-1-59616-124-5
ISBN-13 ePub: 978-1-59616-125-2
ISBN-13 Kindle: 978-1-59616-126-9
LCCN: 2022949879

Printed in the United States of America
First Edition
November 2022

Dedication

I want to thank Bob and my daughters—Jenifer, Torey, and Alison—without your steadfast love and encouragement none of this would have been possible.

Kathryn Knight and Barbara Dena, thank you for your friendship. It means the world to me!

Dana L Brown

The Beginning of Summer

She picked up her phone with nervous apprehension, hoping there would be a message, even after just praying for the strength to totally end the relationship. *Relationship?* Could it even be called that? It was really just two people who'd gotten to know each other on a social media app, so why did her heart *and* her stomach hurt so badly?

The trip to California had been wonderful, well wonderful in all ways but one. And now here she was, back home in her beloved New Smyrna Beach, trying to sort through the unresolved feelings that she thought she'd left in L.A.

Seeing that there were no new messages, she laid her phone down and headed to the laundry room. Grabbing a load of clothes to throw in the wash, she felt the tears coming, and she was totally out of control to stop them. *How did this happen?* she asked through the sobbing. She'd heard about people who got caught up in a social media romance, but she never believed it could happen to her.

The laundry going, Summer grabbed another cup of coffee and sat down to think about how she could have handled things differently. Her hand was trembling from too much caffeine and emotions that she wanted to express but couldn't, so like a spy in the night she picked up her phone and pulled up Jake's Facebook page, looking for any new friends or posts about women. Because that's what he was looking for, a woman to share his life with, and it couldn't be her; they both knew that. She had pledged her heart to another years ago, and the vow was clear. "What God has joined together, let no man put asunder."

Chapter 1

There was nothing special about this day. No kids to chase after, or projects to get excited about, only the normal day of a middle-aged woman who had lost the enthusiasm for her life. She was blessed, she told herself so every day, but despite knowing how fortunate she was, she couldn't let go of the sense of wanting more. *But what?* Memories of her youth were holding her hostage, running through her mind like an old movie reel, and no matter how hard she tried she couldn't turn them off.

I have everything I ever wanted, she thought. *How did I go from being a woman in control of her life, to one consumed with thoughts of the past?* Her smile was bittersweet as she looked around the kitchen that Michael had designed for her when they'd moved to Florida from Celina, Ohio. She loved this house, and she'd loved her life, but something had changed within her, and even within their marriage, and she wasn't sure how to fix it. She had everything that most women her age could ask for, but she craved more. Attention and romance from her husband, and maybe to be thirty again. Was that too much to ask for?

Michael had already left for work and by nine o'clock she was showered, dressed in her stay-at-home work attire of shorts and a T-shirt, her thick chestnut-colored curls in a knot on top of her head. She ready to open up her laptop. After entering the password, and waiting for the system to boot up, she looked at her reflection in the monitor and cringed. It seemed as if every day brought a new crease to her forehead, despite how well she took care of herself.

Sighing, she made a mental note to schedule a facial as soon as possible, and to definitely put on some makeup before Michael came home from work.

The computer ready, she logged into her website and beamed, as she did every time she saw her logo. Her son Riley had been the one to suggest the name for her company, and *The Four Seasons of Summer* was the one place she still felt needed and seen. Now, designing eclectic websites for people who were looking for something original, without spending a fortune, was one of her greatest pleasures.

Opening her inbox first, she found several emails from existing clients whose projects were in the works, and one from a name she had never seen before: Jake Ross. The name seemed familiar somehow, but it wasn't unusual for her to receive emails from strangers. In fact, almost every day she received emails that were advertisements or requests for money, so she opened the emails from her clients, and flagged the one from Jake Ross to read later.

Around one she took a break and had an apple and a pouch of tuna. Her stomach was begging for a chocolate chip cookie, but even though she was five nine, Summer had to work hard to keep her figure in check. With each pregnancy she had gained over thirty pounds, and until ten years ago hadn't been able to totally get rid of them. Now she watched every morsel that went into her mouth and did her best to exercise daily. She hated both, but she hated being overweight more, so she made do with fruit, vegetables, and protein during the day so that she could enjoy a nice dinner with Michael.

The rest of the afternoon was spent working on designs for a new florist that was opening in Edgewater and returning most of the emails in her box. A little before five she stopped to put dinner in the oven, and then, remembering her lack of makeup, headed to the ensuite bathroom they had added to their house when the boys were both out of college. Deciding it was too late in the day for the whole nine yards, Summer swiped on a little blush, mascara, and lipstick, and went back to work.

By the time Michael was pulling into the driveway at six thirty, the computer was off, the table was set, and dinner was about ready, giving

Summer time to switch from her role as entrepreneur and business owner back into her real life. The one she wasn't sure she even wanted anymore.

Chapter 2

"Something smells good," Michael said, setting down his briefcase. "Meatloaf?"

She smiled and nodded and then picked his briefcase up from the kitchen counter and took it to the den. She'd asked him so many times to please not leave his expensive Gucci briefcase on the kitchen counter, especially when she was in the middle of cooking, but it seemed to go in one ear and out the other. To save an argument, she found it was easier to move it the ten feet between rooms than to wait for him to do it himself.

"How long before dinner?" Michael called from the stairway. "Do I have time for a quick shower?"

No, actually dinner was ready to go on the table, but instead she called back, "Go ahead, it can wait a few minutes."

Frustrated, she put the plates of food back into the oven and shut the door, hoping it was warm enough to keep the food from getting cold. Michael was usually starving when he walked through the door at night, so she had made it a priority to have dinner ready as soon as she heard the whir of the garage door opening. Another ten minutes or so wouldn't really hurt anything, it was the principle of it that bugged her.

A few minutes later, Michael came down the stairs, his hair damp, wearing an old pair of jeans that hung low on his waist. A white T-shirt clung to his sculpted chest, and for a minute Summer just stared at him. *This man is my husband*, she thought. *This is the man who used to turn my world inside out…when did that change?*

After talking about their respective days, Michael suggested a walk on the beach after dinner. Instead of cleaning the kitchen, Summer left the dishes and the mess, and walked the three blocks with him to one of her most favorite places on earth.

Cars had to be off the beach by six, making early evening their chosen time of day for a stroll. The tide was high, and the surf was playing *catch me* with their toes, and they both laughed when the sand seemed to disappear beneath their feet. On the walk home Michael took her hand and once again Summer thought about her life, and how she hoped the sweetness of the evening would turn spicy for the night.

But once they got home, Michael went directly into the den to do some online banking, and Summer cleaned the kitchen. The food left on the plates was dried and difficult to remove, but finally everything was in the dishwasher, the counters were spotless, and Summer turned off the light and joined Michael in the den.

"I'm headed up to bed," she said, lightly massaging his neck. "You coming?"

"Yeah, just give me a few minutes," he answered without lifting his head.

Summer let out a soft sigh and climbed the stairs to their beautiful master bedroom. She had offered more than once to take care of their finances, after all she was on the computer most of the day, but Michael somehow felt it was a *man's job* to make sure the bills were paid, and their accounts were balanced, and like the briefcase issue, it just wasn't worth arguing about. Slipping out of her clothes, she pulled a short, gauzy blue nightgown over her head. She liked that it was long enough to cover her problem areas but still showed off her long, lean legs. As a child she had taken tap and ballet from Miss Eleanor, and all that time *shuffling off to Buffalo* and doing plies at the barre had paid off.

As she climbed into bed, Summer luxuriated in the eight hundred thread-count sheets, and for a moment she lay there, tired but still hopeful for a connection with her husband. She had her eyes closed when Michael entered the room, but she opened them, wanting him to know she wasn't asleep. Of course, he took that as the go ahead to turn on the TV.

5

Snuggling under the covers with Michael had always been one of Summer's simple pleasures. She settled on his shoulder as he stroked and massaged her back, a mindless comedy blaring in the background. Hoping she could pull his thoughts away from the TV, her fingers played with the soft black hairs on his stomach, and gingerly she moved down his *happy trail*, where the hair became curly and coarse. There was a time when Michael would have become aroused at this little bit of attention, but now there was no acknowledgement at all. Summer knew that if she stroked him, or took him in her mouth, he'd come to life, but that wasn't what she wanted. She wanted him to be desperate with desire for her, just like he used to be, but those days seemed to have disappeared.

A few minutes later she turned over, without even saying goodnight, and did her best to conjure up her mantra; my life is blessed.

Chapter 3

Every morning was like a rerun of the one before, and today was no exception. Summer watched her husband walk out to his vehicle, thinking how good he looked in his new Hugo Boss suit. Michael was still an extremely attractive man who took great care in his appearance, and sometimes she had a hard time believing that they'd been together for over thirty-five years.

The Land Rover out of sight, she filled her favorite mug and settled in the rocker for her morning routine. After reading a couple of devotionals she talked to God, prayed for the people in her prayer journal, and headed upstairs to prepare for her day.

One of the things she liked best about being her own boss was that as long as she kept her clients happy, she could begin and end her day on her schedule, not someone else's. And working from home in their charming Craftsman cottage just blocks from the Atlantic Ocean? It was more than she could have ever asked for.

The computer up and running, she turned to her email first and realized she hadn't opened the one from Jake Ross the day before. Clicking on the envelope she was pleasantly surprised to see that it was an actual request for a website, and not just junk mail. Taking a sip of her now cold coffee, Summer read:

Dear Ms. Alcott,

My name is Jake Ross and I'm an acquaintance of Franklin Burnett, whose website you designed last fall. I met with Franklin recently to discuss a business idea, and he shared with me what an amazing job you had done in designing his site.

I would love to talk with you as soon as possible and see if we can come up with a manageable business arrangement. I know I'm behind, but my new blog, *Pushing the Plate*

Aside goes live in two months, meaning I need to know right away if you have an interest or not.

Best,

Jake Ross

She read over the email two more time before googling Jake Ross. The moment his picture came up she remembered why his name sounded so familiar. Jake Ross had been one of the world's leading restaurant critics for over ten years when he and his wife Beth were involved in a motorcycle accident. Riding without their helmets, on a winding road in California, they had been hit head on by a pick-up truck. Jake had suffered numerous broken bones and extensive injuries and was in the hospital and rehab almost a year. But his wife, Beth, had broken her neck and sustained massive head trauma, going from a beautiful California girl to a paraplegic with brain injuries in minutes.

She stared at the picture of the lovely young couple taken at their wedding and realized the article she had been reading was five years old. Wiping back the tears that were welling up in her eyes, she looked for a more recent article and found one.

> *Beth Anderson-Ross, wife of former Restaurant Critic, Jake Ross, died today at the age of forty-four following complications from pneumonia. Ms. Ross was a passenger on a motorcycle driven by her husband, which was involved in a tragic accident in 2013 while they were riding on California Highway 1. Since the accident Ms. Ross has been cared for at home by her family and a team of round the clock nurses. Ross is survived by her husband, parents William and Mary Anderson, and a sister, Chris.*
>
> *The family asks that in lieu of flowers donations be made to the Beth Anderson-Ross Foundation for Missing and Exploited Children.*

Summer pushed herself away from the computer and let the tears roll down her face. The obituary was dated from 2018, which meant that

Beth Ross had just died the year before. She knew she needed to respond to Jake Ross with an answer, but she wasn't honestly sure she could work closely with someone who had to still be dealing with so much grief.

Deciding that what she needed was a pick me up, she reached for her phone and dialed the one number she knew by heart: Bree's.

Chapter 4

Hey girlfriend!" Bree answered cheerfully. "To what do I owe this pleasure in the middle of the morning?"

Summer relaxed just hearing her voice. Bree had been the first real friend she had made when she and Michael had moved to NSB fifteen years ago, and Summer knew she had her back and could be counted on to be honest with her. "Have you ever heard of Jake Ross?" Summer questioned tentatively.

"The famous food critic Jake Ross? Yeah, he actually reviewed *The Garlic,* but it's been quite a few years ago. Don't you remember all the hoopla around town about him coming to New Smyrna Beach?" Bree replied.

"I knew I'd heard his name someplace," Summer told her. "Well guess what? He's asked me to design a website for his new blog!"

"Oh, Summer that's amazing!" Bree squealed. "If I remember right, he's gorgeous. Any chance he'll be paying you a personal visit?"

Summer's sigh said it all. "Is there a problem?" Bree asked.

"A big fat problem," said Summer. "He and his wife were in a bad accident about six years ago, and she was an invalid up until her death last year. From what I can find online he gave up his job and had been home caring for her until she died, but now he's going into the food blogging business."

"I'm still waiting for the problem," Bree smirked. "You're a web designer and he needs a website designed. It sounds like a match made in heaven to me."

Summer giggled a little at her friend's analogy, but then became serious again. "I'm just concerned that with all the tragedy he's lived through that he'll be morose, and I don't work at my best when people are unhappy."

"Look at you using big words like morose," Bree laughed. "But honey, if there's anyone who can work with someone whose been through a tragedy, it's you. You've got a heart the size of Texas, and I've never known anyone to not come away feeling better after talking with you."

For the first time since opening the email from Jake Ross, Summer felt positive about the possibility of working with him, so she told Bree she loved her, hung up the phone and went back to the computer to work out her strategy.

Chapter 5

Summer was so busy the rest of the morning that she didn't even take time for lunch. By four o'clock she had received some preliminary information from Jake Ross, as well as a verbal commitment to sign with *Four Seasons of Summer*, and her head was spinning with ideas. Finishing up a quote for a dog walking service, *Delila's Dawgs,* she hit the send button and logged off her computer.

Grabbing a bottle of water from the garage refrigerator, she did a few stretches and then started walking towards Flagler Avenue. Normally just thinking about a run in the hot afternoon sun made her break out in a sweat, but today her endorphins were on high alert, and she was filled with restless energy. As soon as she hit the beach, she picked up her pace and quickly was at a full-on jog.

Forty-five minutes later she was limping home, wondering what in the world had made her think she was still up for jogging. But, after a cool shower and a cold glass of iced tea, she was feeling human again and started working on dinner. Michael was treasurer of the hospital foundation board and had a meeting at seven thirty, which meant an easy meal, and tonight it would be chef salads.

Everything was chopped and shredded when Michael arrived home at six thirty, and after his routine of setting his nice Gucci briefcase down on the kitchen counter, he headed upstairs to change.

Big plates of salad, homemade parmesan ranch dressing, and a small basket of crusty rolls were sitting on the kitchen island when he came down. And of course, his briefcase had been moved to the den.

"I thought we'd eat in here tonight," Summer said cheerfully.

Michael nodded in agreement, sat down, and immediately started to eat. Summer wanted so much to share her news about Jake Ross with him, but he only had thirty minutes to eat before he needed to leave, so she kept quiet, planning to share the news when he got home from his meeting.

Taking the last bite of his salad and rinsing it down with a gulp of iced tea, Michael hopped off his bar stool and looked around for his briefcase. "It's in the den," Summer said with a sigh before starting to clean up. The look on Michael's face was one of confusion but Summer wouldn't allow herself to be goaded into retrieving the briefcase for him. Instead, she hummed as she rinsed the dishes, thinking it was a better alternative than being bitchy.

Looking around for something to read, she picked up *The Middle Passage,* the first book in the Fate and Freedom series by K.I. Knight, when the phone rang. Seeing the name in the caller ID brought a huge smile to her face as she answered, "And how is my baby boy tonight?"

Riley groaned. "He's twenty-three, Mom," he said with a little chastisement in his voice. "Can't we drop that baby crap?"

"John Riley Alcott! Did you just say crap to your mother?"

"I did, and I'd say it again, but you wouldn't listen," he laughed, "so let's change the subject. Do you have your cell phone handy?"

"Right here, why?" Summer asked.

"Open up my Facebook page," Riley instructed her, "there's a picture I want you to see."

Now it was Summer's turn to groan. "You know I don't like that social media stuff Ri; can't you just send me a picture?"

"Mother," her son said sternly. "You design websites, you're more than tech savvy so why do you fight social media so much?"

"I don't know," she replied honestly, "it just seems so invasive, I guess. Don't people keep anything private anymore?"

"Mom, will you please just do this for me? It's kind of important."

Summer opened Riley's Facebook page and there standing next to her six-foot three-inch dark haired, gray eyed replica of his father, stood a petite blonde staring up at her son with love in her eyes.

Her heart was racing and there were tears in her eyes, but Summer knew how important it was that she say the right thing. "She's beautiful, Riley," was all she could get out.

"Her name's Olivia, Mom, and I really, really like her." Riley waited for it to sink in and then asked, "Mom, are you still there?"

"I am honey, and I wish your dad was, too. You haven't shown me a picture of a girl since you were in the fifth grade, so this is big time stuff. Is it serious?" she asked and inside she was praying, *please don't let it be serious.*

Summer waited and then Riley answered, "I don't know, Mom, but it could be. We met in a bookstore, just like you and Dad. That's karma, isn't it?"

Summer sighed. "You know that I want the best for you Ri, and I know that you'll make the right decision. All I ask is that you be careful and don't rush into anything, okay?"

"Are we going to have the birds and the bees talk now Mom?" Riley teased her. "Because I'm pretty sure I know how everything happens, and even how you prevent things from happening, but if it will make you feel better, I'm all ears."

"You're a brat sometimes, you know that, right?" Summer laughed.

"I do Mom, but I also know that you love me and that I love you."

Summer thought her heart would literally break in two. How many twenty-three-year-old boys, no men, would so easily say "I love you" to their mother? "All the way to the moon and back, kiddo," she answered, using the phrase she had always used when putting her sons to bed at night.

"Tell Dad I'm sorry I missed him, okay?" Riley told her, "and be sure to show him Olivia's picture. He'll think she's hot!"

Chapter 6

Summer put the phone in the cradle and let her mind roam back to the days when she was twenty-three. She and Michael had been going out about four months after meeting at a book reading on campus. Michael was finishing his master's degree and she had recently graduated from Ohio State with a Liberal Arts Degree when she found out she was pregnant. To say that Michael had been less than thrilled was an understatement.

But they were in love, and neither one could imagine aborting their child, so they got married; big fancy wedding and all. Michael had been too far into his degree to drop out of school, so instead of a honeymoon they had spent the weekend after their wedding at his parent's cottage at Indian Lake. The weather had been too chilly to be out in the water, so they made love between Summer's bouts of morning sickness, ate a lot of boxed macaroni and cheese, and took walks around the lake, dreaming and talking about their future.

Marriage had been harder for Michael to adapt to than it had been for Summer. He had been living off campus in a bachelor pad with three of his fraternity brothers, and the move to a small two-room walk-up cramped his style. Summer, on the other hand, had the nesting instinct and loved decorating their small space with treasurers from the local thrift stores. She even found a florist who threw away flowers when they started to fade, so every morning she scrounged their trash until she had a bouquet of fresh flowers to help the ambiance of the tiny space.

They had both found part time jobs, hers at the bookstore where they had met, and his at a discount department store, stocking shelves overnight. It wasn't an ideal start to their life together, and Michael whined a lot, but somehow, they made it work.

But when Cooper was born, seven months after their wedding, and Michael held his son in his arms for the first time, his demeanor had completely changed. Michael Cooper Alcott was his father's son from the minute he was born, and while Summer was secretly envious of the attention Michael lavished on their son, she loved the difference the baby had brought to their marriage. The guy who missed his frat house lifestyle had suddenly become a man.

Summer stretched and looked at her watch. She wished Michael had been there when Riley called, but to be honest, she wasn't sure it would have mattered. Michael agreed with her that their sons needed to experience life before settling down, but he also felt that Riley was an adult and needed to make his own decisions. Now had it been Cooper? Well, that would have been a different story all together.

Heading into the kitchen for a glass of water, Summer thought about the Ben & Jerry's Chunky Monkey ice cream in the freezer, and immediately it called out to her. Right now, she wanted nothing more than to fill a big bowl with the rich gooey decadence and drown herself in it, but thankfully she saw her reflection in the open storm door and remembered that being thin felt better than ice cream tasted.

Instead, she grabbed an apple and settled back into her chair. She was just getting wrapped up in Margaret's story, and the horrors she was facing in Angola, when she heard Michael pull-up. Marking her page and putting the book down again, she went to the kitchen to greet him.

Hospital board meetings were long drawn-out affairs, and Michael repeatedly came home tired and grumpy. Knowing this, Summer met him at the door with a smile and a cold beer. He exchanged the briefcase in his hand for the beer, and after a long drink, gave Summer the response she was waiting for. "Thanks, Summer, I needed that."

Together they walked into the living room, but Summer allowed Michael time to vent about his meeting before sharing the call from their son. She was also anxious to tell him about her new client, Jake Ross, but she could tell from the tired look on his face that was going to be a conversation for another day.

"Riley called tonight," Summer told her husband. "He has a new girlfriend he wanted to tell us about." Handing her cell phone to Jake, Riley's Facebook page up, she waited for his reaction.

"She's hot!" Michael said with a chuckle, and that made Summer cringe. Was it even appropriate for a father to think that way about his son's girlfriend? She knew that men had a different code of ethics when it came to women, but she wasn't sure that she liked it at all.

Taking the last drink of his beer, Michael handed Summer the glass and stood up. "I'm beat," he said, wiping his hand through his still thick dark hair. "You ready to go up?"

She really wanted to talk with Michael about her concerns of Riley getting too caught up in a romance at his age, but instead she nodded. After taking the beer glass to the kitchen and turning off the lights, she followed him up the stairs. She wasn't sleepy, she was too excited about having Jake Ross as a client, but rarely did she and Michael not go to bed at the same time, so she tucked her book under her arm, hoping that reading would help her relax.

By the time she had washed her face and brushed her teeth Michael was on his side softly snoring. Not wanting to bother him she turned off the seashell chandelier above the bed, clicked on her reading lamp, and snuggled in. "I guess I will find out what is going to happen to Margaret tonight," she told herself with a sigh, and opened the book to the page where she had left off.

Chapter 7

Sometime during the night, the rain had started back up. When Michael's alarm went off at six, Summer was deep in sleep, dreaming about a dark handsome mystery man. More than anything she wanted to burrow back under the covers and see if she could get her dream to return, but hearing the water turn off at the same time as a huge clap of thunder, she knew that sweet dreams would not be coming her way.

Slipping on a lightweight robe she stepped into the bathroom to splash her face with water and pull her hair into a bun. Michael was just getting out of the shower and when Summer caught sight of him in the mirror, she felt a little warm all over. At sixty her husband was still a gorgeous man. His almost black hair was a little thinner on top, but for the most part was as thick as when she had first met him. There were a few wrinkles around his gray eyes now, but overall, Michael Alcott looked pretty much the way he had on their wedding day, thirty-five years ago.

Seeing her watching him, Michael smirked. "Like what you see?"

Summer tried not to blush and replied as casually as possible. "Sure," she said, "but it isn't something I haven't seen before."

Michael smacked her with his towel and pulled her close. "I'll meet you back here tonight after dinner," he whispered in her ear. "We haven't showered together in a long time."

Not sure how to respond, Summer gave him a very unsexy peck on the cheek and headed downstairs to start the coffee. She may have been tingling from head to toe, but Michael needed breakfast, and after all, it's what June Cleaver would do.

Summer was grinning from ear to ear as she sat down at her computer after Michael left for work. She realized that she hadn't told him about Jake Ross yet but decided it would be good dinner conversation that night at Breakers. *And then we can try that joint shower he'd suggested,* she thought. Almost giddy with excitement, she said out loud, "what a way to celebrate!"

Purposely forgoing lunch so she could indulge in a couple of Blue Moons at dinner, Summer worked fervently to get her slate as clean as possible. Jake had already told her that he was on a time crunch, and needed lots of help, and with the publicity she would get from this type of project, it was imperative that she bring her A game to the table.

The rain stopped around one, and at four thirty, Summer decided to call it a week. She and Jake had emailed back and forth several times and had finally agreed on a color palette as well as some teaser notices to start going out the next week announcing *Pushing the Plate Aside.* Summer knew it was going to be a big challenge, but she knew she was up to it. But for now, it was date night, and the thought of her date had been simmering between her thighs all day.

Stepping into the shower and thinking about being with Michael there later made Summer break out in goosebumps. She knew it wasn't the water temperature because it was more than warm, but Michael hadn't suggested anything as erotic as a joint shower for a long time, and she was more than ready to take him up on his offer.

After washing her hair, Summer slathered it in conditioner, and then exfoliated and shaved her legs. By the time they were silky smooth, so was her hair. Wrapping Egyptian cotton towels around her hair and body, Summer grabbed a jar of Josie Maran Lavender Citrus whipped Argan oil and smoothed it all over, until her sun kissed skin gleamed.

Her hair dry and hanging softly around her shoulders, Summer moved to the closet to find just the right outfit to wear. They had been going to Breakers for dinner almost every Friday since they had moved from Ohio, so she knew that anything would work, but tonight she wanted to knock Michael's socks off. Selecting a form-fitting turquoise cold-shoulder Tee with a scooped neckline and three-quarter length sleeves, Summer admired the way that it showed off her toned midriff.

As much as she had hated the rowing machines at the Y, she was always thankful for them when she saw the results.

Pairing the shirt with a pair of snug white Woman With Control ankle length pants, and her new TOMS champagne-colored Majorca cutout sandals, Summer looked in the mirror and smiled. *Not bad for fifty-eight*, she thought, turning to get a good view of her backside. The pants held everything in place and that was the one thing all the exercise in the world hadn't seemed to help.

After doing her normal makeup routine Summer added a little bronzer to her cheeks and added IT Hello Light Illuminating powder to her forehead, cheekbones, and down her nose to her chin. A healthy swipe of Josie Maran Bee Sting on her lips, and Summer was ready to go. Hearing Michael in the kitchen she gave herself a generous spray of Jo Malone, Orange Bitters cologne, and headed downstairs.

Chapter 8

When Michael walked in the door Summer was posed by the island with her hand on her waist and her hip slightly jutted out. She'd never been very good at the whole seductress thing, but after Michael's comments this morning she felt she owed him a little something. He looked her up and down and smiled before saying, "Don't you look nice."

Summer willed herself to melt into the floor, but it didn't work. *Don't you look nice.* What kind of a lame-assed comment was that for a husband to make to his wife who was standing before him, obviously trying to look sexy? She could feel the tears trying to move from behind her eyeballs but the last thing she wanted was for Michael to know that his words had hurt her. Instead, she slowly straightened up and turned the other way hoping that he didn't notice. And sure enough, he didn't.

Laying his briefcase on the counter Michael headed up the stairs calling out, "Give me ten minutes and we'll be out the door."

Summer had half a mind to leave his very expensive briefcase lying where it was, but with a sigh, she picked it up and moved it to the den. She wanted to scream, she wanted to throw something, but instead she opened the refrigerator looking for a bite of anything sweet to put in her mouth. Of course, the closest she came to sweet was a jar of black raspberry jam, and even though she contemplated eating a big spoonful, the worry over dropping some on her white pants kept her from a humiliating experience.

"I'm ready," Michael said, coming up behind her with a kiss on her neck. Oh, was she glad she hadn't let the whole raspberry jam decision go south! Turning slowly in his arms she looked into his stormy gray eyes and realized he didn't have a clue that she had even been upset. *Why can't he ever tell me I'm beautiful?* she thought. *Or maybe even that I look hot, like he thought Olivia did. He used to tell me I was beautiful all the time, why was it so hard now?*

Unless it was raining, they always walked to Breakers, and tonight the sky was clear and bright. Michael held her hand as he always did, and Summer took deep breaths to get her emotions under control. They both loved Breakers, it had been the first restaurant they had gone to after moving to New Smyrna Beach, and the Key Lime Grilled Mahi Mahi was still one of their favorites. Deciding to concentrate on the evening ahead, Summer took one more deep breath and relaxed.

Sitting on the beach at the end of Flagler Street, the atmosphere at Breakers was always eclectic. Filled with everything from local families to college students on break, you couldn't beat one of their signature burgers or the glorious view. Just walking in helped Summer's mood lighten, and the tall Blue Moon that Michael ordered for her didn't hurt either.

Their orders placed, they toasted to the weekend, and just as she was about to take a big gulp of her Friday night indulgence, Summer heard a familiar, but not necessarily welcome voice behind her.

"Well look who's here," the boisterous voice said slapping Michael on the back, "Our local web designer and her architect husband." The man continued to chuckle at his joke, and Summer was sure she heard Michael groan. Anyway, she hoped she did.

Michael stood up to shake the man's hand, just as his wife sauntered in and wrapped her arms around him. Obviously embarrassed, Michael gently pried her lose, and sat back down next to Summer.

Elliot Stevens owned the Cadillac dealership in New Smyrna and was on the hospital board with Michael. Alone he was loud and obnoxious, but when his child bride Lacey was with him, it was more than Summer could stomach. Still though, she tried to smile and play nice, but just as their food arrived, so did Elliot's evening ruining question.

"It looks like all the tables are full tonight. Whataya say to us sitting right here with Y'all?" And without even waiting for an answer Elliot held a chair for Lacey, right on the other side of Michael. Summer was seething!

The delicious dinner that she had been waiting for all day was sitting in front of her and she couldn't even eat it. Even though Elliot told them to go ahead, Summer just didn't feel right eating while the Stevens didn't even have a drink. Thankfully that was rectified when the waitress came by for their order, but at that point Summer was defeated.

"I'll have a Mai Tai and a dinner salad," Lacey purred. "And put the dressing on the side, I'm watching my figure." With that she winked at Michael, and Summer looked at her fries, knowing they would be going to waste.

Chapter 9

An hour later, after nibbling a few bites of her fish, and guzzling another Blue Moon, Summer was ready to call it a night. Michael had about consumed every flavor of dark beer in the place, and she was concerned that he wouldn't be able to make the three blocks walk back home.

Excusing herself to head to the ladies' room, she bent down to pick up the napkin that had fallen off her lap and what the hell? Lacey was running her high heeled sandal up Michael's leg.

Throwing the napkin on the table hard enough that even the people at the next table looked up, Summer grabbed her purse and headed towards the door. She had almost made her escape when Michael grabbed her arm.

"Where are you going?" he demanded. "And what was that little tantrum about?"

Summer could see people looking their way, as she pulled lose from Michael's grip and stepped outside. "I'm going home," she declared. "But you feel free to stay and party with your friends."

Michael shook his head, not used to dealing with an angry wife. He told her he needed to pay the check and they would leave together. Unfortunately, before he could even make it back inside, Elliot and Lacey were there, saying they had paid both checks and would drive them home.

Summer was on the verge of hysteria and wondered what good old Elliot and Lacey would say if she puked in the back of their fancy white Cadillac. Just the thought of it had her giggling. Very quickly the car pulled up in front of their house and afraid that the Stevens might invite themselves in, Summer gave a little wave, opened the side door, and ran upstairs.

The thoughts that were running through her head were anything but comforting and the one thing she knew was that there wasn't going to be tag team showering anytime soon.

Locking herself in the bathroom, Summer turned the faucet on full blast so that Michael wouldn't hear her sobs. She felt guilty wasting the water, but she wasn't about to let him know how hurt she was, and besides, it was still probably less water than they would have used in the shower.

Within minutes Michael was pounding on the door. "Summer," he yelled, "open this damn door and tell me what's going on."

Her emotions as under control as possible, she turned off the water and looked at her blotchy face and puffy eyes. "I just need a minute, Michael," she said as calmly as possible. "Go ahead and get in bed and I'll be there in a second." She could hear her husband growling in the background, but at least he'd quit rattling the doorknob.

A little cold water splashed on her face, and a healthy dose of eye drops later, Summer turned out the bathroom light and stepped into the bedroom. And there lay Michael, still in his clothes, either asleep or passed out; she wasn't sure. And the tears started all over again.

Pulling on a pair of leggings and slipping her arms into her NSB sweatshirt, Summer turned off the overhead light, and quietly crept downstairs. Grabbing a throw from the back of the couch, she curled up in her rocker and tried to make sense of what had happened tonight, and where her life had gone so off track.

Chapter 10

Light was just filtering through the windows when she tried to open her eyes again. All the crying had left them scratchy and swollen. Certain that she'd never be able to keep Michael from knowing how much he had upset her if she didn't get moving, Summer moved towards the kitchen and her favorite appliance, the coffeepot.

Saturday mornings were usually Michael's time to take over in the kitchen. He'd let Summer sleep in and bring her favorite mug, filled with strong black coffee, to her in bed. Sometimes he scrambled eggs, and sometimes he made pancakes. Standing there waiting for the coffee to brew, Summer realized that he really was a good husband, even if he wasn't very good with flowery compliments.

The problem was, now she was mad! Or hurt or humiliated, she wasn't sure which, but she was not a happy camper. Did she think there was something going on between Michael and Lacey? Not really. Stunning, professional women surrounded Michael all day long. Surely if he was going to stray, it wouldn't be with a teenybopper with a man-made rack, but then men did stranger things every day.

Taking her coffee, and settling back in her rocker, she thought about the past thirty-five years of their marriage and wondered if she really knew her husband at all.

Chapter 11

April 1984

"Come on, Summer, push," Michael instructed her. "You can do this; the doctor says just a couple more and you're there."

She wanted to push, she wanted to please her husband, but truth be told, Summer was exhausted, and more than a little scared. They had only gotten married because of this baby, and Michael hadn't made any pretense of not being happy about it. Now that their child was about to make an entrance into the world, would it rock the boat she had worked so hard to keep steady?

"One more big push, Summer" the kind nurse told her, and just like that, she was a mother. The doctor laid the baby on her stomach and said, "Congratulations, it's a boy."

Summer looked up at Michael, unprepared for the smile that was covering his face. "We have a son, Summer," he beamed with tears in his eyes. "I have a son."

The nurse took the baby to clean him up and for the first time Summer wished her mom was there. She felt as if she'd been run over by a truck and she needed someone to hold and comfort her, and apparently that wasn't going to be Michael.

Clean, fresh, and swaddled, the nurse handed the little bundle to Summer and suggested she try nursing him. In all honesty, she had only decided to breastfeed because of the cost of formula, and now that the time was here, she was scared and uncertain.

"Open your gown, honey," the nurse told her. "Let's get this little guy started." Summer was mortified at the idea of putting her breasts on display, but the baby was starting to fuss, which left it out of her hands.

"So, does this young man have a name?" the nursed asked as she placed the baby's mouth by Summer's nipple.

"Michael Cooper Alcott," her husband said looking at Summer. And just as she was about to say something, Baby Alcott latched on!

With a look of both joy and discomfort on her face, Summer was finally able to speak. "We never really discussed names Michael," she said guardedly. "When did you decide on this one?"

For the first time Michael sat down on the bed and snuggled next to his new family. "Well," he admitted, "I always thought if the baby was a boy we'd name him Michael, but the minute I saw him I knew I wanted your name in there as well. Anyway, I think Cooper will be an awesome name for a boy, and look at him Summer, he looks just like you."

So even though she was secretly hoping to name the baby John after her dad if it was a boy, she knew that making Michael happy was the key right now. And for the first time in their short marriage, he did seem happy.

Chapter 12

Summer sat up with a start when she realized Michael was squatted beside her chair. She blinked a few times, not sure if she had really been asleep, or daydreaming. His thick dark hair was rumpled, what her sons would call *bed head,* but it was the confusion in his eyes that bothered her.

"What's going on?" he asked, trying to grab her hand. "I get that you're mad at me, I just don't know why," and that was her undoing.

"Are you freaking kidding me, Michael?" she yelled, pushing him back so she could get up. "Are you really going to sit there and act like you don't know what happened last night and why I'm so furious!"

Scrubbing his hands over his face, Michael thought before answering. "I had a lot to drink, I know that, but other than that I don't remember much else."

Summer started to laugh and was on the verge of a meltdown. "You're unbelievable, Michael, do you know that?" she spat at him. "I've seen you drink way more than you did last night and still be coherent, so don't give me that bullshit."

For a moment they just stood there, each willing the other to say something when Summer finally spoke up. "There's coffee in the kitchen if you want some, but now if you'll excuse me, I'm going to go get ready and get the hell out of this house!" Grabbing the mug of her now cold brew, Summer held her head high and climbed the stairs, leaving Michael in a state of bewilderment.

Summer quickly put on a pair of tan walking shorts, a red striped sleeveless blouse, and her Sketchers. She wasn't sure where she'd end up, so she put sunscreen and tinted moisturizer on her face, followed by bronzer and two coats of mascara. Her mane of chestnut hair was pulled into a low ponytail, and she was good to go.

Michael was sitting in her rocker with a mug of coffee in his hand, watching a fishing show when she came down. He looked at her with a slight smile, but she just ignored him and went into the kitchen. Grabbing her Kate Spade clutch and car keys, she headed to the garage. Did she mean for the kitchen door to slam? Maybe or maybe not, but one way or another, it felt good.

Summer didn't drive her baby a lot, but oh did she love it! A 1965 navy blue Mustang convertible, V-8 with a white rag top, it had been left to her by her Uncle Toots. A confirmed bachelor, without a family of his own, Summer was more like a daughter to him than a niece. She closed her eyes for a moment remembering the days Toots would pick her up after school and take her to Kewpies for a chocolate soda. The outings and the car were their special bond, and neither one of them ever forgot. When Toots had become too ill to drive his prized possession, he had it restored and kept protected in his garage, always telling Summer it would be hers someday. As much as she loved the car, and what it represented from her childhood, she would gladly give it away to have Toots back again.

Jason's Corner Restaurant in New Smyrna proper was one of her favorite places for breakfast, but with the limitations she put on herself as far as food was concerned, she rarely went there. But now, a plate of their Eggs Benedict was exactly what she needed. It was early yet so she was able to park on the street near the restaurant and sit at one of the outside bistro tables, so she could keep an eye on her car while she ate.

Food ordered and hot coffee in front of her, Summer thought about how she was going to spend her day. She hadn't been out by herself on a Saturday morning in so long that it was a little terrifying to think about doing something *she* wanted to do, so she sipped her coffee and worked on a plan.

The old fort at Saint Augustine was always a fun adventure, but leaving her car parked in the hot sun in an overcrowded lot wasn't very appealing. *Maybe a trip to the outlet mall*, she thought, but the dangers to her car were there as well. Finally, her food arrived, and she put all thoughts of the day out of her head.

Chapter 13

The Eggs Benedict had been scrumptious, but way more than Summer could eat. Even without much in her stomach from the night before, she pushed away from the table with her meal only half finished. She handed the server her debit card, left a nice tip, and walked towards her car.

It was such a nice day that putting the top down seemed appropriate, even though a lot of work. She had just finished snapping the soft top into its cover when an attractive man stopped beside her.

"This car sure is beautiful," he said, "original or restored?"

Summer looked at the man and blushed a little. Normally the people who inquired about the Mustang were more Gen X, but this guy looked to be closer to her age. "A little of both," she admitted. "The interior is all original, but the body has had a little work done to it."

The man nodded, smiled, and then said, "I'm Alex Bailey, by the way. I just moved here from Michigan and was looking for a good place for breakfast. Any recommendations?"

Summer extended her hand as she replied, "I'm Summer Alcott, and you're in luck. The best place for breakfast is Jason's Corner and you're practically standing in front of it."

Alex Bailey had a nice firm handshake, she was thinking, and when he spoke it caught her off guard. "I don't suppose I could talk you into joining me," he said with a smile. "You're the first person I've met since I got here. Well except the manager of the bank, that is."

Looking at the man in front of her Summer tried to appraise him without him noticing. He was tall, maybe six feet or so, with dark blond hair and brown eyes that looked warm and caring. Age wise he could be anywhere from fifty to sixty, he just had that youthful look that didn't seem to grow older.

"So, what do you say?" he asked again. "I'd love to have someone to talk with over breakfast."

"It sounds lovely," she told him honestly, "but I just finished eating and was on my way out. I do recommend the Eggs Benedict though, and if you sit at one of the outside tables, you might make a friend. People are really nice here."

"So far they have been," Alex told her with a smile, and Summer wondered if he was flirting with her.

"Great," she stammered, "and it was nice meeting you, but I've really got to run."

Jumping in the car before she had a chance to embarrass herself, Summer looked at him through the rearview mirror and smiled. *Maybe I'm not invisible,* she thought, and then she pulled away from the curb.

***

As soon as the Mustang roared onto the highway Summer realized she had nowhere to go. *Am I just so out of practice talking to a man that I freaked?* She thought. But now that she was on the open road, she decided to just enjoy the beautiful Florida morning and pushed the accelerator to the floor and let all eight horses do their thing!

Of course, ten minutes into her run for freedom she looked in the rearview mirror and saw red flashing lights were right behind her. Pulling over to the side of the road Summer grabbed her driver's license and registration and prepared herself for the worst.

The deputy who pulled her over looked as if he had just graduated from high school, and that made Summer smile. Watching his face get red from having a woman driving a car older than he was smiling at him, was the young deputies undoing.

"Uh, ma'am," he stuttered. "I need to see your license and registration, please?"

Summer obliged, still smiling at the young man. He took her information back to his squad car but returned just a few minutes later.

33

"You have a clean record Ms. Alcott," he told her. "So, I'm going to let you off with a warning, but do you have any idea how fast you were going?"

Trying to look chastised and remorseful Summer replied, "About a hundred?"

Shaking his head, the deputy gave her the warning ticket with a verbal caution of his own. "That's a beautiful classic car, and I'd hate to see the two of you wrapped around a tree somewhere. Keep it under eighty, okay?" And just as he turned around, he winked at her!

Summer was smiling and singing to her Eric Carmen tape as she cruised down the road. The quality wasn't nearly as good as it would have been on a CD, but she had been adamant that she didn't want to ruin the original dashboard of her car, so as long as she could get them, eight tracks were what she listened to.

Up ahead she saw signs for a farmers' market and decided it would make for a fun break in her day. There were a lot of open parking spaces for her baby, and the stalls were situated so she could keep her eye on her precious car the whole time. After filling bags with some delicious looking heirloom tomatoes, peaches, and lemons, she saw a table laden with scrumptious looking baked goods, and even though she had eaten a big breakfast, she allowed herself one white chocolate macadamia nut cookie.

The cookie was melt-in-your-mouth delectable, and Summer wouldn't let herself have one moment of guilt over the splurge. She licked every crumb from her fingers before getting in the car and heading back onto the open road.

Within minutes she saw an old church surrounded by ancient looking headstones, and her curiosity got the better of her. Walking through the old cemetery was peaceful on a sunny Saturday, or at least it was until she came upon the graves of two children, and her special day came crashing down around her.

"Babies shouldn't die," she said softly to no one in particular as she lovingly caressed the two headstones. The air out of her sails, Summer walked back to her car and got in. Her lovely day on her own had turned dark and melancholy, and now she wanted nothing more than to go home, wrap up in a quilt, and cry.

Chapter 14

Not even bothering to put the top up on the car, Summer closed the garage door and quietly entered the house. She could see Michael on the deck, his long legs propped up on the railing, an open book laying on his stomach. One of the things that had attracted them to each other in the beginning was their love of reading, but while she always had a book going, Michael rarely read anymore.

She really didn't want a confrontation with him now, her heart was still too raw with emotions, but she knew they had to get it over with. Opening the slider, she stepped out onto the deck, and Michael immediately jumped up.

"Summer," he said softly, "I've been so worried about you." He tried to pull her towards him, but she backed away. Trying a different tactic, he picked up the bottle of Summer's favorite Mango Mamma wine that was chilling and said, "Let me pour you some wine."

Accepting the glass, she took a big sip and blurted out, "Are you fucking Lacey Stevens?"

Watching his face the whole time so she could gage his reaction, Summer had to admit that he seemed genuinely shocked.

"What?" he growled. "Why would you even ask such a question?"

"Because she was all over you last night, and when I bent down to pick up my napkin, I saw her running her foot up your leg. That's not the move of a woman who isn't looking for more." Summer crossed her arms over her chest as a defense mechanism but didn't take her eyes off Michael's face.

Michael let out a big sigh and ran his hand over his face. "I'll be honest with you," he started, and Summer could feel her whole world closing in on her. "Lacey has made it more than clear that she'd be interested in a fling, but, Summer, she holds no interest for me at all, and I would never betray you like that."

She'd known Michael Alcott for over thirty-five years and was pretty confident she could tell when he wasn't being honest, but this wasn't one of those times. So when he reached out for her hand, she let him pull her into his arms.

"Is this what you were so upset about last night?" he asked, gently running his hands up and down her back. "You should have just asked me instead of jumping to conclusions."

Deciding it was time to go all in she swallowed hard and replied, "It was more than that Michael. You got a little flirty in the bathroom yesterday morning and I liked it. We don't make love like we used to, and after last night, I decided it was because you had someone else."

"Summer," he said, cupping her face and drawing out the way he said her name. "I'm not a kid anymore. I'm under a lot of stress at work and things just don't work like they used to. Doesn't mean I don't think about the hot monkey sex that we used to have. In fact, I was thinking about it yesterday morning when I made the shower offer, but a few beers, and an evening of the Stevens, took all the lust right out of me."

Afraid to look at him for fear she would cry, Summer nodded, but she didn't quite accept what he was saying. She worked hard to keep herself attractive for him, and more than anything, she wanted to see the proof of his desire because *hot monkey sex* was just what she was looking for.

Taking the last sip of her wine and reaching for the bottle for more, Summer did a one eighty and dropped a bomb that Michael was not at all prepared for. "Do you ever think about them?" she asked.

"Do I ever think about whom?" Michael responded guardedly.

Summer couldn't keep her lip from quivering as she answered, "Our daughters, Michael, our baby girls."

Chapter 15

June 1990

Summer loved being pregnant with Cooper and had expected this pregnancy to go as well, but almost from the beginning things seemed different. With Cooper she experienced the normal first trimester morning sickness, but if she was careful what she ate, it usually wasn't too bad. But this go around was altogether different.

It seemed as if she was hanging over the toilet morning, noon and nighttime, and nothing she ate, even saltines, stayed down. Between throwing up and running after an active five-year-old, Summer was on the verge of exhaustion. Michael had just started a new job and was putting in lots of hours, which meant he wasn't even around to help with Cooper, a task he normally looked forward to.

Dr. Sparks was concerned immediately when she went in for her three-month visit, and even suggested hospitalizing her because of his fear of dehydration, but Summer wouldn't hear of it. Her parents were on a trip out west, and Michael's parents ran their own business, so there was no one to watch Cooper while Michael was at work.

Finally, after a shot to calm the nausea, and a promise from Summer to drink lots of Gatorade and other high electrolyte drinks, Dr. Sparks relented. He did insist however that she come back the next week for a follow-up, plus he said his nurse would be calling daily to monitor how Summer was feeling.

Within a few days Summer had to admit that she was feeling stronger, so when the nurse called to check on her, she tried to get out of the follow-up appointment the following week. But the nurse wasn't having any part of it and reminded Summer that she would be calling the next day.

By appointment day Summer was feeling almost human again, except that she was so tired. Still blaming it on running around after Cooper and taking care of everything else while Michael worked, it never occurred to her that something might be wrong. Dr. Sparks seemed to concur, so Summer went home from the appointment exhausted, but happy.

But around her seventh month of pregnancy, Summer woke up in the night to go to the bathroom and found blood on the tissue when she wiped. Trying not to panic she called out for Michael. The bleeding didn't seem to be slowing down, which made Michael put in calls to Dr. Sparks and his parents, and within thirty minutes they were on their way to the hospital.

Contractions started before they even arrived at the emergency room entrance, and even with a shot by the ER resident on call to try to slow them down, it was obvious that Summer was going to have her baby that night. She and Michael prayed, and even discussed with the nurse the survival rate of a baby born at around thirty weeks, but they were not prepared for the outcome. No one was.

In hindsight, Summer wondered if she should have had the ultrasound when Dr. Sparks suggested earlier in her pregnancy, but even if she had known then what she knew now she wouldn't have agreed to an abortion. After a very quick delivery Summer was holding twin baby girls, no bigger than Barbie Dolls, wrapped together in a striped hospital blanket. They each had a soft pink face, and Michael's dark hair, but below the shoulders instead of two bodies and four legs, there was one pelvis, with two stick thin legs attached.

Looking at the babies in her arms who were barely holding on to life, Summer started to sing to them the song she sang every night to Cooper. "Hush little baby, don't say a word, momma's gonna buy you a mockingbird," came softly from her lips, as she stroked their tiny downy heads and did her best not to lose control. More than anything, she needed Michael to stand by her side and share this moment with their daughters, but he stood alone in the corner, anguish written all over his face.

Katherine and Maryanne Alcott, named after Summer and Michael's mothers, died just fifteen minutes after their birth. At that moment, Summer realized that she was going to have to be the strong partner in their marriage, and that as much as she needed him to comfort her, Michael just didn't have the strength.

Chapter 16

Michael pulled her in tightly before answering. "Of course, I do Honey, but what brought this up?"

Tears running down her face, she told him about her stop by the old country cemetery, and the two children's graves she had seen. How they were just three years apart in age but had died on the same day. She didn't know why they had died, but it had broken her heart all the same.

Summer loved the warmth and security of Michael's arms, but when he didn't say anything more, she stepped away. "I'm not really hungry," she told him, pouring herself another glass of wine, but there's a pizza in the freezer I can fix you."

Michael didn't like meals out of the freezer, Summer knew that. It was wrong on her part to need to punish him in some way but being served frozen pizza didn't seem like that big of deal to her, even though she knew he wouldn't be pleased. To his credit, Michael just nodded and went to the kitchen for a beer.

To absolve some of the guilt she was feeling over the frozen pizza dinner, Summer mixed some greens for a salad, even using one of the heirloom tomatoes she had purchased at the farmer's market. Michael was still sitting on the deck, so she took the food out to him, then turned to go back into the house.

"Sit here with me," he said grabbing her hand. "You know I hate to eat alone."

Summer sighed and sat down in the Adirondack chair beside him, all the while tempted to tell him she was aware of a lot of things he hated.

Like talking about their daughters, or anything without a happy ending, but she kept her mouth shut by sipping on another glass of wine.

When Michael was done with the pizza and salad, he suggested a walk on the beach, but Summer begged off. Right now, she wanted a hot bath, her soft bed, and some relaxation. Her body was tired, her head was throbbing, and to be honest, her heart hurt as well. If Michael wasn't interested in romance, she might as well lose herself in in her own fantasy.

After filling the big garden tub with steaming water and several squirts of her Philosophy Lemon Custard shower and bath gel, Summer eased her body down into the decadent smelling water. The heat felt good on her aching spirits, and the fresh lemony fragrance refreshed her aching heart. She closed her eyes as the relaxation took over, and without even realizing how tired she was, fell asleep.

She dreamt that she was dressed in an evening gown, walking into a spectacular ballroom on the arm of the mystery man. Everything around her was beautiful and exciting, and just when she thought the mystery man was going to kiss her, Summer woke up with a start.

The bath water had turned cold, but her body was on fire. Summer hadn't even thought of kissing another man since her first date with Michael, but now her heart was pounding, and she was filled with lust and shame.

It was only a dream, she thought to herself, but still, she felt an odd kind of uneasiness creep over her. Pulling the plug on the drain, Summer grabbed a towel and roughly dried herself off. It had been one of the strangest days she had experienced in a long time, and she wasn't sure whether to blame it on her fight with Michael, too much wine, or the longing in her soul that she kept trying to push out of her thoughts.

Dried and slathered with lotion, Summer crept into the bedroom, afraid that Michael might already be in bed. But the room was quiet and empty, and with a sigh of relief, she pulled back the covers and climbed in. She thought that her nap in the tub would keep her from falling asleep, but she was wrong. No sooner did her head hit the pillow than she was out, thankfully this time without any spicy dreams.

Chapter 17

Summer woke up on Sunday morning to the aroma of coffee brewing and bacon frying. Instinctively she reached over to Michael's side, even though she wasn't expecting him to be there. The extra hours of sleep had been just what she needed, so after a big stretch, she climbed out of bed.

The clock said it was seven thirty, and church wasn't until ten, so she slipped a pair of yoga pants on under her nightgown and headed downstairs. For a couple of seconds, she watched Michael mixing batter, and she couldn't help but smile. Michael Alcott was a man of few words, but she could tell he was trying to atone for any wrongs he had caused her, and that made her heart soar.

Quietly walking up behind him she put her arms around his waist and breathed in the smell that was her husband. A little bit of citrus and a little bit of spice, but one hundred percent male.

"Good morning," Michael said, reaching for the arms that were holding him. "Did you sleep well?"

"I did," Summer answered, "really well in fact. How about you?"

Michael turned around, so they were standing face to face before answering. "Like shit," he told her, as he ran his fingers through her hair. "Just as I deserved. Summer…" he started, but she cut him off.

"Let's just enjoy the morning, okay? We can talk later if you want, but right now I'm starving, and I need coffee. Can we just call a truce for the time being?" Summer looked into her husband's eyes, and what she saw there made her happy.

"Coffee and breakfast at your service," he teased, and then giving her a chaste kiss, he moved back to mixing the pancake batter.

Michael and Summer had been going to the ten o'clock service of the First Methodist Church since they had moved to New Smyrna Beach, and they both enjoyed it. It's where the boys had gone to Sunday School and Bible School, and where they had met Bree and her husband Dan. The building was small and quaint, like the town they now called home.

After service Bree met Summer in the vestibule and asked if she and Michael wanted to come over for an early dinner. "I thought we'd just throw some burgers and corn on the grill and let the guys do the cooking, does that work for you?" Bree asked.

"It works great for me," Summer laughed. "Michael made breakfast and cleaned up the kitchen this morning. I haven't had a day off KP duty in years!"

"Well," Bree sighed, "we'll probably have to do the clean-up, but if we use paper plates, it shouldn't be too bad."

The women hugged, and Summer walked out on the church lawn where Michael was waiting. Looping her arm through his she took a few steps and then stopped. "I got a new client this week," she told him, "and I'm pretty excited about it."

"That's wonderful, Summer," Michael told her sincerely. "Someone local?"

"Actually," she told him, "It's Jake Ross. You know, the food critic from the Food Channel."

It took Michael a minute to put everything together and then he smiled. "No shit, Summer? Jake Ross wants you to design his webpage?"

"Michael!" she exclaimed. "We're still on church property; you can't talk like that."

"Sorry," he replied to her reprimand, "but Summer, this is big stuff. Jake Ross was a major player a few years ago."

The reminder of what had happened to take Jake out of the limelight put a damper on Summer's mood, so she nodded and kept walking. "The last five years have been really rough for him," she said softly, "but now he's starting a new business and came to me for help. I'm anxious to tell you all about it so let's go home and I'll show you what the *Four Seasons of Summer* plans to do for his new business and blog."

Chapter 18

Summer could see the pride and excitement on Michael's face as he looked over the preliminary designs for Jake Ross' website. "This is amazing, Summer," he told her, giving her a tight squeeze. "I can't tell you how proud I am of you for going after your dream. You're a pretty special woman, you know that?"

It was all Summer could do to keep the tears that were welling up in her eyes from running down her cheeks. Michael had never been given to compliments, but when he gave them, they were sincere. Looking into his dove gray eyes, she beamed, holding on to his words as if they were covered with gold.

After closing down the computer and changing out of their Sunday finery, Michael suggested that they call their sons. It was kind of a weekly tradition that they talked with the boys sometime each Sunday, and even though it wasn't usually this early in the day, Summer was all for it.

As with most everything in the Alcott family, birth order took precedence, so Michael picked up the landline, put it on speaker and tried Cooper first. Michael Cooper Alcott, thirty-four years of age, was definitely his father's son, even though his looks favored his mother and her side of the family. Cooper was a bachelor, living in Los Angeles, and like his dad, was an architect.

"Hey, what's up?" was how Cooper always answered their calls, and today was no different. Summer felt as if someone Cooper's age, and with his educational background, should be a little more respectful, but Michael loved it, along with Cooper's free loving lifestyle.

After a minute of small talk Cooper asked if they had seen the picture of Riley's new girlfriend, Olivia. "She's one hot piece; I'll give her that," he chuckled, "but my baby brother needs to just bang her, not fall in love with her."

Summer cringed at the crude way Cooper was talking, but hearing Michael laugh along with their son, she kept her mouth shut. While she listened to the two men discuss what was going on with Cooper's life, and what was going on in the world of architecture, Summer thought about what Michael's life might have been like if she hadn't gotten pregnant with Cooper. Would he have still been a bachelor at thirty-four, jumping in and out of bed with every woman whom he met?

Hearing her name, Summer snapped back to reality. "So, Mom," Cooper said, "Dad tells me you've snagged a big new client. Jake Ross is still pretty famous around here, but you do know that he's kind of a broken man, right?"

Summer sighed. She didn't want to discuss Jake Ross' personal life with Cooper and Michael, because in her mind it was just that, personal. She was thrilled that they were happy for her, but for now she wanted to leave it at that.

"I know that he's had some problems Cooper," she stated guardedly, "but I'm just designing a website for him; we're not going to become friends." Weeks later Summer would remember those words and realize how quickly they had changed.

They finished up the call with Cooper and Michael dialed Riley's number. Summer was still feeling the sting of Cooper's comment about Jake Ross, but the minute she heard Riley's voice, she softened.

Eleven years younger than his brother, Riley Alcott looked like his dad, but had a soft heart like his mom. He had graduated from his parent's alma mater, Ohio State University, the year before and was working on his masters and interning at a publishing company in Boston. Riley had always been kind and thoughtful, and just hearing how he answered the phone made Summer acutely aware of how different he was from his brother. Even though she was sure he looked at his caller ID before picking up, Riley was courteous to a fault.

"This is Riley," he answered, almost as if he was at work and not at home.

"Wow aren't you proper," Michael chided him. "It's okay to just say hello you know."

Riley laughed and then explained that he was indeed working on his new at work phone etiquette but then asked how they both were doing before bringing up Olivia.

"Did mom show you the picture of Olivia, Dad?" Riley asked.

"She did, and you're right, I said she was hot. I can't say that your mother cared much for that however," Michael chuckled. "Truthfully Ri, she's a very lovely young woman."

"Thanks Dad," Riley continued. "It means a lot to me that you approve."

"I didn't say I approved of you getting serious right now Riley, I just admitted that she's very pretty." Michael waited for Riley to say more and when he didn't, Summer took over the call.

"When are you coming for a visit, Ri?" she asked. "We haven't seen you since graduation."

"It's not that I don't want to come home, Mom," he answered her truthfully. "It's just now with grad school ahead and the internship, well, its just not a good time. But you could come here."

"Dad and I will talk about it," she told him. "Everything else okay?"

"Everything is great, Mom, you don't need to worry about me. But, if you could get my big brother off my back about Olivia, I'd appreciate it."

Summer could hear the frustration in his voice, and it broke her heart. Her sons were as different as night and day, and although she loved them equally, it was Riley that she understood the best.

"I'll do what I can," she told her son, and after a few more minutes, the call was ended.

Normally the Sunday calls to her sons made Summer feel joyful and blessed, but today's calls had felt uncomfortable all around, and it wasn't a feeling she relished at all.

Chapter 19

After hanging up from the calls to their sons, Michael grabbed the Sunday paper and headed out to the deck. He stopped first in the kitchen for a glass of iced tea, where he found Summer looking at her iPad.

"I thought we were grilling out with Dan and Bree," he said, watching her flip through screens covered with fancy looking sweets.

"We are, but I thought it would be nice to take a dessert. Anything sound especially good to you?" she asked without looking up.

"Well, I've really been craving one of those delicious Molten Lava cakes you made last Easter, but is that too much work?" Summer turned and smiled at her husband. Michael had a sweet tooth; she knew that, but he suffered in silence because of her issues with food. She decided right away that she'd make him that rich cake that he loved, and the best part was she could leave the leftovers with their friends.

"I'd be happy to make you a Molten Lava cake, Michael," she told him, "but I'm going to need to run to Publix for a few things. While I'm gone, you can read your paper in peace, and if you need a snack, there's some cheese and grapes in the fridge."

Giving him a quick kiss, Summer grabbed her purse and headed to the garage. The first thing she noticed was her beautiful Mustang still sitting there with its top down. Deciding that it was too dangerous to leave her baby in the busy grocery store parking lot while she shopped, she quickly put the top up, and climbed into her everyday car, a Toyota Camry.

The Publix in New Smyrna Beach was almost always busy, and Summer was thankful she hadn't driven the Mustang when she saw how full the lot was. Grabbing a cart and trying to get around the baked goods and deli area without running over a child, she ran instead right into Lacey Stevens.

"Why Summer," Lacey said in her fake little girl, sultry voice. "Where's that big sexy husband of yours?"

Summer wanted to punch her in the face, but seeing that it was Sunday, and she was a respectable member of the community, she decided to take the high road. Or at least the middle road. Returning Lacey's fake smile she replied, "Well the last time I saw him he was sitting on the toilet reading the Sunday paper," and with that she walked away. *Let that image stick in Lacey's bobble head*, she thought to herself, and moved on through the store.

Groceries purchased and safely packed in the car, Summer smiled all the way home thinking about how she had handled Lacey. For the first time since Friday night, she was feeling more like her normal, positive self, looking forward to a fun evening with friends, and getting back to work the next day.

Calling out, "I'm home," when she walked in the door, Summer was met with silence. Michael was not in his den, which meant he was probably still on the deck. Lying back in the lounge chair, the newspaper on his chest, she found him sound asleep.

Not wanting to disturb him, but worried that he was getting too much sun, Summer lowered the awning so that it covered him and went inside to start the cake. The whole time she was mixing and measuring, she hummed to herself and wondered what Michael would say when she told him about her encounter with Lacey Stevens? He wouldn't like what she had said he was doing; she knew that, but Lacey had it coming, right?

She was just pulling the cake out of the oven when Michael walked into the kitchen, his face red and wrinkled from sleep and sun. "Hey," he said, running his hands over his face. "Why did you let me sleep so long?"

"Because you said you didn't sleep well last night," she reminded him, "and because I know how hard you work." Setting the cake down on the cooling rack, Summer put her arms around her husband and pulled him in close.

"Let's not fight anymore," she whispered in his ear.

"Were we fighting?" he said, rubbing his hands up and down her spine.

"Well, we might be after I tell you about seeing Lacey Stevens at Publix, but before you get too upset, remember that I made you your favorite cake."

The evening with Bree and Dan was just what she needed, Summer thought as they were driving home. Good friends, good food and a beautiful Florida sunset was enough to put anyone back in a happy mood. Michael held her hand as he drove, even pulling it to his lips for a kiss, and once again she thought, *My life is blessed.*

After turning off the downstairs lights, they moved quietly up the stairs, neither speaking so as not to break the spell. As soon as they were inside their bedroom, Michael pulled Summer into his arms and gave her a long passionate kiss. She could hardly breathe as the kiss moved to her neck and the top of her shoulder, and as she melted into him, the need she had been feeling broke free.

Michael hadn't made love to her like this for months, and Summer couldn't get enough. Sure, they'd had sex occasionally, but not the hot, steamy, you turn me on kind that she was so desperate for. He took special care to kiss and caress all her sweet spots, and when it was over, they were both gasping to catch their breaths. Pulling her onto his shoulder, Michael kissed his wife's hair and stroked her supple back. "I know I don't say it often enough, Summer, but I love you; I love you so much."

Smiling in the dark, Summer stroked Michael's chest, and told him that she loved him, too. It was a magical moment, and one that she had been waiting on for such a long time. Closing her eyes, she thought, *there'll be no mystery man dreams tonight*, and those thoughts took her into deep sleep.

Chapter 20

Monday morning dawned bright and clear, and Summer stretched and sighed before getting out of bed. She could hear Michael in the shower as she moved into the bathroom to wash her face and was pleasantly surprised when he called out to her.

"Good morning sunshine," he said, through the shower door. "Did you sleep well?"

Summer almost purred she felt so good. "I slept amazingly well," she answered, pretty sure that Michael could hear the smile in her voice. "And how about you?"

He opened the steam-covered door and stood unabashedly naked, starring almost through her soul. "Best night's sleep in months," he winked. "I think maybe we've found an alternative to sleeping pills."

Summer laughed and threw on her robe, agreeing that a good orgasm, or make that two good orgasms, was better than taking a pharmaceutical.

Once downstairs, she started the coffee and opened a package of fresh blueberry bagels for Michael's drive into Daytona. The coffee was hot, and the bagel was cooked to perfection when Michael appeared in the kitchen, and like every weekday morning she handed them to him, he kissed her cheek, and patted her behind, and was out the door.

For a moment after Michael left for work, Summer stood there perplexed. The night before they had the best sex she could remember for a long time, and in the bathroom, they had teased and flirted with each other, so what had changed in the fifteen minutes she had been in the kitchen fixing his breakfast?

Pouring her own cup of coffee, she went into the living room and got comfortable in her rocker. Confused over how quickly her husband's persona could change, she rocked and sipped her coffee, before picking up her devotional and starting her morning.

She had always loved the quiet of the morning. In the winter, the sky was dark, and she huddled up with her coffee and a quilt, thinking about Michael and the boys, and occasionally even let her mind drift back to the short time she held her twin daughters. In the spring and summer, she liked watching the light dance across the windows, almost like it was inviting her to come outside and play.

Today the light was doing all it could to catch her attention, but Summer was in her own little world. *Does romance mean so little to men?* she asked herself. *How can Michael not feel how important that connection is to me?* Receiving no answer, she picked up her devotional, and started reading about the goodness of God, and before long she was back in her zone.

Devotions and coffee finished, Summer went upstairs to get ready for the day. She was fighting off some nervous energy because today was the day she and Jake Ross were going to start work in earnest on his website, and she wanted things to go well. After throwing on a pair of yoga pants and a tank top, she headed to her computer and logged in.

As with every morning, emails were the first thing to be checked and getting rid of advertisements and trash; she scrolled down to one from Jake.

Good Morning, Ms. Alcott,

I truly appreciate your willingness to taking on my project at such a late date, and I'm committed to helping you in any way that I can. I would love to discuss some more ideas with you today if you're available.

My plan is to be in the office all day and I would like to hear from you as soon as possible. I'll be at my desk and ready to get started.

Best,

Jake Ross

Summer read the email again, wanting to make sure she handled this in just the right way. She had known from the onset that the project Jake Ross had in mind was going to take most of her time, but she needed him to be aware that she had other clients besides him. After answering emails from a couple of other customers, she went back to the one from Jake Ross and replied.

Dear Mr. Ross,

Why don't we set nine o'clock Pacific time each morning as our time to connect? That will give me mornings and late afternoons to work on your website and my other commitments, and it will give you time to market your new blog. I know we are on a time crunch here, but I too am committed to making this project exactly what you have in mind.

Sincerely,

Summer Alcott

The Four Seasons of Summer

407. 756.3510

She hit send, and then stared at the computer for a moment like an immediate answer would appear. And then it did! Summer felt a little shaky as she opened the new email from Jake Ross, knowing that in the business world a response to an email could take hours, sometimes even days. *Was he just sitting there waiting to hear from me?* she thought. It was before six in the morning in California, but as she read the email a smile came across her face.

"Deal! I'll be on at 9:00a.m," was all it said, but for Summer it meant so much more. Maybe Jake Ross wasn't as broken as Cooper thought he was, because his response was light and easy, and nothing like she was expecting.

With a sigh, Summer filled her Outlook calendar with appointments for Jake, and then began looking through the rest of her emails.

Just before noon in Florida, she finished the last of her email correspondence and went to the kitchen for another cup of coffee. She knew she had probably had enough, after all her hands were already trembling a little, but she also was certain that was more about her upcoming online meeting with Jake Ross than an over indulgence of caffeine.

Chapter 21

The meeting with Jake Ross went well, and Summer was eager to get started on some ideas by the time they signed off. He had seemed very relaxed in his emails, and she took that as a good sign. Maybe her comment to Bree about him being *morose* had been unfounded.

It was almost two o'clock before she found time to take a break for a snack. A big container of her famous homemade paella base was thawing out in the fridge for dinner, so that meant an extra light lunch. A few baby carrots and low-fat cheese stick in her hand, she grabbed a can of Diet Coke and headed to the deck.

Summer loved their backyard, and even with the stifling heat of Florida, she felt peaceful and content. The food didn't quite fill her stomach, but the beautiful cerulean blue skies and the bougainvillea blooming around the fence more than filled her soul. *Was it possible to feel anymore gratified than this?* she wondered.

Taking the last sip of the now warm soda, she grudgingly got up from the Adirondack chair and headed back inside. It wasn't that she didn't love her web design business or that she was averse to hard work, but for some reason Jake Ross had gotten in her head, and she wasn't sure that was a good thing.

By four thirty, Summer had several things put together for Jake, as well as helping a new hair salon owner who was struggling with the vision for her new website. Feeling as if her afternoon had been successful, she climbed the stairs to the bedroom, hoping that a shower would help with the kinks in her neck.

The shower felt wonderful and so did the Philosophy Hula Girl body wash. The smell of Hawaii filled her senses, and for a moment she was back in Maui with Michael, where they had celebrated their twenty-fifth wedding anniversary. Oh, what a wonderful time they had! Strolling the streets of Lahaina, driving the Road to Hana, and making love, glorious, uninhibited love! It was a memory that was etched in her heart forever.

After drying off, Summer slathered herself with Hula Girl Whipped Body Soufflé and followed it with several big squirts of body spritz in the same fragrance. "Maybe Michael will want to create some of that Maui magic," she said out loud, and then for good measure, gave herself another dousing of the light and delicious smelling scent.

Stepping into a black thong and red shorts, Summer pulled a form-fitting white T-shirt from her dresser and slipped it over her head, sans a bra! *Let's see what Mr. Alcott things about this,* she giggled, and then with a swipe of strawberry lip gloss and a dusting of blush, she was running down the stairs with ideas of being the antipasto before dinner!

A pitcher of Sangria was chilling in the refrigerator along with a big green salad, and flaky, buttery bread was ready to pop in the oven while the saffron rice cooked and the sauce simmered on the stove. Summer was feeling a little giddy with her seduction plan and decided a small glass of sangria might help calm her nerves.

The cool, fruity concoction was smooth and delicious, and she was about ready to pour herself another glass when she heard Michael pull into the driveway. Shifting gears, she fixed a glass for each of them and stood by the kitchen door, waiting to give her husband a proper welcome home.

Sometimes surprises were good and sometimes Murphy's Law took over, and this was one of those times. Michael pushed the door open with his shoulder, his hands filled with big black binders, running right into Summer and spilling sangria all over her white T-shirt. And if that wasn't enough, behind Michael stood Elliott Stevens.

The two men just stared at her, and Summer was pretty sure she had died and gone to hell. The wine had soaked in quickly and she now looked like a contestant in a wet T-shirt contest. Realizing that her boobs were on display for the slimiest man in town, she covered her chest with her arms while giving Michael a glare that would scare the dead.

"Did I forget to tell you that Elliott was coming over tonight, so we could work on the hospital board books?" he asked sheepishly.

Summer was irate! No, he hadn't told her about Elliott coming over, if he had she would have gone to Bree's and let them order takeout. Instead, here she stood, smooth and smelling like coconut and mango, sangria covering her almost naked chest, and Michael's favorite dinner ready to go. And that didn't even cover her little seduction plan.

Summer shook her head and scurried up the stairs as fast as her feet would carry her. She hated that she was this emotional in front of Elliott because she knew he would go home and tell Lacey, but she couldn't help it. Another minute in the kitchen and she would have burst into tears or hit her husband upside the head. Sadly, she was afraid it might have been both.

Michael was right behind her, but one look at his wife's face told him he'd better keep his mouth shut. He watched as Summer angrily pulled the now ruined T-shirt over her head and then said, "I was sure I had told you."

Throwing her shirt at him Summer growled, "Go back to your guest, Michael," she hissed, "I'll be down in a minute.

Summer heard him mumble, "Women." as he closed the door, and that was all it took for the sobbing to begin.

Chapter 22

"When did I become such an emotional mess?" Summer asked herself out loud. Several of her friends had confided that they had mood swings when they went through the change, but Summer had been lucky in that respect. One month she had a period, and the next month she didn't, and that had been the end of that. No hot flashes, or any of the uncomfortable parts of growing older, but was she having them now?

Putting on a bra and a loose-fitting blouse, Summer added some concealer under her now puffy eyes, let out a big sigh, and headed downstairs. Maybe if she acted normally around Elliot, he would forget to share her little meltdown with Lacey. Sure, and maybe manatees could fly!

Michael and Elliott were enjoying the pitcher of Sangria in the dining room, folders and reports spread out around them. Like a southern gentleman, Elliott stood up when Summer entered the room, but Michael just looked up at her, almost afraid of what she would do. But despite growing up in Ohio, Summer knew how to be a lady, so she just smiled, and got the dishes out of the china cabinet.

"Dinner will be in about forty-five minutes," she said as sweetly as possible. "Will you be done by then, or should we eat in the kitchen?"

Elliott looked at Michael, obviously not used to a wife who actually made dinner for him and waited for his response. "I'm not sure if we'll be done, but we'll move all this to the den, so we can eat in here," Michael told her, his voice dripping with charm. "Your dinners deserve to be eaten in the dining room, not the kitchen."

Damn him! Summer thought. *Why did he have to be so thoughtful when she was still so mad?* But needing to keep up the pretense with Elliott, she gave Michael's shoulder a soft caress, and nodded. But before leaving the room she grabbed a large wine glass, and the pitcher of Sangria. If you can't beat them, you might as well join them, right?

By the time the rice was perfectly cooked and added to the fragrant paella medley, and the bread was toasty and brown, Summer had downed three glasses of Sangria, not caring that Michael and Elliott hadn't even gotten a refill. She knew overindulging in alcohol was not a good thing for her, but the fruity beverage went down smoothly, and after the first glass, well, really the second if you counted the one before the men got home, she was feeling no pain.

Michael came into the kitchen to see if he could help and found his wife twirling her now empty glass in her fingers. Seeing that the pitcher was empty of anything other than some wine-soaked citrus fruit, he took the glass from Summer's hand and pulled her in close to him.

"Did you enjoy the Sangria?" he asked with a chuckle. He was certain all the imbibing was her way of defusing her anger, but boy, Summer Alcott was fun when she was tipsy.

"As I matter of fact, I did," she said trying to act indignant, "and I'd like a refill, please," she added, trying to retrieve the glass from the counter.

"Unfortunately, the Sangria has run out, but it looks like dinner is ready, so how about we eat?" Summer tried to wiggle out of his clasp, but Michael held on.

"I really am sorry about tonight, Summer," he told her, nibbling gently on her neck.

The heat from the wine and the heat from Michael's nuzzling was enough to make her lose her resolve, and just as she was ready to give her husband a full-on kiss, Elliott appeared in the kitchen.

"Everything okay in here?" he asked. And like that, the spell was broken.

***

Summer did her best to stay pleasant throughout the meal, but it wasn't an easy task. Elliott was slurping his paella, and even with one of her good linen napkins tucked into the collar of his shirt, little flakes of sauce and rice were flying everywhere. The noises he was making reminded her of a bad porn movie, and if she hadn't been so mad it would have been comical.

She looked up one time to see Michael rolling his eyes but wasn't sure if that was for their guest's poor manners, or because he knew Summer was unhappy. Regardless, she kept her thoughts to herself and did her best to rush things along. Normally she would have offered coffee and dessert, but tonight she just started clearing the table the moment Elliott laid down his fork.

"That was the best meal I've had since dinner at Mama's," he told her sincerely. "I need to get that recipe, so Lacey can have the cook make it for us." With his napkin still around his neck, and sauce dripping down the front of his shirt, Elliott Stevens looked like anything other than a man who had a cook. But it didn't really matter because her sauce was her secret, and the last person Summer would share it with was Lacey.

She smiled at him as if to say "of course," but no actual words came out of her mouth as she picked up his plate. Michael stood up and tried to help, but Summer shooed him away. She was still mad at him, and it was hard to keep that fire fueled when he did something nice.

The dishwasher running and the food all put away, Summer crept upstairs without even stopping to say goodnight. She could hear the men in the den discussing hospital business, so she knew her getaway would go unnoticed. What a day it had been. The online meeting with Jake Ross had been great, the dinner with Michael and Elliott not so much.

After throwing her clothes in a pile on the floor, instead of taking them to the laundry chute, Summer climbed into bed and thought back over the events of the last twelve hours. She was just about to turn out the light and close her eyes when she heard an odd ping coming from her dirty clothes. Realizing that her cell phone was still in her shorts pocket she got up to see what the noise was.

"A message?" she questioned, looking at the blue circle inside a white square with a white lightning bolt in the middle. Clicking on the app she read that Jake Ross wanted to connect with her on Messenger. Thinking that something must be wrong she accepted the message only to read, "I really like your ideas for my website. Can't wait to talk with you tomorrow. Jake"

Summer turned off the phone and got back into bed, a huge smile covering her face. *He likes my ideas*, she thought to herself with a smile. She could hear Michael coming up the stairs, and because she didn't want the euphoric feeling she had to be replaced by an argument, she closed her eyes and did her best imitation of sleeping.

Michael turned off the light on her side of the bed and went into the bathroom to change. He climbed into bed quietly, as if he didn't want to wake her, and then said, "I know you're not asleep, Summer, but we don't have to talk about this now if you don't want to." He gave her a kiss on the cheek, rolled over, and went to sleep.

Chapter 23

In her haste to feign sleeping the night before, Summer had forgotten to set the alarm on her bedside table, and for some reason her internal alarm hadn't gone off either. Instead of waking up to the usual soft music, she heard instead Michael's swearing as he jumped out of bed.

"The alarm didn't go off," he yelled as he rifled through his closet. "I won't have time to wait for coffee, so you might as well stay in bed."

Like I could sleep, Summer thought, hearing the shower door slam. But even though she wasn't sleepy, laying in their big bed felt pretty indulgent, so she stretched, and yawned turning on her side so she could see Michael coming out of the bathroom.

He was rushing around when he realized that his wife was still curled up in bed. "You really aren't getting up?" he asked with a confused look on his face.

"Isn't staying in bed what you told me to do, Michael?" Summer responded. "I would have been happy to get up and make you coffee and…" Michael cut her off before she could finish her sentence.

"Never mind," he growled, "I'll get something at the coffee shop downtown."

"Suit yourself," she told him and turned over away from him.

Summer waited until she heard the garage door close and Michael's vehicle pulling out of the drive before she finally got out of bed. She truly did feel badly about forgetting to set the alarm, but judging by Michael's reaction, she knew that was one mistake she wouldn't own up to.

Between waking up late and the extra time in bed, she had just enough time to throw on some clothes, brush her hair, and make coffee for herself before a scheduled call with a longtime client. Taking a sip of the steaming brew from her favorite mug, Summer thought about Jake's message from the night before while she waited for her computer to come to life.

She knew that her cell phone number was on every email that she sent, so it was no mystery as to how he had found it, but why had he sent a message instead of a text? And why send her anything in the evening that wasn't an emergency when they already had a standing appointment every day? Summer was still contemplating the situation when she opened her email and saw the unopened envelope from Jake.

After his message last night, she hadn't been expecting to hear from him so soon, and for some reason that made her nervous. With apprehension Summer moved the mouse to Jakes unopened email, but as soon as she read the words, she smiled.

Dear Ms. Alcott,

I apologize if I was out of line sending you a message tonight, but I haven't been this excited about a project in a long time, and I just really wanted to tell you how much I like your ideas. If you don't feel that it was appropriate you can block me, and I won't be able to message you again.

However, if it's not a problem, you can send me a Facebook Friend request and we'll be able to chat whenever we need to. I'll let you make the call and I'll be fine with whatever you decide. But I hope that you agree.

Jake

Friend him on Facebook? The only Facebook friends she had were family members and Bree, did she want Jake to be able to send her messages? Deciding that it was all part of the job, Summer found her cell phone and sent Jake an invitation to be her friend. Her heart was racing, and it seemed as if she had just hit the send button when his confirmation popped up. *Welcome to the world of social media*, she thought to herself.

It was hard to contain the smile on her face when she got back to her computer and read a brand-new email from Jake. He told her again how much he liked what she had done so far and asked what else she had up her sleeve. Having someone appreciate her work and telling her that were huge ego builders, so teasingly she replied, "Just wait and see." But the kicker was when he told her that her picture on Facebook was gorgeous. And that was the moment that Summer Alcott and Jake Ross went from being business associates to being friends.

***

Summer tried to devote the rest of the day to work, but Jake was persistent with his messages. Since she had done as he asked and friended him on Facebook, they were now truly connected. Summer wasn't big on social media posting, but she found lots of posts on Jake's. So many in fact, that she wondered if his social media accounts were taking the place of actual friendships.

After finally telling him that she had work that needed attention, they typed in their goodbyes, but instead of putting her phone away she pulled up Jake's Facebook profile and began looking at the pictures. Immediately, visions of his late wife Beth filled the screen, and Summer was overcome with both sadness for the loss of such a vibrant woman, and awe for the beauty she had been.

How does someone ever get over such a tragic loss? She thought and wondered what she could do to help him heal. The words *just be a friend*, came to her, and she decided right then it was what she would do.

She put her phone away and worked for about an hour, and then realized she was hungry and needed a break. The refrigerator held nothing enticing but the leftovers from last night, and Summer knew she'd never be able to eat paella again without seeing Elliott Steven's smarmy face. Packaging everything up, she decided to take the leftovers to Bree and then make a needed run to Publix. She grabbed the keys to the Toyota and headed out the door, thinking about the toasted coconut yogurt she was going to buy for her lunch.

Just seeing Bree always brought a smile to Summer's face. She loved her friend like a sister and knew that all of her secret thoughts and feelings were safe in Bree's hands. "Hey, Lady," Bree said, pulling her in for a hug. "What brings you here in the middle of a work day? Does the boss know you're playing hooky?"

It was a big joke between them that Summer was the only employee, thus making her the boss as well as every needed position in *Four Seasons of Summer*. Handing her friend the sack of goodies from the night before, Summer shared the whole Elliot Stevens incident with her.

"I know I shouldn't laugh," Bree said, trying not to crack a smile, "but I'd have given anything to see Elliott's face when you were standing there with your wine covered T-shirt. That man hasn't seen a pair of real boobs in so long he probably didn't even know what he was looking at."

At that point, both women were laughing, and Summer realized it was just what she needed. "I wish I could stay and we could make fun of Lacey some more, but I want to pick up some salmon for dinner, and I may wilt away to nothing if I don't get some yogurt in me soon."

"You and your diets, Summer," Bree scolded. "One of these days you're going to take it too far."

"You are definitely good for my ego, Bree," Summer said truthfully, "but my husband works with young, gorgeous women every day, and weight has a way of creeping up on me. But you don't need to worry, I always eat healthy, I just don't overdo."

The women hugged again, and Summer headed out into the sultry Florida afternoon. She needed to buy groceries, she was behind in her work, but first things first. No longer able to wait until she got home to have something to eat, she ran through the local drive through and ordered a cheeseburger and a Diet Coke. Sometimes a girl just had to do what a girl had to do. And what Bree didn't know wouldn't hurt her, right?

Chapter 24

It was still a little early for the afterwork grocery rush, which made it easy for Summer to maneuver down the aisles. Deciding on asparagus with a Dijon-Lemon sauce, roasted fingerling potatoes, and fresh grilled salmon for dinner, Summer grabbed her needed items and headed to the check stand. She was just about to get in line when her unfortunate lunch choice crossed her mind. Pulling the cart back, Summer headed to the dairy isle where she grabbed a four pack of Lite and Fit Toasted Coconut Greek yogurt, and then back to produce for a bag of her favorite Pink Lady apples.

Food emergency taken care of and groceries safely in the back seat, Summer headed for home. She really wanted to get in a little more work, but as Bree had pointed out, she was the boss. After unloading her purchases and putting everything away, Summer decided to close down her computer, freshen up, grab a glass of pinot grigio, and read for a little bit before Michael arrived home.

Before logging off, she made sure there were no important emails waiting for her, and fortunately there weren't. That meant no emails from Jake either, and for some reason that bothered her. It wasn't like they were bosom buddies or anything, but she had enjoyed their communication that morning and was secretly hoping for more. *Oh well,* she thought, *now I can spend more time getting engrossed in* The Middle Passage.

After stepping out of her workday outfit and giving herself a nice spritz of her favorite rosewater spray, Summer felt fresh and rejuvenated. After the fiasco the night before, she put on a pair of stretch capris and a tank top, not about to try the whole seductress bit again.

She didn't know if Michael would bring up the incident with Elliott Stevens or not, but she had decided not to if he didn't. She'd had a great day, and the last thing she wanted was to think about Elliott slurping up her fabulous paella, or worse yet, ogling her wine drenched boobs.

A cold glass of pinot in her hand, Summer grabbed her book and her phone and headed for the deck. The air was still hot and heavy, but positioning an Adirondack chair under the awning, the temperature felt ten degrees cooler. She took a big sip of the fragrant wine and was just about to lose herself in the amazing story of Margaret and John's journey across the Atlantic, when her phone dinged, signaling that she had a message.

It was hard to keep the smile off her face because she knew the message was from Jake. No one else had ever sent her a message, so it had to be from her new client and friend.

I have a dinner to attend tonight for one of Beth's charities, but I wanted to tell you how much I enjoyed our talk this morning and I hope you have a great evening. J

The smile that had started on her face was working its way down her body and Summer felt trembly all over. It wasn't a big deal, just a message from a business associate, yet for some reason Summer found herself back in high school and being passed a note from the cute boy sitting next to her in French class.

She finished the wine and would have gone back for more, but the garage door going up signaled that Michael was home. No more daydreaming about messages from Jake Ross or losing herself in the life of a beautiful anthropologist, it was time to greet her husband at the door and go back to her role as Michael Alcott's wife.

When Michael stepped into the kitchen, Summer was more than surprised to see a bouquet of beautiful yellow tulips in his hand. Michael had never been a *flowers* kind of guy, and for a moment Summer just stared at him. With the smile of a boy getting his hand caught in the cookie jar on his face, Michael handed her the flowers without saying a word. Not sure if he was expecting her to start the conversation or not, Summer took the bouquet and turned around to get a vase.

"Uh, Summer," Michael stuttered awkwardly, "I'm really sorry about last night. I thought I had told you about Elliott coming over, but I realize the thoughtful thing to do would have been to call and remind you. I know you were embarrassed, and anyway, it was my fault."

Summer looked at her husband as if he had sprouted wings. Michael Alcott was not one to admit he might have made a mistake, and the fact that he had made her suspicious.

"I understand, Michael," she said with a smile. "You're a very busy man with lots of responsibilities, it's only natural that sometimes things slip your mind."

"Yes!" he exclaimed. "That's what Jana said." Michael looked at his wife triumphantly, as if he had just answered the fifty-thousand-dollar question, and then he realized his mistake.

"Jana, your assistant?" Summer asked coolly. "You told your assistant about last night and my humiliation in front of Elliott Stevens? You took what was already a mortifying evening for me into your place of business and shared it with your coworkers? Oh, what a good laugh they must of all had." By now Summer's voice was getting louder and her hurt was getting deeper.

"It wasn't like that, Summer," Michael told her. "You need to let me explain."

Summer crossed her arms over her chest, her knees shaking, and her voice quivering. "Okay," she answered, "explain."

Chapter 25

Summer was seething as she listened to Michael's explanation as to why he had felt it was okay for him to discuss their private life with his coworkers, his female coworkers at that. Not once did she interrupt, or question something he said, and when he was finally done talking, she held her head high and walked out of the room.

"Summer!" Michael yelled after her. "That's it? You're going to walk away without saying a word? What the fuck is going on with you?"

Michael wasn't really given to swearing, so Summer knew he was at his breaking point. The thing is, she didn't care. As far as she was concerned, their marriage was out of control, and she didn't know how to rein it back in.

Squaring her shoulders to her full five-foot nine-inch height, Summer did her best to look Michael in the eye. Jabbing him in the chest with her finger she let loose on all the emotions she'd been holding inside.

"I'll tell you what the fuck is going on with me," she hissed. "I'm your wife, your partner, the mother of your children, but I deserve so much more. What happened to passion and romance, Michael, to flirting and being playful? I feel like your mother most of the time, or as you call me, June Cleaver. I want to be your lover, the person you cherish over all others, but lately that feeling has been few and far between."

When she stopped to catch her breath, Michael retaliated. "How about the other night?" he questioned, "Or the morning in the bathroom?" He smirked, thinking he had one upped her, but Summer wasn't backing down.

"I'll agree, Sunday night was wonderful, but by Monday morning you were back to being the man of the house and I felt like the hired help. And do you really want to relive the promises you made on Friday morning when you were too drunk, and too blindsided by Lacey Stevens to follow through with them on Friday night?"

Michael scrubbed his hands over his face, realizing he was in dangerous territory, but he couldn't let it drop. "What does any of this have to do with me mentioning to Jana what happened last night? Isn't that what you're really upset about?" The look on his wife's face told him he had just gone too far.

Summer spoke so softly that it was almost frightening. "I've loved and supported you for thirty-five years Michael Alcott, knowing that marrying me was not in the plan for your life. But I'm fifty-eight years old and I'm tired of always thinking of you and how things will affect the mighty Michael. Maybe none of this makes sense to you, and maybe my thoughts are all over the place, but it gets down to this. Before I get another day older, I want romance and passion and sex so hot it will burn your skin. I don't want to get old being filled with regrets, so I'm telling you now what my expectations are. Now it's up to you to tell me whether you can live up to them or not."

Summer was shaking she was so angry, and from the color of Michael's face she could tell that he was, too. "I had salmon ready to go on the grill," she told him, "but I think I'll put it in the freezer for another night. I'm going to fix myself a peanut butter and jelly sandwich and a glass of milk and go upstairs to read. I'm sure you can find something to eat around here, but just in case you're looking for the leftovers from last night, I took them to Bree's."

Michael mumbled something about not being hungry, went into the kitchen for a beer, and headed to the deck.

***

By the time Summer got upstairs with her sandwich and milk, she realized that her book was still out on the deck, and facing Michael was the last thing she wanted to do. They rarely even had arguments and now

71

twice in one week they'd had real fights, and that bothered her. It bothered her a lot. Was their marriage in trouble, or was she really going through some kind of a midlife crisis?

The peanut butter was sticking to the roof of her mouth, and the milk wasn't really helping, so with a sigh Summer put her dishes on the dresser and lay down on the bed. *Maybe there's a good movie on*, she thought, but unfortunately at this hour it was all game shows or gossip TV, masquerading as news. Flipping through the channels she stopped when the words BREAKING NEWS ran across the screen.

The picture of a car, the front end smashed beyond recognition, was etched in her mind as she listened to the reporter talk about the tragic accident on US Highway 4 outside of Orlando. A family on their way to Disney World had been cut off by a driver in an SUV trying to go from the far-left lane to the far-right lane to exit, causing the car to flip several times before hitting the cement median. According to the reporter, no one in the car had survived, but the driver of the SUV had walked away without a scratch.

The emotion of the day was more than she could handle, and before she could even catch her breath, Summer was sobbing into her pillow. It was at that minute that Michael came into the bedroom.

"I'm sorry, Summer," he said, pulling her towards his chest. "I had no idea you were unhappy or needed more attention. I love you; don't you know that? And as for my plans to marry you, they were always there, just maybe not as quickly as they happened."

Summer nodded against his strong warm chest, the tears starting to slow down. "I do know that you love me, Michael, intellectually that is, but that doesn't mean that I don't need you to show me that love. Do you understand what I'm saying?"

She looked up at her husband's deep gray eyes and saw confusion in them. "I need more attention," Summer continued. "In the bedroom, yes, but just in our everyday life. Our marriage has always been strong, but let's be kids again and just have fun."

Michael kissed the top of her head and pulled her in tighter. "I'll try," he said softly. "I promise I'll try."

"That's all I ask," she said lifting her face to smile at him. "We have so much, Michael. I feel selfish to want more, but I still do. Now how about we go downstairs, and I make us some scrambled eggs? I'm sure you're starving, and my sandwich didn't quite cut it, either."

"Or," he said with a sly grin, "why don't you get into bed, and I'll bring a tray up that we can share."

"It's the best offer I've had all day," she beamed, as she headed to the bathroom to get ready for bed.

Less than twenty minutes later Michael entered the room carrying a tray holding a plate of fluffy scrambled eggs, two English muffins smothered with Summer's favorite black raspberry jam, one fork, and one large glass of orange juice.

"It's breakfast in bed for supper," he told her, "like we use to have when we first got married."

Summer had forgotten those late-night suppers they had shared in bed while they tried to work around each other's schedules. And more than that, she had forgotten about the very special dessert they had enjoyed afterwards. Watching her still handsome husband trying to scoop up the eggs for her to taste, she hoped that he still remembered.

Chapter 26

For several days everything was close to being perfect. Michael was affectionate and attentive, and during their Friday night date to Breakers he didn't look at the TV once. And when Summer told him it was okay to catch the score of the game; he took her hand and shook his head. Even between the sheets he was really trying, and although it took him a few minutes for her to see evidence of his desire, Summer believed him when he told her it was more of an age thing, and nothing to do with her.

On Saturday morning Michael fixed French toast and sausage, reminding Summer that she'd worn off a lot of calories the night before and needed to keep up her strength. She blushed and gave him a sly smile, thankful for this wonderful new version of her husband.

"I hate to leave you," Michael told her as they cleaned up the kitchen together, "but I have a big client meeting on Monday, so I need to get some work done today."

Summer nodded and tried not to let him see the disappointment she was feeling. They'd been talking about getting new living room furniture, and her plan had been to suggest they drive to Deland this afternoon and start the search. But she knew how important being prepared was for Michael, and if he had to work on a Saturday, she was going to be understanding and supportive.

"I could catch up on some things, too," she said, trying to sound cheerful, "you go on and get your work done and I'll have wine and cheese waiting on the deck when you get home. Anything sound good for dinner?"

"How about that salmon you put in the freezer the other night?" Michael said with a wink. "It should be a nice enough evening we can eat outside."

Summer snapped him with the dishtowel and then gave him a big kiss. "Get out of here," she teased. "Go make beautiful buildings that our grandchildren can enjoy."

Hearing the word grandchildren wiped the smile off of Michael's face. "You don't know something I don't know, do you?" he questioned. Neither of their sons were married and while he would have been fine for Cooper to be thinking long term, he knew if either of them was close to parenthood, it would be Riley.

"Oh, for heaven's sake!" Summer laughed. "It was just a comment and nothing more. I mean I hope we have grandchildren one day, but I don't see that in the near future."

Michael gave a relieved sigh and headed to the den for his briefcase. Amazingly, since their blowup he had taken it to the den every evening when he came home, without Summer saying a word. She watched him grab his things and then wondered if any women would be working today. In his dark washed jeans and light blue button-down shirt, he looked sexier than in one of his expense suits. And that was saying a lot.

He kissed her goodbye, lingering a little longer than usual, swatted her on the behind and walked out the door. Summer grabbed another mug of coffee and headed to her rocker for her morning devotions. How was she feeling? Only one word described it. Blessed.

Devotions read, coffee mug empty, Summer bowed her head and prayed. She had always been a believer and tried her best to be a good faithful servant, but like most people, she struggled from time to time. She had asked for forgiveness every morning since lashing out at Michael, but she had also given thanks. The words she had said had been hurtful; she knew that, but the results had been amazing. At the end of the prayer, she asked for discernment in the way she discussed conflicts with her husband, and then headed to the computer to get in a little extra work herself.

***

It was three o'clock before she knew it and Summer was proud of the work she'd accomplished. She had a first draft of the website ready for Jake to look at on Monday morning and had completely wrapped up *Delilah's Dawgs.* Hoping that Michael might be home soon, she put a bottle of Mango Mama wine and two wine glasses in the freezer so they would be extra cold and took a wedge of their favorite cheese out to soften. The salmon had been thawing in the fridge for several hours, so all she needed to do now was prepare the vegetables and plan for a wonderful night.

Summer was humming all the way to the bathroom, daydreaming about the evening ahead. Her favorite wine and cheese on the deck, Michael grilling the salmon while they each talked about their day, and then later, one piece of Key Lime pie for them to share. It would be a magical Florida evening, and it was making her feel hot and cold all over thinking about it.

When Summer came down the stairs, the first thing she noticed was Michael's briefcase sitting on the island in the kitchen. She decided not to read too much into it but when she moved the briefcase to the den, she found Michael slumped over his laptop, a beer sweating profusely on the beautiful teakwood desk, no coaster in sight.

Summer stepped up behind him and put her arms around his shoulders. At her touch, Michael immediately tensed up. "Is everything alright?" she asked.

Michael rubbed his hand over his face and turned around. "No, everything is not alright," he replied in a snarky manner. "Bob Lucas called an emergency meeting for the hospital board on Monday night, and that's the day of my big client presentation. The meeting wasn't supposed to have been until next Monday, so Elliot and I thought we still had another week to go back over the books and have all of the financial information together, but now it looks like I'm going to be working night and day if I want to be prepared. On top of that, I still don't have my client presentation all the way done."

"Maybe if you explained to him…" Summer started, but Michael cut her off.

"I already told him Monday was a disaster for me, but he doesn't give a shit. He's retired and doesn't have anything else in his life but being mister big shot president of the hospital board and that makes him feel important." Michael reached for his beer and took a big swig. "Looks like I'm going to be working all weekend, so you may want to put the salmon back in the freezer."

As much as she hated to say it, Summer asked if having Elliott come over to help wouldn't be the answer, but Michael shook his head. "I've already tried," he said with a huff. "He took Lacey away for the weekend." Summer shook her head, knowing that it was either cook the salmon tonight or throw it away. "You go ahead and work on your books," she said, trying to keep the hurt out of her voice, "and I'll grill the salmon. I'll even bring you a plate when it's done." Before turning away, she picked up his beer bottle and tried not to focus on the ring it had left on the desk. Laying a coaster down beside it she gave him back the beer and walked out of the room.

By now the wine was frosty cold and Summer thought, *why not?* She opened the bottle and filled her glass to the brim, loving the icy crystals that had formed. She knew that wine connoisseurs would not approve of her chilling methods, but as far as she was concerned on a warm Florida evening, nothing beat sharing a bottle of Mango Mamma wine on the deck with the man she loved.

She cut herself a few thin slices of cheese, grabbed a handful of crackers, and her wine, and went outside. Yes, her plans had been ruined, but it made her remember the words from a Robert Burns poem, *the best laid plans of mice and men often go awry.* Not wanting to ruin the wonderful days they'd been having, Summer plopped down in a lounge chair to enjoy her snack before starting the grill.

The late afternoon sun was still warm and bright, the wine was smooth and cold, and the cheese was soft and delicious. Summer let out a sigh of frustration and closed her eyes. No matter what, she loved her life, and yes, she was blessed. Right?

Chapter 27

When Summer took Michael his dinner, he barely acknowledged her. She set the plate to the side of the desk along with a glass of cold iced tea. She knew Michael was frustrated, but too much beer was not the solution to his problem. She gave him a light kiss on the top of his head and then settled in the kitchen to eat her own dinner. Alone.

The salmon that had sounded so fabulous a few hours ago didn't even register on Summer's taste buds, and in her stupor over Michael having to work on a Saturday night, she'd let the vegetables overcook. "Oh well," she said out loud, "It won't hurt me to miss a meal."

After tossing the food in the kitchen trash and taking the bag out to the garbage in the garage, Summer cleaned up the kitchen and poured herself another glass of wine. It was when she was putting the bottle back in the fridge that Summer spied the pie and thought, *why not?* Afterall, she had barely eaten any dinner and since Michael hadn't touched his plate, she was sure dessert wasn't on his mind. Besides, the pie was to have been a surprise, he didn't even know she had bought it.

Michael was still slumped over the laptop when she went in to tell him she was going up to bed to read, but he mumbled something back that kind of sounded like, "Goodnight." Summer grabbed her wine and her pie and put her cell phone in her pocket. Ever since she had friended Jake Ross on Facebook she took it with her everywhere, and tonight was no exception. After climbing the stairs to the master suite, she slipped out of her clothes, pulled on a T-shirt, and plopped into bed. Her dog-eared copy of *The Middle Passage* was laying on the nightstand, and taking a big sip of the now warm Mango Mamma wine, she settled into the captivating story of Margaret and John.

She was just getting lost in the historical story full of fear and hardship when she heard the now familiar ping, signaling she had an incoming message. She smiled knowing the message was from Jake, but as soon as she opened it, the smile quickly faded.

Tonight's dinner was another evening with a group of boring socialites, all telling me how wonderful Beth had been and how was I able to go on without her? Yes, she was wonderful, more than wonderful, and living without her is the hardest thing I've ever had to do, but don't they realize how difficult it is for me to keep having these conversations? I'm mentally and physically exhausted but for some reason I just needed to talk to you.

Summer thought long and hard before replying. After all, Jake Ross was her client, and she wasn't his confidant, but knowing that he had turned to her when he was hurting did something to her heart. She took a deep breath and then responded.

I'm so sorry this happened, Jake. People can be unthinkably cruel sometimes, and I'm sure that's the case here. I won't tell you that I understand what all you're going through, but I will tell you that if I can help in any way, I'm happy to.

And so, it began. Jake sent a message about his life, and how hard the last few years had been since the accident, and Summer gave him all the strength and the comfort she could. They communicated through messenger for almost two hours, and it was only when Summer looked at the clock and started to worry about Michael that she finally told Jake she needed to say goodnight.

Jake thanked her for spending time with him, telling her how much it had meant and ended the conversation by saying, Thank you for listening. Summer read the words and then went downstairs in search of her missing husband.

To be honest, she expected to find Michael with his head drooping over the computer, but instead she found him going over spreadsheets, a pencil in his mouth and his fingers pecking on the keyboard.

"Michael?" Summer questioned. "Don't you think you need to give it a rest and come to bed?"

If he even heard her Summer would be surprised, but he did manage a small nod. Of course, he didn't stop or even slow down, so she took his glass into the kitchen and filled it with ice and water. Leaving it in the middle of the coaster, Summer sighed and headed back upstairs. Thoughts of Jake Ross and their conversation were swirling in her head like the eye of a hurricane, and she wanted nothing more than to lie down and put them to rest. But she had no sooner turned off the light when her phone pinged again. Reaching for it she saw the message, Goodnight my beautiful friend, and the tsunami in her heart broke free.

Chapter 28

Summer knew that it was probably wrong for her to feel so much pleasure at Jake's words, but she couldn't help herself. It wasn't as if they had done anything wrong, but this was the first time since meeting Michael that she had talked intimately with a man, and it felt delicious and shameful, all at the same time. As she turned off the light, and burrowed under the covers, Summer told herself that this would be a one-time thing that she wouldn't allow to happen again.

But happen again it did. Sometime in the night Michael had come to bed, she knew because his side was messy and had that *slept in* look, but he wasn't there when she got up. She found him in the kitchen, a mug of hot coffee in his hands,

"Oh Michael," she said as she looked at his tired face, "did you get any sleep at all?"

"I tossed and turned for about an hour and then decided it was better just to get up and go back to work. The good news is I should be done with the hospital report and my client presentation sometime this afternoon."

Summer got her own mug of coffee and took a drink before saying anything more. "Does that mean you're not going to church with me?" she asked softly.

"I can't stop now," he replied. "I think the Lord will understand."

Summer nodded and after another swig of coffee, turned towards the refrigerator. "Do you want eggs with bacon or ham?" she asked innocently.

"I had some cheese and crackers a couple of hours ago and I'm really too wired to eat anyway," he told her.

"You need a real meal, Michael," Summer protested. "Your body needs fuel."

"I said I'm not hungry," Michael snapped, took his coffee, and headed back to the den.

Summer tried to stop the hurt in her heart from forming at Michael's hateful words. She knew he was tired, or he wouldn't have reacted that way, but still she didn't feel as if she deserved them. Not interested in cooking for herself, she found the stash of cookies that she had put in the freezer for Michel and grabbed one of the giant-sized, pecan, chocolate chip delicacies and immediately bit into it. Even frozen it was delicious, and after refilling her mug, she went back upstairs to get ready for church.

Peeking outside the bedroom window, Summer could tell that it was going to be another beautiful Florida morning. She was about to pick out her clothes for church when she spied the piece of uneaten Key-Lime pie on the dresser. Her cheeks heated as she remembered it was because of her long talk with Jake that she had left the pie untouched, and as much as she hated throwing away more food, the pie was definitely past it's yumminess.

After cutting the pie in small chunks so she could flush them down the toilet, she moved to the large walk-in closet to find something to wear to church. Did she feel guilty about disposing of the pie like a thief in the night? Maybe, but not enough that she was ever going to disclose her secret to her husband. Michael liked her thin, and he didn't understand why food was such an issue for her, which was the reason she tried to keep her eating habits to herself.

Deciding on an Ann Taylor flutter-sleeve wrap dress, and tan strappy sandals, she got in the shower, careful not to let her shoulder length curls get wet. She loved her long hair, and even though her mom told her she was too old for the style she had, Summer knew that today age didn't define how a woman wore her hair. Wiping the steam off the mirror, Summer dropped her thick fluffy towel and saw her naked reflection staring back at her. *Not bad for fifty-eight*, she told herself.

And then out of nowhere, Jake Ross was in her thoughts, and the blush that started on her face went all the way down to her toes.

Chapter 29

"I'm sorry that you can't go to church with me," Summer told Michael as she carefully put in her earrings. "But I understand how important all this is to you." Gently touching the back of his head, since he was continuing to pound away on the computer, Summer told him goodbye and headed to the garage.

Before closing the door, she yelled in, "Anything special sound good for dinner?" Michael just grunted. Deciding to try to recreate the dinner on the deck that hadn't happened the night before, Summer mentally told herself to stop and pick up steaks on her way home from church. Surely, he would have all of his work done by suppertime, and they could enjoy a nice evening together.

It was a lovely sunny morning and Summer decided to drive the Mustang to church. Soon the rainy season would begin, and her baby would stay safely locked in the garage, but today she wanted to be behind the wheel of her convertible, and smell of the fresh ocean breeze. Starting the engine, she backed out carefully, mindful to turn off the tape deck, and the music she'd been jamming to the last time she'd taken the Mustang out for a spin.

In most small churches in America people seem to sit in the same pew week after week, and Summer's church was no different. After parking as far away from other cars as possible, she walked up the steps to the greeters, one standing on each side of the church's front door. Taking a bulletin and explaining why Michael wasn't with her, Summer hurried up the aisle to where Bree and Dan were waiting for her.

"Good morning, Sunshine," Dan greeted her, using the nickname he had bestowed on her when they first met. "Where's your hubby this morning, playing hooky from church?" Dan laughed, and Summer knew he was teasing, but she wished Michael was there beside her. In all their years of marriage they had rarely missed attending church together, and it just felt weird. She was about to explain to Dan why her husband wasn't with her when the processional began and Reverend Marks asked them to stand and sing Hymn Number One Fifty-Three.

After the processional was the time for meet and greet and when Summer turned around to shake hands with the people in the pew behind her, there sat Alex Bailey, the man she had met at Jason's Corner. She wasn't sure why she felt so uncomfortable, but when Alex took her hand, it felt like more than a handshake. Quickly introducing him to Dan and Bree, she sat back down as the minister started to talk. Bree was trying to get her attention, but with Dan between them, Summer kept looking straight ahead, pretending that she was engrossed in the service.

Just after eleven, Reverend Perry asked the congregation to stand as he led the benediction. Summer had never been so ready to make a getaway from church, but she fussed with her purse and talked to old Mrs. Green, hoping that when she turned around Alex would be gone. But nope, there he stood, shaking hands with a group of men, with his eyes directly on her. Staying close to Bree she walked towards the line of people waiting to talk to the reverend, which gave Alex just enough time to catch up with her.

"Do you have a minute, Summer?" he asked. "I was hoping we could talk."

When she thought about it later, Summer never knew where her response came from, but the first words out of her mouth were, "I'm married."

She could swear that she could see a smile forming on Alex's face when he answered, "Good, I am too, and I'd love you to meet my wife when she gets here."

By now they were both standing in front of Reverend Perry, and Summer was as tongue tied as she'd ever been. "Summer," the kind pastor began, "I see you've met Dr. Bailey, our new veterinarian. He

85

asked me if I knew someone to help him with some advertising, and I thought of you right away."

Summer wanted to hide. Here she thought Alex Bailey was hitting on her in church, and instead he wanted to discuss hiring her. Talk about a faux pas. Was she so needy for male attention that she was starting to imagine men wanting her? Doing her best to stay calm and professional, Summer smiled and pulled one of her business cards from her purse.

"Why don't you call me tomorrow," she said with a forced smile, "and you can tell me more about what you're looking for." She handed him the card and walked away before she embarrassed herself further. Then deciding she was being childish turned back and added, "And I'd love to meet your wife, Dr. Bailey; in fact, I'll be looking forward to it." Then without another word to anyone, she dashed to her car.

Chapter 30

By the time she had stopped by Publix, taking care to park her Mustang as far away from other cars as possible, and purchased two nice fillets and ingredients for Caesar salad, Summer was feeling the heat from the scorching summer sun that beat down. She wanted to strip down, throw on a swimsuit, and cajole Michael into going to the beach for a swim. But when she arrived home, the Land Rover was gone. The house was quiet, and Michael was nowhere to be found.

She wasn't really concerned, but it was out of character for either one of them to go out without leaving a note. Realizing that Michael had been under a lot of strain, Summer sighed and went upstairs to undress. *Maybe he had to run into the office*, she thought, *or maybe Elliott got home and he's over there?* She was going over scenarios in her head when the landline beside the bed rang.

"Hello?" she answered anxiously, hoping the call was from Michael. As soon as she heard his voice the panic that had been rising up in her throat started to slip away, but the moment he started talking, the panic was replaced with frustration.

"Hey Baby," he said with a cocky tone, "you just get home?"

Baby? Michael never called her baby. It was only a little past noon; had he been drinking already? Taking a deep breath, and doing her best to compose herself, Summer replied.

"Yes, Michael, I just got home, and what a surprise it was to find that my husband who had been working so hard that he couldn't go to church wasn't here when I arrived."

"Look," he said so quietly that she knew he was whispering, "Tom Jenkins called and needed a fourth for a round of golf, and I thought it would be a good way to blow off some steam. I've been working day and night if you remember, plus when did I start needing your permission to leave the house?"

"I'm done with this conversation, Michael," she said with enough force that his golf buddies could probably hear. "Go play with your friends; I'm going to the beach." Slamming the phone down to blow off her own steam, Summer quickly got out of her clothes and grabbed her swimsuit. The phone rang again but she refused to answer it. *Let him worry for a while*, she thought.

They had an unwritten rule in the house that no one would go swimming in the uncertain ocean alone, but right now Summer didn't care. She was hot, both inside and out, and she wanted to feel the cool waves of the Atlantic, and she was going to, with or without her husband. All she wanted was to cool down, but the way she felt inside she was afraid that was an impossibility.

Summer grabbed her always loaded beach bag, threw in two bottles of water, and slipped her feet into a pair of Croc Sandals. Seeing her book and her cell on the table by the chair she picked them up and started walking to the beach. But the closer she got, the more she remembered why weekends weren't her favorite time on New Smyrna Beach. Cars and people were everywhere and even finding a spot where she wouldn't be surrounded by teenagers and families with squalling toddlers was impossible. Finally, she gave up, turned around and went back home.

Summer's heavy hair was dripping with sweat, and her feet were gritty with sand. She walked the three blocks slowly, trying to decide what she'd do when she got to the house. She was still upset with her husband, plus now she was a hot mess. Literally. But a cooling towel on her neck and a tall glass of iced tea helped her calm down, and taking her book and phone, she got comfortable under the awning on the deck. She opened the book but instead of reading looked at her cell phone and thought *what the heck* and sent a message to Jake.

You up yet? She asked. And immediately he responded.
I was just thinking about you.

Chapter 31

It was amazing how having a conversation through e-communications could feel as real as talking in person, but it was, and Summer was enjoying every minute of it. They talked about their shared love of food, where they attended college, even the differences between Florida and California, but there was no mention of Michael, even though Beth's name came up a few times.

Intellectually Summer knew that she was treading in deep water, but her heart was floating so she pushed all the negative thoughts aside. It wasn't until the landline started to ring that she realized how long they'd been talking. Looking at her watch she saw that it was after three and using the truth about needing to answer the home phone, Summer reluctantly typed in Goodbye.

Waiting for Jake to sign off, Summer kept her cell in her hand. She was totally floored when she read his words.

You're a gorgeous woman, Summer Alcott, and if you weren't happily married, I'd ask you out.

Summer was thankful to be alone because she knew her cheeks had to be as pink and hot as she felt all over. To top it off, he had ended the message with three red hearts, and damned if that didn't make her own heart beat faster. Trying to catch her breath she went inside for a refill on her tea, just as the landline started to ring again.

Seeing the name in the caller ID, a smile lit up Summer's face. "Hey, Ri!" she said with enthusiasm, "how's your day going?"

"It's going fine, Mom," he replied, "but the question is, how's yours? I've called three times and you've never been home. I even called your cell, and you didn't pick up, is everything okay?"

Summer had never lied to her sons, and she wasn't going to start now, but there wasn't any harm in stepping around the truth, was there? "I'm fine Riley, and your dad is fine, too, but he's been working a lot of hours and decided to play golf this afternoon to unwind. It's been really hot and humid, so I walked down to the beach for a swim and just missed your calls. I'm sorry if I worried you."

Riley laughed. "There's so many things wrong in that answer," he told his mom. "First of all, I didn't know dad even liked golf, I mean, he never talks about it. And you, young lady, weren't you the one who installed the *Buddy at the Beach* rule when Coop and I were kids? Breaking your own rule, Mom, that's major."

"Okay wise guy," she retorted. "When did the child become the parent? I'm not ready for Shady Pines yet, so mind your manners. And just to set the record straight, I walked to the beach and walked back home, not even one toe went in the water."

"You'll never be ready for Shady Pines, Mom," Riley said with love. "Summer Cooper Alcott will go down in history as the Foxiest Mama ever."

It was all she could do to hold back the tears. Riley was a great man, and he deserved a great life, which brought her thoughts to Olivia.

"So, tell me what's going on with you, Ri," she said. "Still seeing Olivia?"

"I'm not sure people still *see* each other, but yeah, we're still together. I think she may be the one, Mom."

Summer caught herself before she gasped into the phone. As much as she wanted Riley to enjoy himself before settling down, she was determined not to drive him away with her nagging. "Then why don't you bring her home for Thanksgiving?" Summer asked. "We can have a big old-fashioned holiday."

"It sounds great," he said hesitantly, "but I kind of told Olivia I would go home with her for Thanksgiving. You understand, don't you?"

Understand? She and Michael had never spent a Thanksgiving away from their sons, and she wasn't ready for that to happen yet. But being a good mother, she held in her hurt and said, "Of course I do Ri. Where does Olivia's family live anyway?"

"They live in New York City," Riley answered. "Her dad is an investment banker, and her mom runs some kind of charity. They're really great people, Mom. I know that you and Dad will like them a lot."

Summer needed Michael and she needed him now! Riley had already met Olivia's parents and they'd only heard about her a week ago? But again, trying to be the mother that Riley depended on, she replied, "I'm sure we will."

After that the conversation became a little awkward, and finally Riley said he had some laundry to do and to tell Dad he said hello. Summer told her son that she loved him, to which he said he loved her too, and they hung up.

For some reason, Summer wanted to message Jake, but she thought better of it and called her best friend instead. The minute Bree answered the phone Summer began to cry, "I think I'm losing him."

Chapter 32

1993

"I want to have another baby," Summer said one evening while she and Michael were sitting by a roaring fire in the cozy little house in Celina, Ohio. "Cooper's almost nine and we always planned to have a houseful of kids." She looked into her husband's deep gray eyes, knowing what he was going to say, but this time she was ready to move the conversation in her direction.

"Summer," Michael said calmly, used to getting his way, "we've been through this before. I can't go through the heartache that happened last time. You can't go through it either, and Cooper's old enough now to know when something isn't right with one of us."

She cringed, hurt that Michael couldn't even mention their daughter's names, let alone the tragedy of their birth, but this time she had ammunition and she intended to use it. "Michael, when Kathryn and Maryann were born, we were both too grief-stricken to ask the right questions. But I've done my homework and talked with one of the leading specialists in the country on conjoined births, and everything I've been told is that what happened with our girls was a terrible act of nature, but it doesn't mean it will happen again."

Summer stopped, waiting to hear what Michael would say, but he sat there stoic and unmoving. Deciding to try another tactic she added, "You promised me babies, Michael Alcott, and I want them. I'm thirty-two years old and I can't wait forever. The girls would be three years old now, and hopefully I'd be pregnant again. I've let your doubts keep me from having the one thing I always wanted, and I'm not waiting any longer."

"Really?" Michael said, letting out a snarky laugh. "You have a daddy picked out because I've told you before I'm not taking the chance with any more pregnancies."

Summer looked him in the eye and for the first time saw tears welling up in the corners. "What's really going on here, Michael?" she asked, taking his hand in hers.

"I feel like it was somehow my fault, Summer," he said, "I was working so much that year and you were home alone with a rambunctious little boy, and you both got the flu. What if all that caused a problem?"

Why had he never told her that before? Taking a deep breath Summer looked at the man who had melted her heart on their first date and cupped his cheek with her hand. "Michael, what happened to our daughters was no one's fault. I don't know what happened or why, but it did and it's time we let go. Cooper is a beautiful, healthy child and there's no reason to think we won't have another one just like him. I want another baby, Michael, please don't deny me any longer."

Michael nodded his head and pulled his wife into his arms. "I want another baby, too, Summer," he told her, with tears running down his face. "I've just been so afraid that you blamed me, and I couldn't stand to see that suffering on your face again."

She kissed him long and hard, and he kissed back, but John Riley Alcott wasn't conceived that night in front of the fire. It was almost a year after their talk when Michael had come home for lunch and Cooper was at school that Summer met him at the door in nothing but one of his dress shirts. When she pulled the plackets open to reveal her nakedness, lunch was totally forgotten.

Six weeks later Summer took her first sip of morning coffee and immediately ran to the bathroom. She didn't need a test to tell her why the taste of coffee had made her throw up; she knew. When Michael found her, she was leaning over the toilet with tears of joy running down her face.

Chapter 33

By the time Summer calmed down enough to tell Bree that it wasn't her husband, but her son who she was worried about losing, Michael was home. Seeing the anguished look on his wife's face he rushed to her and immediately asked, "What's wrong Summer, is it one of the boys?"

Summer told Bree she'd call her later and did her best to tell Michael about her conversation with their youngest son. "He's too young to be this serious about a girl, Michael, he still has his master's to finish, and he's always wanted to backpack through Italy. How can he do that with a wife?"

"Oh honey," he said, wrapping his long arms around her, "is it possible you're jumping the gun a little bit? I don't think Riley has any intention of walking down the aisle just yet."

Summer tried to remember being twenty-three, before she found out she was pregnant, and all that came to mind was dreaming with her girlfriends about wanting to get married as soon as they graduated from college. She had known the minute she met Michael Alcott that he was the man she wanted to make those dreams come true with, but she had never imagined it would happen the way it had. Being a pregnant bride was never what she wanted, although she used to wonder if Michael thought she got pregnant on purpose so he'd have to marry her.

She snapped back to reality when she heard his voice. "What's going on in that pretty head of yours Mrs. Alcott? I never have been able to read your mind."

"I was just thinking about what it's like to be young," Summer sighed, "and how we don't even know how old Olivia is. She could still be a teenager, and we've never met her, that just doesn't seem right."

"First of all, I don't think Riley would get involved with a teenager, and from her picture I'd say she's about his age. Secondly, let's not jump to conclusions here. Riley's a smart young man who knows what he wants, and I don't think he has marriage on his mind." Michael stopped long enough for Summer to blow her nose before he continued. "What I really think's bothering you is that for the first time you may not be the most important woman in Riley's life, and that's a painful reality. Am I wrong?"

Summer nodded her head and blew her nose again. "It's just that he's my baby, Michael, and if he's all grown-up, where does that leave me?"

"Right here with me, just where you belong." He gave her a squeeze and asked, "Are you still mad about me playing golf this afternoon? And if you are, just wait until you hear what I have to say about you swimming in the ocean by yourself."

That was enough to crack the shell that was trying to encase Summer's heart, and she laughed. "How about we call it a draw, okay? You had every right to get out with your friends this afternoon, I just worried when I came home, and you hadn't left a note. And I didn't actually go swimming, so you can save the lecture. Instead, let's take a bottle of wine to the deck, and try to relax a little before dinner. Tomorrow is your big day, and I don't want you tense."

"How about we take the wine upstairs, and we can work off some of the tension together," Michael said with a wink, and taking her hand they walked together into the kitchen, grabbed a chilled bottle of Beach House Sauvignon Blanc and two glasses, and climbed the stairs to their room.

Deciding to try the showering together they had missed the week before, Summer realized that it really wasn't all those romance novels made it out to be. She remembered when they were first married, when Cooper was just a bump, they had showered together often, and it had been deliciously sexy, but now neither one of them was quite as agile as they had been in their twenties, and finally they gave up.

Drying each other off and slipping naked into bed, Michael kissed her passionately, before moving his lips to her breasts. Summer used to feel she was on the verge of an orgasm when Michael licked and gently bit down on her nipples, but for some reason today she wasn't getting that thrill. He moved from one to the other, lavishing them with attention, but the arousal she was waiting for wasn't happening.

Not wanting Michael to know that his spur of the moment lovemaking wasn't turning her on, Summer gently pushed him back and started nibbling and licking her way down his chest to his thick erection. Part of her mind was on pleasing her husband and the other part was wondering what was wrong with her. She'd always loved sex, and hadn't she just told him she needed more attention in that area, yet when he tried to give it to her, her body wouldn't respond. She was working so diligently, sucking, and licking, and rolling the delicate skin of his scrotum, that she didn't hear Michael when he told her to stop, and he erupted in her mouth.

Michael was trying to compose himself. Pulling her head down on his chest he said, "Are you okay?"

To be honest, she wasn't sure. She had been so lost in thought that she let him go too far, and when she realized what the problem was, she almost couldn't breathe. Because it hadn't been Michael in her mind, she was making love to, it was Jake Ross.

Chapter 34

Michael was determined to show Summer the pleasure she had given him, but she was able to convince him that she wanted this afternoon to be all about him. They lay in their big king-sized bed covered with a silky, high, thread count sheet, gently touching and caressing each other. After a few minutes, Michael's movements slowed down, and when she looked over at him, she realized he was asleep.

Carefully slipping out of bed, she threw on a pair of Lululemon leggings and an oversized New Smyrna Beach T-shirt, grabbed the bottle of wine, and quietly climbed down the stairs. There was still a beautiful late afternoon sky, so she reached for her favorite wine glass—the one with the turquoise beads on the stem she had purchased at *TaDa*—and headed to the deck. She had just poured herself a big glass of the crisp, refreshing wine when she heard the ping of the Messenger app. Summer panicked, not knowing where she'd left her phone, and breathing a sigh of relief when she realized she had left it on the patio table when she went in to talk to her son.

The message was from Jake, of course, and it was short and sweet.

I wasn't sure how to tell you this earlier, but I have a date tonight. I've had a few in the last six months but they've never gone too well. I've already decided that I'm going to stop trying if this one doesn't work out. Wish me luck!

She felt as if she was hyperventilating. Less than an hour ago she had been thinking about Jake during one of the most intimate moments with her husband, and now he was telling her that he had a date! And wish him luck? She knew that's what a good friend would do, but if Jake became involved with a woman, where would that leave her?

She was just thinking about pouring another glass of wine when Michael put his arms around her from behind and she almost jumped out of her chair. "You scared the crap out of me," she said, trying to gain her composure. "Did I wake you up?"

Michael pulled the hair off of her face and softly kissed her cheek. "No, you didn't wake me," he said, caressing her shoulders, "but you promised me steak and I'm starving. Plus, I thought maybe we should talk about what happened earlier."

Summer was up in a flash. "There isn't anything to talk about, Michael," she said as confidently as possible. "I'm hungry too, so why don't you start the grill and I'll go make the salad?"

"Summer…" he started.

She put a finger to his lips and said, "Do you want a beer or a glass of wine?"

"I'll have wine," he answered, "but I'd still like to talk."

"You start the grill, and we can talk during dinner," she said sweetly, pouring them each a glass of wine. Taking her wine, she stepped into the house, drinking as she went. She wasn't sure what part of, "what happened earlier," her husband wanted to talk about, but as far as she was concerned, there was nothing she wanted to discuss.

Thankfully she didn't have to because they no sooner sat down than the phone rang. Summer felt a weight being lifted when she heard Michael say, "Hey Cooper, sorry we didn't call earlier. It's been a strange weekend."

By the time the call with Cooper ended and the now cold steaks and warm salad had been pushed around on their plates, Summer's head felt as if a snare drum was beating inside. She got up from the table and wrapped up what was left of the steak, thinking she could use it for stir-fry, and looked forlornly at the salad. The once crisp romaine was now limp and gooey, and looking at it made her stomach hurt as much as her head.

"We've got to quit wasting so much food," she told Michael as she dumped the remains down the disposal. "There are people all over this world starving, and twice this week we've thrown away meals because we got too involved to enjoy them. We should be ashamed."

"I've never quite understood how cleaning our plates helps people who are hungry, but I agree, it's wrong to be so wasteful," Michael told her. "Maybe we should stick to bread and water for a few days as our penance."

Summer could tell he was trying to cut the tension with a joke, but she wasn't interested. "It's not funny, Michael," she scolded, "and my head hurts so badly right now that I can't even talk. There are some cookies in the freezer if you want dessert, but I really just need to go to bed. Can I do anything to help you for tomorrow before I go up?"

Michael shook his head. "Thanks, but I'm just going to go over my presentation for the new client once more and then I'll be up. Summer, this afternoon was…, well it was great," he stammered. She could tell he wanted to say more about their afternoon tryst, but instead he gave her a half smile and turned towards the den.

Her head still pounding and her heart aching, Summer climbed the stairs to their room. She was ashamed of herself for thinking of Jake when she was in bed with her husband, but she knew she had to hold it together. Tomorrow when she emailed Jake Ross, she would be nothing but professional and this nightmare would go away. But the moment she saw the bed with the rumpled sheets, her mind immediately pictured him; young, sexy, golden-haired, blue-eyed Jake, the man who was consuming her thoughts and invading her fantasies.

By morning Summer's headache was gone and her resolve had returned. She would be polite to Jake but not allow any personal conversation between them. She was a married woman, with a business to run for heaven sakes, and even though she and Jake were only talking, Summer's time and attention belonged to her husband. Knowing that she had made the right decision, Summer hurried downstairs to get Michael's coffee and bagel ready for his drive into work.

The cinnamon raisin bagel was toasted and covered with soft, honey vanilla cream cheese by the time Michael got downstairs. His Yeti was filled with steaming hot coffee, and Summer smiled when he kissed her and patted her behind as he headed out the door. This was her life, she told herself, and taking her coffee headed to her rocker for her morning devotions.

She had just sat down for her first sip of fragrant, dark roast hazelnut, when she saw the message on her phone. Knowing it was from Jake, she hesitated, but when curiosity got the best of her, she opened it.

You still awake?

The evening went really well, and you're the person I wanted to tell. For some reason, your kind and caring spirit has traveled through cyberspace, and I feel as if we have a real connection. Anyway, my date was with a book publisher who shares her time between New York and L.A. We had a nice dinner and then sat outside in the moonlight and talked. It was all very romantic.

You haven't responded so I guess you're in bed.

Tell you more tomorrow. J

Summer dropped the phone in her lap and started to sob. "NO!" She shouted to the silent room; *this can't be happening*. If Jake had found a real woman, someone to touch and to hold, what would happen to her? As the tears continued to flow, all she could think about was how special Jake made her feel, and more than anything she knew that she wasn't ready to let those feelings go.

Chapter 35

Summer was restless and on edge waiting to see if Jake would message her again before their daily email. As she put on her makeup, she paid particular attention to her eyes, adding soothing moisturizer to the delicate skin around them. All the crying made them puffy and sore and, it made her feel older than her fifty-eight years.

Finally dressed, and with more makeup than usual for a weekday, Summer tried to come up with a way to get Jake's attention. She knew that he was on Facebook a lot, so she took a chance and created a post. Not something directed at him, but something she hoped would catch his attention.

Earlier in the summer, she and Bree had gone to the beach, and Bree had taken a candid picture of Summer walking along the shoreline. She had been wearing a gauzy, deep purple wrap slung low around her hips with a white and lavender floral bikini. Summer loved the way the picture made her feel; young and spontaneous, and even a little sexy. Of course, she hadn't told Bree that, but once Summer had the picture in her phone, she had looked at it whenever she needed to boost her moral. And today was one of those days.

Now what reason could she come up with for posting a picture of herself in a swimsuit? After a few minutes of thinking, she found pictures of herself at Thanksgiving, Christmas, and Easter, and made a collage to use with her Four Seasons of Summer logo. Jake had told her more than once that she was beautiful, so now was the time to cash in on those sentiments.

Summer had been so busy working on her *get Jake's attention campaign* that she almost jumped out of her skin when the phone rang. "Hello," she said breathlessly into the receiver.

"I'm looking for Summer Alcott of Four Seasons of Summer," the voice on the other end said. "Is this the right number?"

"This is Summer Alcott," she replied. "How may I help you?"

"Good morning, Summer," the voice continued. "This is Alex Bailey, we talked yesterday at church. Is this a good time for you?"

And so, they talked for about forty minutes with Summer making notes and asking questions about Alex's vision for his website and ending the call with Alex making a verbal commitment. Summer promised to get a contract sent that very day. After the distress of the morning, it was a great change of pace, and Summer hung up feeling in control once more.

Until she grabbed her phone and saw the message from Jake.

Good Morning my beautiful Summer!

The publisher sent me a Facebook Friend request and she's invited me to dinner tomorrow night! What do you think of that? And by the way,

I think I like "Summer" best!

Can't wait until nine. J

She wanted to crawl in a hole. Jake had seen the Facebook post, Summer was sure of that, but he was teasing her at the same time he was gushing about his next date with the book lady. Things were not going as planned; they were not going as planned at all.

Work was the one thing that helped Summer get her mind off of her problems, but today, it wasn't doing the trick. She put together a contract for Bailey Veterinarian Clinic and emailed it to Alex Bailey but waiting until noon Florida time to talk with Jake was agony. She knew he was awake. He had messaged her for heavens sake, but he had said he couldn't wait until nine. She was going to wait, even if it killed her.

Remembering that she'd had only coffee that morning and that she hadn't done her prayers, Summer peeled an orange, poured herself a glass of iced tea, and sat down to read her devotional. But instead of reading she started to daydream, and pretty quickly her thoughts were of

Jake and what it would be like to sit and talk in the moonlight with him like he had with his new friend, and how his voice would sound. They had messaged so much that she felt as though she could hear him through his e-communications, and his voice was always rich and deep.

Sitting up with a start Summer realized she was in big trouble, and when she was in trouble, there was only one person she could talk to: Bree. Putting her orange back in the refrigerator as not to waste food, she grabbed her keys and headed out into the bright Florida morning.

Chapter 36

Summer knocked so hard on the door that she was afraid she might damage it. She hadn't called to make sure that Bree was home, and the idea that her friend might not be available brought more anxiety than she was already feeling. Pounding one more time she heard Bree yell from inside, "Hold your horses I'm coming."

Bree heaved the door open, ready to jump on whomever was waiting to sell her something, but instantly drew back when she saw her best friend standing on her doorstep, tears running down her face. "Summer, what is it," Bree said, pulling her in for an embrace. "Are you still worrying about Riley?"

Summer shook her head and pulled back from her friend. "This isn't about Riley, but I do need to talk with you. Do you have a minute?"

Bree gave her a genuine smile as she escorted Summer into the kitchen. "I always have time for you girlfriend, now get comfy while I fix us some lemonade. It's going to be really hot today for fall."

While Bree fixed their drinks, complete with a fresh slice of lemon off of the tree in the backyard, Summer tried to get herself under control. She looked around the cheerful kitchen where she had spent so many hours chatting with her friend and wondered if this would be the last time Bree would welcome her in with open arms. After Summer shared with her why she had come for help, would Bree be too disillusioned to even want to stay friends?

Bree sat down on a bar stool and said, "Okay Summer, spill. And I don't mean your lemonade because I just mopped the floor."

That little bit of levity reminded Summer of just how perceptive Bree was, and that she was making a joke to lighten the mood. Taking a drink of lemonade, and heaving a big sigh, Summer jumped right in.

"I've met someone, Bree," she stammered, "someone I was just trying to help through his loss, but now I realize that I really like him, and I want him to like me. What am I going to do?"

Bree put down her glass and engulfed Summer in her arms. "Are you telling me that you're having an affair, Summer, or that you're thinking about having one?

Summer couldn't hold back the tears any longer. "No Bree, of course I'm not having an affair, in fact, I've never met the man face to face. He's a new client and we've become close friends, but last night he had a date and he really liked her and if he has her, where does that leave me?"

"It's Jake Ross, isn't it?" Bree asked.

Summer looked in her friend's eyes and nodded. "You know about all the heartache he's been through, and I just wanted to help him, and be a friend. Bree, he makes me feel young and vibrant and desirable, and I haven't felt this way in a long time. He tells me I'm beautiful and I want his attention all for me, but now I'm afraid I'm going to lose it. Is it so wrong for me to have these feelings?"

Bree got up and put her glass in the sink. The way she was staring out the kitchen window made Summer afraid that she was going to lose her best friend as well as Jake's attention, but when Bree turned around, with tears in her own eyes, Summer knew something else was wrong.

"Do you remember when I quit working?" Bree asked cautiously.

"Sure, you said with the housing market down real estate wasn't fun anymore, and with Dan's new job you were able to live on just his income. But what does that have to do with my situation?" Summer had no idea where her friend could be going with this.

"I didn't leave because the housing market was down, Summer, I can sell a house in any economy," Bree said confidently. "I left because I became involved with one of my co-workers, and Dan found out."

Summer's hand began to twitch, and she desperately need something to do with them. "Tell me what you mean by involved, Bree?" she asked.

"I thought I was in love with another man, and we became more than friends. Much more." For a few seconds, the room was totally silent, and then Bree told Summer the whole story.

"I know that you're worried about Riley being too young to settle down, Summer, and I agree, but he's twenty-three and a college graduate. I started dating Dan when I was sixteen, and we eloped the day after my eighteenth birthday. It all seemed so romantic back then, two young lovers running off to start a life together, but believe me, that euphoria didn't last."

"But Bree," Summer interjected, "you and Dan seem so happy, so secure in your life and your marriage. I just don't understand."

"We are happy now, Summer, but it's taken a lot of work to get here. Dan is the best man I know. He's a great dad, and he'd help anyone who asked, and he loves me, of that I've never had a doubt. But once the kids came along, we had trouble finding time for us, and at some point, we just stopped looking for it. Oh sure, we still had sex, but it was pretty much for physical release and never with any passion. I thought I was content until Gabe Barrett bought the real estate business I worked for, and from then on things changed. He offered all I was looking for in my life, and I fell, hook, line, and sinker."

"I don't know what to say," Summer told her friend. "I guess I'm kind of in a state of shock."

"I understand, Summer, truly I do," Bree said. "I also understand what you're telling me about your feelings for Jake Ross. Just like you imagined that Dan and I lived some kind of magical existence, I guess I thought the same about you and Michael. But marriage and real life aren't fairytales, even if the front we show the world appears to be."

Then Bree added, "Do you think less of me now that you know my sordid story?"

"I could never think less of you Bree," Summer answered honestly. "You're the best friend I've ever had. But I'm just so sorry that I always come to you to whine and all this time you've been dealing with your own issues."

"I love that you come to me Summer, and I don't want you to ever stop. Maybe it's because of my *issues,* as you call them, that I'm a good shoulder to cry on. You came here today with a real problem, and I think it's time we dealt with it," Bree told her. "What do you say?"

"Okay, "Summer answered hesitantly, knowing that what Bree told her would not be the answer she was looking for.

"Plain, hard facts, my friend. You're married, and even though you don't think you're doing anything wrong having this online friendship, at some point it's going to blow up in your face. The best thing for you would be if Jake Ross falls in love with this woman he's met and for you to let him go."

Summer nodded in agreement, but inside her heart refused to listen. *I can't let go yet,* she thought, *I just can't.*

Summer and Bree talked for a few more minutes and when Bree got up to offer lunch, Summer looked at her watch. "Oh crap!" she shouted, grabbing her things and heading to the door. "I'm late for my client appointment! I've got to run Bree, but thanks, thanks for everything." Giving her friend a quick hug, she jumped in her car, anxious for her online meeting with Jake.

Chapter 37

She practically flew home, afraid that Jake didn't wait, but when she arrived, there was an email from him filled with concern.

"It's not like you to be late for our meetings, Summer," she read. "I hope that everything is okay?"

Summer started to type while she tried to catch her breath. Intellectually she knew that Bree was right about her feelings for Jake, but Bree just didn't understand. Jake lived thousands of miles away. They weren't going to have an affair; they were just friends who enjoyed each other's company. Granted, it was all online, but that's what made it safe, right?

"Sorry Jake," Summer typed. "I had some errands that ran longer than I expected. I've attached the final draft for your website; what are your thoughts?"

"Your designs are amazing," Jake answered, "Everything you do is amazing, I'm so glad you agreed to take my project on."

They emailed back and forth for about twenty minutes and then Jake said he had an appointment and needed to go. They agreed to keep this time slot open for a couple of weeks in case something came up and then signed off.

Summer moved away from the computer not sure what her true feelings were. She was pleased by the nice things Jake said about her work, and he hadn't once brought up the book lady, as Summer was calling her, but Bree's words were starting to sink in. She had a husband and a family she loved, if she was really a friend to Jake, wouldn't she want him to have the opportunity for the same? As much as she knew the answer should be *yes*, she couldn't bring herself to admit it. She needed Jake Ross, and the attention he so freely gave her, and she wasn't ready to have him out of her life.

With no more appointments for the day, Summer went to the refrigerator to see what she could round up for a light lunch. It was almost one thirty and she didn't have any idea what to fix for dinner either, so taking the orange out from earlier, she peeled off a section and stuck it in her mouth while she looked over the options.

There was broccoli, yellow peppers, and grape tomatoes in the refrigerator, and onions and bowtie pasta in the pantry, which she could throw together with a light parmesan lemon sauce and make a healthy Pasta Primavera. She even found a few of chicken tenders in the freezer to add, to keep Michael from accusing her of trying to make him a vegetarian. That decided, she took what was left of her orange and popped the top on a can of Diet Coke. What she really wanted was a glass of wine, but a day drinker was one thing Summer Alcott was not.

She tried to remember where she had left her book, and once it was found she sat down to read. Thirty minutes only, she told herself, and then I'll do some work on Alex Bailey's website. But the trials and tribulations of Margaret and John's life in *The Middle Passage* ended up consuming the rest of her afternoon.

Summer checked her computer for any important emails, and then closed it up for the night. She knew that Michael had to go to the finance meeting for the hospital board, and that today had been his big client presentation, so she wanted everything to look nice when he got home. Including her.

She set the dining room table with her Grandmother Cooper's stoneware and toyed with the idea of wine with dinner, however, knowing Michael was going back out, she thought better of it. She snipped some begonias and arranged them in a pretty vase and put a new pair of white tapers in the crystal candlesticks Michael's mother had given them for their last anniversary. Stepping back for one last glance, Summer was pleased with the way everything had come together.

Leaving just enough time for a shower and a change of clothes, she started for the stairs as she heard a ping come from her phone. Opening the app, she read the message from Jake.

I'm leaving for my dinner with my publisher friend, whose name is Leda, by the way. I haven't been to a woman's house for dinner in close to twenty years and I'm scared shitless. Think of me. J

Doing her best not to cry, Summer went directly to the kitchen and poured herself a big glass of wine. After all, she wasn't the one going back out, and it was after five.

Chapter 38

Michael was in a great mood when he got home and didn't even notice that Summer had been drinking. "The client presentation couldn't have gone better," he exclaimed. "They loved my ideas for the outdoor shopping mall, and I'm confident they're going to sign with our firm." Setting his briefcase on the kitchen counter he walked into the dining room and looked over the beautifully set table.

"Did you do all this for me?" he asked, looking at the vase of fresh flowers and softly glimmering candlelight. "I wish I could stay home, and we could celebrate, but I have the finance meeting tonight."

"I understand," she responded, doing her best not to get close enough to him for him to smell the wine on her breath, "but I knew you'd do well at work, and I wanted to do something special for you. Are you ready to eat or do you want to go change first?"

Before she could react, Michael pulled her into his arms and gave her a deep, slow kiss. "How's the wine?" he asked with a quizzical look on his face. "Were you starting the celebration without me?"

Summer tried to break away, but almost all six foot three inches of Michael Alcott was muscle, and she didn't stand a chance. "The question on the table is are you ready to eat, or do you want to change first?" she told him, completely ignoring his comment about the wine.

Michael let Summer go but continued to stare at her. "When did you become such a drinker, Summer?" he asked. "A couple of beers at Breakers or some wine on the weekends is all I remember you having, and I've been part of your life for a really long time. But lately it seems like you're enjoying alcohol a little too much." Summer could tell he was trying to gauge her reaction, so she stayed as quiet as possible.

"Is there a problem we need to talk about?" he added.

"Since when did you become so touchy feely, Michael?" she asked. "In all the really long time we've been together, you've never been much for talking about emotions, and now all of a sudden, you're Doctor Phil. I'm fine, everything is fine, so now please answer the question. Are you ready to eat or not?"

"I would have liked to have changed, but there isn't enough time now." He pointed to the table before answering. "Let's not let your efforts go to waste."

Summer nodded and arranged the food in front of him, trying to act as cheerful as possible.

"Everything looks delicious," Michael told her, taking a bite of the pasta. Noticing that she didn't have any chicken on her plate he quizzed, "You haven't given up meat, have you?"

Summer closed her eyes and counted to ten. It was a trick she had learned during their first few months of marriage when they were still learning how to live with each other, but she realized that she and Michael normally got along so well she hadn't used it in years. "No, Michael, I haven't given up meat, but it's something I can do without and there were only a few pieces left."

"I'm happy to share," he said with a crooked smile, and that small gesture caused her to smile back.

While they ate they talked about their day, and Summer told him she had gone to Bree's, but she didn't say why. Thankfully, Michael was so used to the two women spending time together that he didn't even question her about it. He told her more about his client presentation, and how excited he was about his project, and before she knew it, Michael was looking at his watch, saying he needed to go.

Summer was prepared for the normal peck and pat Michael always gave her when he left, but instead he pulled her close and kissed her. Really kissed her. "Stay out of the wine until I get home," he said with a wink. "If the finance meeting goes as well as the meeting at work, we can celebrate together when I get home."

She cleared the table and cleaned up from dinner, feeling lighter than she had all day. Men and women could be friends without any romantic attachment, and that's how things would be with Jake. Tomorrow when they talked, she'd ask him about the Book Lady, Leda, she corrected herself, and be the friend that he deserved.

Chapter 39

At noon the next day Summer waited at her computer, certain she would hear from Jake. He hadn't sent her a message since the evening before, and she thought for sure he would want to tell her how the dinner at Leda's had gone. By the time twelve thirty had come and gone, she realized he wasn't going to be emailing during their allotted time, but she scrolled through some advertisements in order to stay online. Finally, she just gave up and went to the kitchen for a bite of lunch.

There had been about a cup of the pasta primavera left the night before and Summer had carefully packaged it into two microwaveable containers. She put one in to heat and poured herself a cold glass of tea, wondering all the time why she hadn't heard from Jake. Was he trying to tell her something, or was he just busy? And if he was just busy, was he busy with Leda? The microwave beeped, and Summer sighed, knowing that the hunger she was feeling wasn't going to be filled by a small dish of pasta. In fact, it couldn't be filled by food at all.

Michael's finance meeting the night before had gone as well as his client presentation, so to celebrate they were going out for dinner at the Sea Food Shack. It wasn't fancy, but they both loved the quirky nautical atmosphere, and their soup was to die for. Sometimes Summer got the Roasted Red Pepper Crab Soup and New England Clam Chowder swirled, because she couldn't make-up her mind about which one she wanted. Unfortunately, right now nothing sounded good, so she put the pasta back in the refrigerator, grabbed her phone and her purse and decided that a walk down Flagler Avenue might fill the void she was feeling.

Flagler Avenue was one of Summer's favorite places in the world to shop. Her mother had taken her to Paris the summer before her senior year at Ohio State, and it had been amazing, but there was something about Flagler that filled her soul.

To begin with, it was an easy walk from her house, but the real joy was all the wonderful boutiques filled with treasures you couldn't buy just anywhere. She always started at Friki Tiki because it was her favorite shop, but she wouldn't allow herself to buy anything until she'd perused every other shop on the street. Of course, something always grabbed her attention at Friki Tiki, which meant she had to stop back by before going home. But that was just part of the adventure of Flagler Avenue.

Today she was almost at the bridge when she realized that not one thing had caught her eye. Summer had always been a frugal shopper, but it was a rare day when nothing in her favorite stores caught her attention. She thought about stopping at Silly Willy's to get some Chicken Chips for her neighbor's Yorkie, but then she remembered that Mrs. Anderson was at her daughter's in North Carolina for several weeks, so Summer just walked on by.

Back at Friki Tiki's she bought a bottle of Mango Mamma wine, just because she couldn't find anything else, and walked home feeling lonely and out of sorts. Twice she had stopped to look at her phone, but there were no messages from Jake.

More than anything Summer needed to talk with someone about her feelings, but whom? Michael and Bree were her two most trusted allies, and she definitely couldn't talk with either one of them. Bree had made it clear that Summer needed to end her friendship with Jake immediately, and she almost giggled imaging a conversation with Michael about him.

"It's like this, Michael," she said in her head. "I've been feeling old and undesirable lately, and I've met a man who makes me feel young and alive. His name is Jake Ross; yes, my client Jake Ross, but all of a sudden, he's met a woman and I feel like I'm losing his attention. Any ideas on what I should do to keep him focused on me and not some book publisher?"

That would go over great, she sighed, walking home with her bottle of wine clutched to her chest as if it were gold. Disappointed that she hadn't found anything she couldn't live without on her shopping trip, she stopped when she saw her reflection in a store window and groaned.

Michael would really worry if he saw me now, she thought, loosening her hold on the bag of wine. "It's not like I'm going home to drink this," she said out loud. "It's just to refill the wine rack."

Chapter 40

Dinner at the Sea Food Shack with Michael was nice, but Summer couldn't get her mind off Jake. Or to be more accurate, the absence of Jake. She had felt a real connection with him and thought he felt the same way, so why hadn't she heard from him?

"Summer?" Michael questioned, "did you hear me? You look like you're a million miles away."

"Sorry, I was just thinking about a client," she told him honestly. "What was the question?"

"I asked how your soup was since you've hardly taken a bite. But tell me about the client that has you so deep in thought," Michael's smile made her feel like a jerk.

"My soup is fine," she started, "and um, did you know we have a new vet in town? He's asked me to design a website for him."

"They mentioned it at the meeting last night," Michael said. "The people who've met him say he's a great guy, but how did you land his business so quickly?"

"Well," Summer started cautiously, "remember the Saturday after our forced dinner with the Stevens' and how I went out for a while by myself? I met Alex Bailey for the first time when he stopped to admire the Mustang."

"For the first time?" Michael questioned with a raised eyebrow.

"Yes, for the first time," she continued. "I met him again on Sunday at church, and Reverend Marks gave us a more official introduction. He had even suggested to Dr. Bailey that I'd be a good option to help with his advertising, and I guess everything just worked out."

Michael took her hand across the table and gave it a squeeze. "I really am proud of you Summer," he said looking in her eyes, "I guess all of your dreams have come true."

Those words were just enough to make her face go from a sun kissed bronze to a sun burned red. Had all of her dreams come true? A few weeks ago, she would have agreed, but now she wanted more, and that more was threatening everything she held dear.

Michael let go of her hand, without even noticing her reaction, and continued to eat his shrimp. He didn't say anything more about Summer and her success, and she breathed a sigh of relief. Everything she had told Michael about Alex Bailey was true, it's just that he wasn't the client that was so heavily on her mind.

After dinner Michael helped her into the vehicle and started down the street. "How about a stop at Treats on the Beach?" he asked cheerfully. "I'm thinking a banana split for two is just what we need to cap off this celebration."

The last thing Summer wanted was a big dish of gooey covered ice cream to try to abstain from, but she told herself this was Michael's celebration, and she would only eat enough to satisfy him. WRONG! When someone loved sugary treats like she did and was a stress eater to boot, and they had a sweet temptation put before them, there was no way they wouldn't pig out, and boy did she ever.

Michael watched as his wife shoved in spoonful after spoonful of rich vanilla ice cream, covered with chocolate and caramel sauce, into her mouth, stopping only long enough to wipe the drips from her chin. "I'm glad to see you have your appetite back, Summer," he chuckled. "After only eating half your soup at dinner, I worried you were coming down with something."

When she realized that he was talking to her, and that she'd eaten most of the dessert for two, Summer blushed and pushed the boat of ice cream in his direction. "I'm done." She said sheepishly and pretended to be watching the people out for an evening stroll.

Chapter 41

By the time they got home, the ice cream was sitting in Summer's stomach like a sinker. She remembered feeling this way as a kid when her dad would take her out for donuts on Saturday mornings. She'd eat two of the nut-covered maple Persians, knowing she'd be sorry later. All she wanted was an antacid and to lay down. Leave it to Michael to have other plans.

She had on an old NSB T-shirt and was pulling her hair way up into a ponytail when Michael came behind her and kissed her neck. "It was nice going out for dinner tonight," he said, moving his hands around to fondle her breasts. "We need to go out through the week more often."

Just hearing the word dinner made her think of food, and Summer was having a hard time keeping hers down. "Ugh, Michael," she said, moving away from his groping. "Can I have a rain check? I've had way too much to eat, and I walked into town today, so um, I really just need to go to sleep." Summer turned and looked into her husband's beautiful gray eyes, hoping to see understanding. Instead, what she saw was confusion.

"Sure," he said gruffly, but Summer could tell he didn't mean it. He was trying to bring some excitement into their marriage, but why did he have to pick tonight? Was he attributing her new fondness for wine to her being sexually frustrated, or did he just think she was having some type of *woman's crisis* so he tried to humor her? Whatever the reason, she couldn't think about it tonight, and she crawled into bed, her eyes closing the minute her head hit the pillow.

Sometime in the night she woke up, her mouth as dry as dust from all the ice cream. Normally she brought a Tervis Tumbler with ice water upstairs, but tonight there was nothing on the stand beside the bed, and she knew the tap water from the bathroom wasn't going to cut it. Carefully getting out of bed so she wouldn't wake her sleeping husband, Summer quietly crept down the stairs to the kitchen.

Two big glasses of cool refreshing water later, Summer's parched throat felt normal again, and she headed towards the stairs. She hadn't been able to check her phone earlier with Michael nearby, so instead of going back to bed, she sat down in her rocker to check her messages. But there were none. At least none from Jake, and his were the only ones she was interested in. She didn't want to care, she didn't want to cry, but she did, on both counts.

Her heart was aching, and the tears were rolling down her cheeks as she pulled a quilt around her shoulders and cried herself to sleep.

The living room was dark and quiet when she opened her eyes. Her phone was still on her lap, so glancing at the time Summer saw it was three o'clock in the morning. *That's midnight in LA*, she thought, and checked her messages one more time. And still, there was nothing from Jake.

When she had gone to bed Summer's stomach hurt, but now the hurt spread throughout her body. As much as she loved her rocker, it was not meant for sleeping, and after hours in an awkward position, her back was stiff, there was a crick in her neck, and her head was pounding. Carefully exiting from the chair, she left her phone on the end table, and tiptoed back up to bed.

Michael snored softly as she entered the room, and this time she was thankful for that rasping noise. It meant that at least for now, he was sound asleep, and she hoped against hope that he had been that way the entire time she was gone. She moved close to his warm body, needing to ward off the chill still wrapped around her heart, and fell into a restless sleep.

The routine the next morning was the same as it was every day. "When did our life become so predictable," Summer sighed, as she headed in to read her devotions.

Her sturdy oak rocking chair and old handmade quilt were just the same as they were yesterday, but when she looked at them now, Summer saw how mundane her life had become. When had she stopped feeling blessed to start longing for more? She had married Michael for better or worse, and while she knew what she was going through didn't constitute worse, what was it? Picking up her devotional, she tried reading the words that used to make her feel so safe and secure, but today they were just words, and the impact wasn't there.

After reading the page several times, she closed her eyes and started to pray.

The food disaster from the night before kept Summer from enjoying her normal morning coffee. She still felt a little like a cannon ball was lying in her abdomen, and the last thing she wanted was to make it go off. Her muscles were rebelling from the hours sleeping upright, so when she went upstairs and put on her comfy pajamas, she was powerless to resist the pull of her big comfy bed. Snuggling up with Michael's pillow, she fell into a deep dreamless sleep.

Chapter 42

Bright light was sifting through the windows when Summer opened her eyes. It had been so long since she'd slept like this during the day that it took her a few minutes to get her bearings and remember what had happened. Thankfully her stomach distress was gone, in fact, all of the aches she had experienced earlier had vanished, so she stretched her long arms and legs, gave a big yawn, and rolled out of bed.

The clock on the table showed that it was eleven o'clock, and she really needed to hurry! She grabbed a pair of yoga pants and a T-shirt and almost ran to the bathroom. Twenty minutes later she emerged, squeaky clean with shiny teeth, her hair in a sloppy knot on her head, and just enough make-up to make her feel presentable.

Once downstairs Summer tidied the kitchen and opened a can of Diet Coke, feeling the need for caffeine. While she waited to log in to the Four Seasons of Summer email, she took a brief glance at her phone and there it was. The blue circle with the white lightning bolt inside the white square indicating she had a message. And not any message, but a message from Jake Ross.

Summer's heart was racing, and her hands were shaking as she opened the message. As much as she had wanted to hear from Jake, after all this time she was afraid of what he might have to say. But when the app opened, the first words she read were, I haven't heard from you in a while. You okay? After that everything was a blur, but it didn't matter to her at all. She had heard from Jake, and at the same time she had worried about him, he had been worrying about her. Taking a minute to plan just the right thing to say, she finally replied.

I didn't want to bother you or get in the way of your new woman. I figured everything must be going well since I didn't hear from you.

To which Jake replied:

No woman is ever going to come between us, Summer. That's not something you have to worry about.

Summer wanted to ask him what he meant by that, but instead she sent a Smiley Face emoji, and he sent her one back. Relieved that their relationship was still intact, she started back to work.

The rest of the day passed swiftly. Summer was able to get the pictures from Alex Bailey that he wanted to use on his website and give him her preliminary ideas. He wasn't looking for a fancy spread, just something to let people know how to find him and what his specialties were. After all, a veterinarian in Florida could be asked to treat pet iguanas or macaws, on top of the regular domestic animals.

Satisfied that she had put in a good day's work in half a day's time, Summer logged out of her computer and started thinking about dinner. *Maybe pork chops,* she thought, rummaging through the packages in the freezer. She also found a dish of hash brown casserole, or what Riley called *potatoes with cereal*, and she knew it would be a good option with the chops.

Thinking of her youngest son brought a smile to Summer's face and she promised herself that she would try to be the cool, understanding mom that he thought she was. Thinking about sons and mothers she wondered for a moment about Jake and his mom. He'd mentioned that he had a brother getting married soon but nothing about parents or other siblings. Oh well, that could be a conversation for another day.

The pork chops were marinating, and the casserole was almost thawed when Summer came back down from changing clothes. She felt like she owed Michael something for her behavior the night before, but exactly what, she wasn't sure. She definitely was going to stay out of the wine and maybe after dinner, he'd be up for a stroll on the beach.

The pork chops were grilled to perfection and resting in a warm oven along with the casserole when Michael walked in. Giving him her brightest smile, she took the briefcase from his hand and put it in the den.

"Are you hungry?" she asked. "Dinner's ready but you have time to change first."

Summer could tell that Michael was appraising her and trying to decide which wife he had come home to. The sweet, loving girl he had married thirty-five years ago, the sex kitten of late, or the one who got angry and yelled. She understood his dilemma, because she wasn't always sure herself, but trying to be the wife he needed, she teased, "I'm having a sense of Déjà vu all over again. What is it, change first or eat first?"

Michael relaxed, thankful that it was sweet, loving Summer standing before him, and he brushed a lock of her chestnut curls from her face as he answered, "I'll go change and be back in ten." He started towards the stairs and then came back and gave her a kiss. Not just a peck like Ozzie gave Harriet, and not a "I can't wait to get you into bed kiss," but a kiss that meant something, and for Summer it stirred her heart.

Dinner was pleasant, and everything was going along smoothly. Michael was more than happy to take a walk with his wife afterwards. They left their shoes on the cement and walked hand in hand through the hardpacked sand, smiling at young lovers wrapped in an embrace. They talked about their boys, the upcoming holidays, and how the sunset was changing with the seasons. It was a perfect evening, and for the first time in a while, Summer felt blessed again.

They no sooner walked in the door than the phone began to ring, and Summer rushed to answer it. The caller was Elliott Stevens asking to talk with Michael, and she handed him the phone and went to the kitchen for a glass of water. The conversation was definitely not going to be a quick one so Summer decided to go upstairs and rinse all of the sand off of her feet.

Her feet were sand free and dry when the ping from her phone caught her attention. The message had to be from Jake, he was the only person who messaged her, but she and Michael were having such a good evening that she was afraid to open it. However, open it she did, and resting on her bed, she ended up in an electronic conversation with the gorgeous man, thirteen years her junior, who made her feel like the most desirable woman in the world by the words he used. And the red heart emojis that he used when they signed off didn't hurt either.

It was almost ten o'clock and Summer could hear Michael still talking to Elliott. There must be some huge problem with the hospital foundation to keep two men talking on the phone for so long. At this point she was more than a little frustrated and didn't know what to do. Finally, turning on the television, she found an episode of an old show from her childhood and settled down to remember the good old days.

Despite her morning nap, it didn't take Summer long to fall asleep, and by the time Michael finally made it upstairs he found his wife still dressed, but dead to the world. Gently trying to remove her capris, Michael did his best to wake her, realizing how soft and sexy she looked.

"Summer," he said, his voice husky as he tugged the pants down far enough that her lacy red thong became visible, "I need some help here." Through the slits in her eyes, she could see the erection rubbing against the zipper of his jeans, but instead of reacting she feigned sleep.

"Summer, can you lift your hips at least?" he urged, as the stubborn capris slipped off. Unbuttoning her blouse, he found a matching bra, and tried to decide his best course of action.

Unfortunately, Summer decided it for him when she pulled up the covers and mumbled, "Night."

***

That night was the first time she dreamed about Jake. They were walking on a beach somewhere in California, and she was wearing a very skimpy red lace bikini. Jake had on respectable board shorts, but no shirt, and the sculpted muscles of his abs, along with the large bulge in his shorts, had her salivating. Jake had taken her hand and pulled her into the most sensual kiss she had ever experienced, leaving her breathless and hungry for more.

Just as she was about to pull him down on the sand, music from the alarm clock filled her ears letting her know it was time to get up.

Her heart was pounding at the realization that she had an erotic dream about a man who wasn't her husband, and it only got worse when she slipped from the bed to see she was dressed in her sexy new red panties and bra. She unhooked the bra and slipped the panties down her long legs, groaning when she became aware of how damp they were. *Have I ever had a dream that aroused me like this?* she thought, and then throwing her lingerie in the laundry hamper, grabbed her robe and headed to the bathroom.

Michael was out of the shower and wrapped in a towel when she entered. He gave her a weak smile and headed to dress, leaving her alone to do whatever it was women do first thing in the morning. By the time Summer emerged he had already gone downstairs.

"I must have hit snooze," Summer told him as she watched him fill his Yeti with hot coffee. "You should have woken me up."

"You didn't oversleep," he answered. "I just needed to get an early start today, and I realized that I didn't mention it to you last night."

Summer wanted to say something, but she didn't know what. The guilt she felt from her dream about Jake threatened to overflow, and she knew she had to push it down. It was just a dream, right? It didn't mean anything. She sighed because she knew that wasn't the truth. It did mean something. It meant that her infatuation with him was getting stronger, and even though she knew it was wrong, she wasn't ready to give it up.

Chapter 43

Summer was curled up in her rocker, sipping her coffee and replaying her nighttime soap opera in her head when her phone pinged. The time read seven forty-five, meaning it wasn't even five o'clock on the west coast. Certain that something was wrong, she immediately opened the message.

Jake: Good Morning, my beautiful Summer! I forgot to tell you last night that my brother is getting married this weekend in Key West, and I've got to leave for the airport in less than an hour. I know this is kind of spur of the moment, but I was hoping you would consider meeting me in Miami on Sunday. I'm sure we could find some appropriate convention for you to sign up for so you have a good reason to get away. What do you say? I'd love to sit down with you, face-to-face, and have a real conversation, without electronics.

Her mind was reeling. Surely, he didn't really think she could up and go to Miami on a whim? There was no way Michael would ever understand it, and besides, Summer wasn't sure an in-person meeting was even a good idea. What they had now was friendly and fun but actually getting together? That was a totally different story.

Taking a deep breath to get herself calmed down, Summer began to type.

Summer: I appreciate the lovely offer, Jake, but my family would not understand me taking off for Miami like this. Conference or no conference, I don't think this is a good idea. Please tell me that you understand.

Jake: I understand perfectly, just don't say you weren't asked. I've still got some packing to do so I've got to run. Talk later, J.

"What the hell just happened?" she asked herself. Was Jake mad at her? Her life felt like one big ocean, and she was stuck in the middle drowning. She loved the attention Jake gave her, it made her feel like a teenager again, but asking her to meet him implied more, and she didn't want more, did she? Did she?

Summer put her head in her hands and willed herself not to cry. There were so many questions that needed answered. Like what about Leda, were they still seeing each other? And if they were, why was he asking her for a clandestine meeting in Miami? But mostly she was wondered what would have happened if she'd said yes?

She took a sip of coffee, but it was now as icy as her heart felt. She started on her devotions, but she just couldn't focus on the words. She needed to clear her head and decided that a bit of yoga might do the trick, even though her body was feeling every bit of her fifty-eight years.

The exercise definitely helped, as did the Cuddl Duds leggings and long-sleeved shirt she put on afterwards. When your heart and your body ached, there was just something about wrapping yourself in fleece that seemed to make everything better.

After getting such a late start yesterday, Summer was determined to get in a full day of work. She fixed herself a cup of hot tea, sat down at the computer, and logged in to her email. Web designing was a little like feast or famine, and the closer it came to Thanksgiving and Christmas, the slower her business was.

But today when she checked her email messages, she found one from a new prospect, an author who had just moved to Florida from Atlanta and needed a website designed. Of course, just thinking about an author took her mind straight to Leda, the publisher of books, and that brought her full circle back to Jake. Taking a big sip of tea in hopes of staying focused, she spewed it all over the keyboard when the scalding liquid hit her mouth.

"Son of a...," she shouted, trying to keep herself from swearing again. How did a nice girl like her get caught up in a mess like this? She was just trying to be a friend to Jake Ross and now not only was their friendship in question, but her feelings for him were definitely more than friendly.

***

By the end of the day, Summer had a signed contract from the author and was excited about designing a website for her. It turned out that Dena Daniels had just debuted her first novel, and the response had more than exceeded her expectations. A teacher for over thirty years, she was good with words and writing but struggled with technology. She had emailed back and forth with Summer most of the afternoon, and Summer had immediately felt a connection.

This is just what I need, she thought. *Something to distract me from my ever-increasing fascination with Jake.*

Summer enjoyed cooking and was good at it if she did say so herself but streamlining her recipes to only feed two had not been successful. Instead, she made meals meant for six or more and froze them for times like this when she worked late but still had a hungry husband to feed. Looking over the options in her freezer, nothing really called out to her. Even with the new relationship with Dena forming, Summer needed comfort food, and she knew what that was.

Dried beef gravy. As a girl it had been her favorite meal, even the one she requested for her birthday dinners. In fact, she loved it so much she'd given it a name that she used, even to this day. White dipping. There was nothing like rich creamy gravy, with little bits of dried beef, poured over buttered toast points to conjure up Summer's memories of home and happiness.

Just as she was melting the butter for the start of the roux, her cell phone rang. Holding it to her ear with her chin so the butter wouldn't burn, Summer greeted her caller with a little apprehension. "Hey, Bree," she said as normally as possible, "this is an odd time for you to call; what's up?"

Summer could tell that her friend was searching for just the right words before speaking. "Well, I haven't talked with you since you came by my house, and I wanted to make sure everything was okay. That we're okay," Bree said.

Summer moved the pan away from the heat, so she could concentrate on the conversation. "Why wouldn't we be okay, Bree?" she asked. "We both shared some very personal information, but that's what best friends do. There's nothing you could tell me that would change our friendship, so please don't worry about it."

"It's more than that, Summer," Bree insisted. "I'm worried that you're playing with fire and don't understand how dangerous it is. Remember in our women's group at church, someone recommended that we all read the book *FerVent*? Did you do it?"

"No," Summer answered. "Did you?"

"I didn't then, but I bought a copy today and I've read most of it already. Summer, I really believe the devil knows where you're the most vulnerable, and that's what he's working on." Bree took a breath and continued. "You want your youth back, and you think that's what Jake Ross offers, but Summer, you need to let him go."

To say she was dumbfounded was an understatement. She and Bree went to church together and talked about church type things, but *the devil?* That was not a topic that had ever come up.

"Bree, I love you, and you're my best friend, but do you really believe the devil is out to get me? I mean I believe in hell and everything, but I'm a good person, aren't I? And I haven't broken my marriage vows or anything." Even as the words came out of her mouth, Summer knew they weren't true. If the situation were reversed and Michael was communicating with a woman, how would she feel? She'd feel just like she did now, like shit.

"Just think about it, okay?" Bree asked. "Tomorrow I'm going to drop my book off, so you can read it for yourself. In the meantime, I'm going to pray for you, and I hope you will be, too."

Summer thought back to Jake's request that morning and how much she wanted to meet him in Miami, even though she knew that it was wrong. Was the devil really hitting her where she was weak, or was Bree transferring her own experience to Summer? One way or another, the thought was in her head, but her heart was still focused on Jake.

"I've got to run, Bree," Summer said honestly. "I was just starting dinner, and you know what a creature of habit Michael is. He'll want food on the table within ten minutes of his arrival home."

They said their goodbyes and Summer went back to her food prep, thinking about what Bree had said, but not buying it. Surely the devil had bigger souls to go after than hers?

Chapter 44

Michael sat down at the table when Summer put a plate in front of him. "Dried beef gravy?" he questioned.

"You don't like it?" Summer asked him, knowing darn well that he did. "It's my favorite meal and I can feel my mom's arms around me every time I eat it," she added a little defiantly. "But if you want something else…"

"Calm down, Summer," Michael responded. "I do like it, and I know that it's your favorite. You usually only make it in winter is all. I guess I didn't realize that it made you think of your mom; is everything okay with her?"

Summer nodded, feeling foolish for getting so feisty, but today her emotions were all over the place. First, Jake had asked her to meet him in Miami, and then Bree had told her she thought Satan was working on her. If that wasn't enough to cause a disruption in her feelings, what was?

The rest of dinner went well with Michael enjoying the white dipping enough to ask for seconds. He even helped her clean up the dishes, for which Summer was grateful. She told him about her new client, Dena Daniels, and that she had already ordered her book, *One Last Love* from Amazon, and he told her that one of the other architects in his firm had become a first-time grandpa. It was a normal evening, with normal conversation, between two long-time married people.

After sitting on the couch together and watching a silly television comedy, Michael said he was ready to go up to bed and Summer agreed. He made sure the doors were locked and she went around turning off the lights. She had left her cell in the kitchen after her talk with Bree, and when she looked at it, the hurt from the day resurfaced. Jake was off at a wedding, and she had no idea when, or if, she would hear from him, and she and Bree had had their first disagreement. Her life was spinning out of control, and she had no idea how to make it stop.

Once upstairs, Summer got ready for bed, not at all sure what to expect from her husband. She'd spurned his attentions the night of his celebration dinner, but that was only because she'd eaten too much ice cream. Last night she'd fallen asleep, but again, not her fault. If Michael would have ended his phone call sooner, she would have been more than happy to show him her new red lingerie, but he hadn't, even though she knew he had seen the lacy pieces of silk adorning her body.

After some reflection she decided that maybe it was up to her to make the first move, and that's exactly what she did. Donning a long, sheer white eyelet nightgown, instead of her normal sleepwear, and leaving her chestnut curls down like Michael preferred, Summer turned off the bathroom light and joined her husband in bed.

"Wow!" Michael exclaimed. "If this is what dried beef gravy does for you, I think we need to eat it more often." He pulled back the sheet and invited her into their bed and into his arms. "I've missed you, Summer," he said in a low, husky voice, and pulling her close enough for a deep passionate kiss, he showed her how much.

Chapter 45

The next morning Summer woke up more satisfied than she had been in weeks. Thinking about all the delicious things they had done to each other gave her goosebumps, and she reached over and snuggled closer to her still sleeping husband.

"Good morning, Mr. Alcott," she purred in his ear. "I trust you slept as well as I did?" Running her fingertips softly over his still flat stomach, she let them slip down to the source of last night's pleasure. Early in their marriage she would have been rewarded with a morning expression of Michael's lust for her, but today, no matter how much she teased, nothing happened.

"Good morning yourself," Michael said rolling towards her, and away from her wandering fingers. "What time is it anyway?"

Summer sighed, knowing that while last night had been pretty close to amazing, Michael was back to his business persona this morning, and nothing she could do would change it. She slipped out of bed and grabbed her nightgown from the floor, wrapping it around her as she headed into the bathroom. Even after all these years, she wasn't comfortable with Michael seeing her naked in the daylight.

Once downstairs the morning repeated itself like every other weekday morning, and soon she had her peck and pat, and Michael was out the door. Taking her cell phone and a fresh cup of coffee, she headed to her rocker for her morning ritual of devotions. When she opened her prayer journal, she stopped to think about what Bree had said the evening before. Was the devil really using her insecurities about her age and attractiveness by bringing Jake into her life? Once again, she didn't believe it and went on with her reading and prayers.

The last drop of coffee gone, Summer pulled out her cell to see if Riley had posted any new pictures with Olivia. She wanted to be supportive and knew her son would appreciate likes and positive comments on his posts. But it wasn't a picture of Riley and Olivia that came up in her newsfeed, but a picture of Jake, wrapped in the arms of a sexy brunette in a slinky black dress. The gorgeous woman had to be Leda, but what was she doing there? Why would Jake have asked her to meet him in Miami if Leda was going with him to Key West?

The pain she was feeling started as sobbing in her heart and ended up as tears covering her face. She knew she was a mess but had no idea how to get control of her emotions. She and Michael had just spent a night having the kind of hot sex she'd been craving, and this morning she was devastated to see Jake Ross with his arms around another woman. One thing was certain, she was in over her head with Jake, but she wasn't ready to lose him. It was time to up the ante.

Summer showered, washed and dried her hair, and with great care put on her make-up. Then pulling out a pink sundress with spaghetti straps and a flouncy skirt, she got dressed. Carefully holding her cell phone up, and angling it down, she started taking selfies until she had the perfect one. Without allowing herself time to think about her plan, Summer sent a message to Jake along with the best picture. "Hope you're having a great time," was all it said.

By the time she got downstairs there was already a reply from Jake.

Not nearly as good as it would be knowing you were meeting me in Miami on Sunday.

To say she was confused was an understatement. He was in Key West with a beautiful woman on his arm, yet he was flirting with her? Yes, she had sent the picture in hopes of making him think about her, but she had never imagined he would bring up Miami again. Was Jake Ross just playing her, or had he been without a woman too long?

She decided not to answer, even though it was killing her. Instead, she changed out of the dress, although she laid it carefully on the bed to wear that night to Breakers and went back downstairs to log into her computer.

After some great emails with Dena, she had an idea that she thought would be perfect for her new website. Since Dena was a romance writer, and her debut novel was titled *One Last Love,* Summer used the whole love and romance theme for the website. Normally she worked on more than one project in a day, but she wanted to really wow Dena with the final design and was so into the graphics that it was five o'clock before she was finished and ready to call it a day.

Not bad, she thought to herself with a smile and rushed upstairs to get ready for her standing Friday night date with her husband. She quickly slipped into her dress, styled her hair into waves around her shoulders, and fastened the straps on her gladiator sandals. A quick swipe of lipstick, a little repair to her make-up, and a big spritz of Amazing Grace, and Summer was ready. Grabbing a sweater to ward off any chill, she was waiting by the door when Michael got home.

"Look at you," he said with a wink. "Give me ten minutes and I'll be ready."

Summer was just this side of devastated. There was no mention of their incredible night, and definitely no complimentary words about her appearance. *What would he think,* Summer thought, *if he knew I had selected this dress to entice another man? And what would he say if he knew about the other man's invitation?* She knew there was no point in thinking this way. Michael was who he was, and there was no changing him after all these years. But still it hurt to think she was going to spend the rest of her life wanting more from a man who had no clue that she was unhappy. And if he did know, he had no desire to do anything about it.

Chapter 46

Friday night at Breakers had always been Summer's favorite night of the week, but tonight her thoughts were miles away, and so was her heart. She knew she wasn't in love with Jake, but she was sure *in like* with him. But the attention he gave her, and the way he made her feel? She was deeply in love with that, and she longed for that feeling from her husband. She ordered her regular Blue Moon, but when she told the server that she wanted the Key Lime grilled Mahi sandwich, she could hardly hold back the tears.

"Are you okay?" Michael asked, the concern showing on his face.

Summer tried to smile and stop the waterworks, but they had a mind of their own. "You stay and eat, Michael," she answered. "I need to go home."

The server brought their beers just as she started to cry in earnest leaving everyone in an awkward position. Michael threw a handful of cash on the table and apologized to the server, saying there was an emergency and they had to leave. By now the people sitting near them were staring at Summer, but she didn't care. She had to get out of there now.

By the time Michael caught up with her, Summer was half a block away, refusing to stop when he called her name. "What's going on with you, Summer?" he demanded. "I'm sure everyone in the restaurant thinks we had a fight, and I'm not sure we can ever go back there again."

Michael grabbed her arm and pulled her close to him. Looking into her tear-filled hazel eyes, he asked once more, "What's wrong? You were fine when I got home so I know it's not something with the boys or our family. I'm worried about you, Summer. Can't you see that?"

Summer let him put his arms around her while she cried, but she didn't say a word. After a couple of minutes, she pulled away and continued the short walk to their house. She could hear Michael swearing and calling her name, but she kept walking in silence.

At home she headed straight for their bedroom and crawled into bed, not even bothering to undress. Michael was in hot pursuit, but when it became clear that she wasn't going to talk, he went back downstairs. The minute she heard him rumbling around in the kitchen looking for something to eat, the tears started to flow again, and she made no attempt to stop them.

How did things get so out of control? She wondered. *A few weeks ago, I was content with my life, and now all I can think about is escaping it.* That realization was enough to really put her over the edge and she ended up crying herself to sleep.

***

When she opened her eyes, it was morning, and Michael's side of the bed had definitely not been slept in. Knowing she needed to apologize she slowly headed to the stairs, trying to come up with the right words to say to him. As she passed by Cooper's room, she noticed the messy bed and knew that's where Michael had spent the night. His clothes from the evening before were in a pile on the floor, and she smiled to herself wondering if Michael was walking around downstairs in his underwear.

But when she got there, Michael was no place to be found. What she did find was a pot of freshly made coffee and her favorite mug beside it with a note inside.

"I've gone into the office for a few hours to give you some time to think," she read. "Enjoy your coffee but when I get home we're going to talk."

Coffee in hand Summer picked up her phone and went directly to her rocker. The first thing she saw was a message from Jake, sent the night before.

Tomorrow is my brother's big day, and I have to tell you it's a lot harder than I thought it would be. I'm happy for Eric and Megan, but the memories of my wedding to Beth are overwhelming. It would hurt a lot less if I had someone special here with me. Anyway, I'm thinking of you, and I'll post pictures on Facebook throughout the day. Jake

What did he mean if someone special was there with him? Summer thought. *Is Leda not special, or is he hinting that I am?* Quickly opening up Facebook to see what she had missed, there was a picture of a man who looked a lot like Jake, kissing the brunette she had seen in the picture the day before. Reading the caption, she almost shouted!

"The happy couple's last kiss before the big day. My brother and best friend, Eric, and his soon to be bride, Megan."

"It wasn't Leda," Summer said out loud. "The beautiful brunette Jake had his arms around was his brother's fiancée!" Not able to hold back her excitement, she immediately sent Jake a message back.

I love having you in the same time zone, and I love the picture of your brother and his fiancée! They make a beautiful couple, and I'm so happy for both. I look forward to wedding pictures and by the way, I wish you had someone special there, too. Or at least, were meeting them in Miami.

Not giving herself time to change her mind, she immediately hit the send arrow, and smiled.

Chapter 47

By the time Michael got home, Summer was in a great mood and had come up with a game plan for their talk. Insisting that she must be experiencing hormonal changes, she assured him she would see her doctor if she had another uncontrollable emotional outburst. Either he believed her or was just happy to have his cheerful wife back, because he accepted her explanation without question.

Throughout the day she checked Facebook for pictures from the wedding, and she even took her phone into the bathroom when she saw she had a message from Jake. It was quick, but flirty and fun, but oh, did it make her heart sing.

She and Michael were talking about what to have for dinner on Sunday when the doorbell rang. Summer remembered that Bree had said she would be over with a book for her to read, and more than anything, she did not want to face her friend right now. Michael opened the door and gave Bree a hug, telling her that Summer was in the kitchen.

"Hi!" Summer said with as much exuberance as she could muster, "is it too early for a glass of wine?" It wasn't even two o'clock, but a glass of wine was just what Summer needed if she was going to have another conversation with Bree about Jake.

Bree shook her head and answered, "It's such a nice afternoon, I thought maybe we could go for a walk?"

"Okay," Summer agreed, realizing that Bree was just trying to get them away, so they could talk freely without worrying about Michael overhearing their conversation.

"We're going for a walk," Summer told her husband. With a kiss on the cheek she added, "We won't be gone too long."

"Have you thought about what I said yesterday?" Bree asked almost the moment the door closed behind them.

"I did think about it," Summer answered honestly, "but Bree, I'm just not ready to give up this thing with Jake. We're just having a good time; that's not a sin?"

Bree reached into her bag and handed Summer the copy of *FerVant* she had promised to bring her. "But you're having a good time with a man who's not your husband; surely you know that's wrong?"

"Okay, I admit it isn't ideal, but Michael and I are going through a rough patch and Jake is helping me through it. I need him, Bree; why can't you see that?" Summer pleaded.

"I see that you're rationalizing your relationship with Jake Ross, and that scares me. It scares me a lot. Do you think Gabe and I met and just fell into bed? We started out as coworkers, then became friends and confidants. I told him about my marriage issues, and he told me his, and after several months of looking for reasons to spend time together, we drove to Orlando, rented a room, and spent the weekend in bed. It was the most exciting and terrifying thing I'd ever done." Bree stopped to see if her words were having an impact before continuing.

"That first time I told Dan I was attending a real estate conference and he didn't question a thing. But I could only use that excuse a couple of times before I had to find a new one. That's when Gabe and I started meeting at houses the company had listings for, and that's when Dan found out. Summer, when Dan walked in and saw me naked on the floor with Gabe, my world almost stopped. It was the absolute worst day of my life, and if you don't stop this game you're playing with Jake Ross now, you're headed for the same pain, and so is your family."

Summer listened and tried to hear what Bree was telling her, but her situation was different. Jake lived a time zone and several thousand miles away, and yes, he had asked her to meet him, but she'd said no, hadn't she? She wasn't going to betray her husband, she was just going to enjoy the way he made her feel, without anyone getting hurt.

After several blocks of walking and talking Bree could tell that she wasn't getting through to her friend. "I love you, Summer Alcott," she said. "You're the dearest friend I've ever had. Just know that I'm here when you need me, and I'll never judge you, no matter what."

Summer had tears in her eyes when she hugged Bree, thanking her for caring. "I can't let go yet, Bree," she said, "but it's good to know you're there when I need someone to talk to."

Bree nodded, walked away, and turned back to look at Summer. "Read the book, Summer," she said. "Please read the book." The rest of the weekend was quiet, with Summer trying to keep things as normal as possible. They grilled grouper and ate on the deck on Saturday evening, went to church and called their sons on Sunday, had pot roast with potatoes and carrots for dinner, and prepared for the week ahead. Several times Summer saw the book Bree had given her lying by her rocker, but not once did she pick it up. She did other reading though, but it was purely for pleasure and not enlightenment.

She could tell that Michael was being cautious about initiating sex, and she did nothing to encourage him. On Saturday night, she stayed up longer than usual watching movies on TV, and when she finally did go to bed, she gave him a kiss that was almost sisterly before turning on her side. It was a little uncomfortable, but Summer felt justified since Michael had done the same thing to her in the past.

On Sunday evening, she got a message from Jake that he was about to board his plane for Los Angeles, and once again he said how much he wanted her to meet him in Miami.

We could have come up with some conference you needed to attend, he told her. Even though it was the exact excuse Bree had given Dan, Summer refused to believe that what she was doing with Jake was the same as what Bree had done with Gabe Barrett.

By the next day she and Jake were sending messages back and forth like kids, and Summer was on cloud nine. One day she was telling him about a special dish she had made, and that she was a pretty good cook. His response had been, "I'll bet you're good at a lot of things." Something about the winking emoji he sent afterwards led her to believe he was referring to her being good in bed. Not sure how to answer, she replied that she was good at anything she enjoyed. Those few simple words were the end to Summer's belief that they were just friends.

Every day she forced herself to spend at least two hours on *Four Seasons of Summer*, so that none of her clients went without attention. In the time span between messages with Jake and doing her own work, Summer read and edited Jake's blogs before he posted them so that *Pushing the Plate Away* was polished and professional. She was extremely busy but extremely happy.

One day in a routine message Jake mentioned Leda, and Summer felt a crack in her fantasy world.

Summer: You haven't mentioned Leda since before your brother's wedding. I guess I thought you weren't still seeing each other.

Jake: There just wasn't anything to say, but yes, we've been seeing each other all along. She thinks we should move in together, and I'm just not ready for that.

And that was all it took for the crack to break the fantasy in two. Summer was devastated and didn't even know what to say. If Leda thought they should move in together, it meant they were sleeping together, and that was more than she could bear.

Jake: Summer, are you still there? What's going on in that gorgeous head of yours?

Summer: I'm just a little confused, Jake. You tease and flirt with me, you asked me to meet you in Miami, and you're still seeing Leda? And obviously you're sleeping with her, so what's going on is that I'm feeling used.

Jake: Please don't be too harsh on me, Summer. I'm a guy and I have guy needs. Leda's been divorced for ten years, and she says she has needs, too. I'm the first man she's been with since her divorce, and even though she's not perfect, she's sweet and we get along well. I'm a guy, or did I say that before?

Summer wrote several replies and deleted them all. *First man in ten years, my ass!* She thought. No woman stays celibate for ten years only to give it up within a couple of weeks of meeting a man. Either she was desperate or smelled money, but Summer didn't believe for a moment Leda was being honest with Jake. But what could she do? Finally, she sent Jake a message that she thought it was better if she just didn't give her opinion, and that she needed to get to work.

He thanked her for not judging him and said they would talk later. Which turned out to be almost a week.

Chapter 48

Summer was hurt, and she was angry, but she had no outlet for either. She needed Bree, but she knew talking to her would just bring another lecture, and she didn't need another reason to feel badly. She went about her days, got lots of work done, and did her best to pretend all was right with the world by the time Michael got home at night.

One bright spot in her otherwise gloomy frame of mind was her new-found friendship with her client, Dena Daniels. Once her website was finished, Summer was afraid it would be the end of their conversations, but it turned out they were very much alike, so a work relationship turned into more.

On the third day of not hearing from Jake, and only talking with Bree at church, Summer knew it was time to give her a call. "Summer?" Bree answered immediately. "I saw your name on the Caller ID and I almost cried. I think about you all the time, and I miss you; are you okay?"

Summer laughed. "Slow down, Bree," she said. "I'm okay and I miss you, too, that's why I called. But I do have some news about Jake Ross that you'll probably find interesting. He's been seeing his book publisher girlfriend all this time, and having sex with her, too. I feel like such a fool."

"Oh, Summer," Bree said, "it's exactly what I've been praying for. You needed something to make you see his true colors and this is it."

Summer wasn't sure how to respond. Yes, Jake wasn't exactly the man she thought he was. He'd invited her to meet him in Miami, and he was more than flirtatious with his comment about her being good at a lot of things, but truly what did he owe her? She was starting to regret ever mentioning Jake to Bree, but how did she back pedal, now?

"You're right, Bree," Summer said, and for the first time ever, she lied to her best friend. "I do see Jake now for what he is, and I hope he and Leda will be happy together."

She could hear Bree crying when she answered. "I'm so glad, Summer," she said between sobs. "I wouldn't want you to ever experience the hell that I went through."

Summer continued to let Bree think she was following her advice about getting out of Jake's life for good, and then told her she needed to return to work. Right before they hung-up Bree said more than asked, "You read the book, didn't you?"

Summer groaned inwardly but couldn't tell another lie. "Not yet, Bree, but I will; promise." And then hung up.

For two more days she held her breath waiting to see if she'd hear from Jake again. She checked Facebook to see what he was up to, but there were no new posts. She checked her email for new blogs to review, but there was nothing. Every hour that passed without hearing from him was agony, and Summer was almost to her breaking point.

On Saturday afternoon the church held an afternoon tea, and she and Bree attended together. She put on her happy face and did her best to enjoy the event. Alex Bailey's wife, Nancy, was introduced, and Summer and Bree both agreed she was a lovely person, and they would enjoy getting to know her better.

The party finally over, Summer dropped Bree off at home and wanted nothing but a glass of wine, a hot bath, and maybe another glass of wine. She'd kept to her commitment to slow down on alcohol, but every muscle of her body hurt, including the big one pounding away in her chest, and she needed relief.

Michael was watching football on TV when she got home and paid no attention when she tried to tell him about meeting Alex Bailey's wife. She hated when he was so engrossed in something that he didn't even acknowledge her, but what the heck, she had a plan to adhere to. Since the red wine glass in the cabinet looked the biggest, Summer filled one with Pinot Grigio and ascended the stairs to her bedroom. Clothes off and hot water making decadent bubbles in the tub, Summer heard the ping of messenger. Grabbing the phone and easing her body gently into the tub of hot foam, she opened the message and read Jake's question.

Jake: Are we still friends?

Summer's heart was pounding. She took a gulp of wine while she argued with herself on what she should do. The rational side of Summer said she should finish her bath, have that second glass of wine, and spend the evening with her husband. After all, Jake had dropped a bombshell on her about Leda and then left her alone for days. But the emotional side of Summer, the side that was kind and caring, the one that had offered Jake friendship in the first place, was a nervous wreck and wanted nothing more than to send him a message.

Summer: Yes, of course we're still friends. Why do you think we wouldn't be?

Jake: I could tell that you were upset about Leda, and I wasn't sure if you'd want to hear from me or not.

Summer: Maybe confused is a better word. I don't understand how you can talk with me like you do, when you're sleeping with another woman. Especially when I thought you were still grieving for Beth.

Jake: For the last five years I've spent days at a time curled up on the floor, sobbing and thinking about Beth, and everything our accident cost us. We wanted a family, and instead the infant I ended up with was my beautiful, amazing wife. No one knows what it was like, Summer, and until you came along, some days I could barely breathe let alone carry on a normal conversation.

Summer: I don't know what to say, Jake. All I did was offer you friendship, I didn't do anything special other than be there when you wanted to talk.

Jake: But you did do something special, Summer. You listened to me, and accepted me, and showed me there was still a life for me out there. I'll never be able to thank you for that.

Summer: So then where does Leda fit in, Jake?

Jake: I'd had a few dates before Leda, but the magic was never there. Friends tried to fix me up after Beth died, but every date was a disaster. I finally signed up at match.com, and that's how I met Leda. You're absolutely gorgeous, Summer, and if you weren't happily married, I'd be on your doorstep with flowers and sappy poetry, but you are, and Leda's available.

Summer: Thank you, Jake. That means a lot to me, even though I still don't understand about Leda.

Jake: You won't have to try much longer, because she's leaving for New York in a couple of weeks. She wanted to stay in California, and move in with me, but I told her I just wasn't ready for that big of a step. I like her, Summer, but I have to be honest with you, she's not the woman I have in mind.

Summer took the last sip of her wine and realized that the water in the tub was cold. *Not the woman he has in mind. Is he telling me that I am?* She pulled the plug, and with one hand, grabbed a towel, wrapping it around the goosebumps covering her body. He'd said that if she wasn't happily married, he'd be on her doorstep with flowers and sappy poetry, so the question for her was just how happily married was she?

The bath and the wine had done nothing to calm her nerves after her communication with Jake, and Summer still had an evening ahead with her husband. The husband she had promised to love and honor until death separated them, but did she still love Michael? That was the question that was haunting her, but she could never really come up with a definitive answer.

The evenings were getting chillier as fall progressed, and even though New Smyrna Beach was still blessed with sunshine and eighty-degree temperatures during the day, Summer opted against shorts and slipped on a pair of soft leggings and a long-sleeved T-shirt. Her hair up in a messy bun, and no make-up save a swipe of lip gloss, she headed downstairs for that second glass of wine.

Michael had just turned off the TV when she walked in the room, and the smile on his face let her know that Ohio State had won the game. "You look awfully comfortable," he told her, "I guess that means we're staying in tonight?"

After the fiasco at Breakers, they had avoided their favorite restaurant, especially since Lacey Stevens was doing her best to share

Summer's meltdown with the world. There were lots of great places to eat in town, but the problem was, Summer wasn't interested in going out. "They gave us little sandwiches and cookies at the tea," she tried to explain, "so I'm really not hungry. When you're ready, I'll put a burger on the grill and make you a salad, okay?"

Michael could tell he didn't have much choice and just replied, "Sure." Watching as Summer poured herself a big glass of wine, he added, "Do you want me to go to Red Box and rent a movie? There's a couple out that you've mentioned wanting to see."

"That sounds good," she answered. "Why don't you go now and see if *Book Club* is in? Someone at the tea said every couple needs to see it."

Michael left on his movie hunt, and Summer sat down with her wine. Still thinking about Jakes's remark that Leda wasn't the woman he had in mind, she sent him a message.

Summer: What are you doing tonight?

Jake: Just enjoying a quiet night in alone; you?

Summer: The same, but where's your little girlfriend?

Jake: Visiting with her sister before she heads back to New York.

Summer: Michael just left to see if he can rent Book Club for us to watch tonight. Have you seen it?

Jake: Yep, Leda and I watched it last night.

"Well crap on a cracker!" she said to herself. "This conversation has sure taken a wrong turn."

Summer: I think I hear Michael, so I need to run. Talk later.

Summer laid down her phone and thought about their conversation. Jake hadn't corrected her when she called Leda his girlfriend; what did that mean? Then she started thinking about Jake and Leda snuggled up together watching a movie, and she didn't like it at all. Since she'd had two glasses of wine, and since this movie was just taking place in her head, she imagined herself on the couch instead of Leda, snuggled up with Jake. She'd be sitting between his knees while he reclined on pillows, their hands exploring each other over their clothes. She could almost feel Jake's fingers moving gently over the seam of her leggings, the lightweight fabric causing friction to her most intimate spot. Another few seconds and she would have combusted sitting alone in her living room, but just as she felt herself start to let go, Michael called out. "I'm home and I got the movie."

"Your face is kind of flushed," Michael remarked as he walked in the room. "Maybe you need to take off those leggings and put on something lighter?"

At the word "leggings" Summer felt the heat rising to her face again. It was bad enough having a sex dream about another man when she was sleeping, but in the middle of her living room when it wasn't even dark outside. She shook her head as if to get water out of her ears, and knew she was in deep trouble.

"Before you get comfortable, why don't you go light the grill and I'll throw the salad together," Summer said, hoping to change the subject. Michael agreed and headed to the deck. She quickly splashed a little more wine in her glass and opened the refrigerator, grabbing everything she could to make a salad. But when she pulled out the ripe, firm cucumber, salad was the last thing on her mind.

"Get a grip," she said out loud, and chugged the last of the wine.

After Michael had eaten and everything was cleaned up, Summer got comfortable in her rocker, and he stretched out on the couch. The movie was hilarious from the start and Summer couldn't help but send a message to Jake.

Summer: This is the funniest movie I've seen in years! That judge character needs to get some down and dirty sex.

Jake: You're my kind of woman, Summer Alcott! I love down and dirty.

Summer knew she was venturing into dangerous territory, but the thrill was too exhilarating to stop.

Summer: Yeah? Me too!

Jake: What are you wearing right now?

Summer: What am I wearing? Why?

Jake: I just want to visualize you while I'm in the shower.

Summer: In the shower? Are you going somewhere?

Jake: Not going anyplace, but this conversation has me very uncomfortable, if you get my drift.

Summer: Oh…

Jake: Yeah, O. Goodnight my beautiful Summer, sweet dreams.

After that it was hard for her to concentrate on the rest of the movie. As much as she wanted to see how it turned out, Summer ended up closing her eyes and thinking about Jake in the shower, his body glistening and wet. With all the wine, and very little food, it didn't take long until she was close to sleep, daydreaming about being in that shower with Jake.

"Summer," Michael said, jostling her out of her thought, "are you awake?"

"Um, I guess so," she answered with an exaggerated yawn. "Did I miss much of the movie?"

"Almost all," he chuckled. "You can watch it tomorrow afternoon. Right now, we need to get you up to bed."

Summer didn't put up a fight as he helped her up the stairs, but when he tried to help her get ready for bed, Summer dug in her heels. "I can finish from here," she said, turning away from him. "Don't forget to close up downstairs."

The minute Michael left the room she was out of her clothes and into an old nightshirt. Her body was on fire, and she needed release but somehow it felt wrong to make love with one man when your mind was on another one. Men probably did it all the time, she told herself, but she'd never been promiscuous, and that's how this felt. But how could you be promiscuous with your husband, she reasoned, and pulled the night shirt over her head and jumped into bed naked, knowing Michael would be surprised. Very surprised.

Chapter 49

As it happened, the surprise was on her because the next thing she knew it was morning, and the smell of bacon and freshly brewing coffee were floating in and out of her mind.

"When did you come to bed?" she asked Michael, accepting the mug of coffee he was handing her.

"Sometime after *Saturday Night Live*," he answered, removing the perfectly crisped bacon from the skillet. "But if I'd have known you had decided to sleep like Marilyn Monroe, I'd have been up sooner." He gave her a wink and pulled the eggs out of the fridge.

"How do you know about the way Marilyn Monroe slept?" Summer questioned. "Didn't she die before you were born?"

"Her picture was the first time I saw a woman naked," he smirked, "That's not something a boy ever forgets. My friends and I found an old edition of my dad's *Playboy* and Marilyn was the Sweetheart of the month. I don't know why I said anything about her except I heard somewhere she liked to sleep naked."

"Thanks for the history lesson," she teased "but I'm starving so give me your best Bobby Flay."

After breakfast they dressed for church, with Summer doing her best to put last night's messages out of her head. She was a little worried that Bree was right about Satan going after her where she was vulnerable and made up her mind to be cautious with Jake and steer clear of sex talk.

Summer always came away from church with a full heart and an attitude of gratitude. She knew how lucky she was to live the life that she did, and that was where her mantra of being blessed had come from.

Michael was such a handsome man, and he treated her well, so why in the world had she ever thought she needed more? They walked hand in hand to their vehicle as she made a mental list of things she wanted to talk with her sons about on their weekly Sunday afternoon calls.

Michael went up to change while Summer added some ham and cheese to the leftover salad for his lunch. He had talked her into ordering pizza for dinner, which for Summer meant carrots and celery for lunch. She was still full of the bacon and egg feast that morning anyway, so she didn't really mind.

Michael took his salad and a box of crackers to the living room and turned on the television. Apparently yesterday he'd watched his favorite college team, his Alma Mater, Ohio State play, and today it was his favorite Pro Team, The Tampa Bay Buccaneers. Summer didn't understand all the hoopla around football, but men seemed to love it. Anyway, her husband and sons did, and having them occupied had always left her time to read.

After changing her clothes, Summer picked up her copy of Dena Daniel's book, *One Last Love*, and went to the deck for some peace and quiet. The cover had a picture of a glorious sunset and a beautiful woman lifting up a glass of red wine, almost as if she was toasting the ball of fire in the sky. Dena had told her it was the story of a woman who had two unhappy marriages behind her when she finally meets the man of her dreams. Dena wouldn't give away anymore clues, but it had nothing but Five Star Reviews on Amazon, and Summer couldn't wait to dive in.

The book was so good that she couldn't put it down. It had romance, conflict, friendship, and sex—lots and lots of sex. Dena had published it herself, a trend that many authors were doing, and Summer wanted to ask her new friend if she had tried the traditional publishing route. For Summer it was every bit as good as some of the big named authors she enjoyed, but that was up to Dena. All she had been asked to do was build her a website.

When Michael came to tell her it was halftime, Summer was ready to take a break and talk with her sons. They had both sent her texts about their week, but like any mom, she loved hearing their voices. Michael put in the phone number for Cooper, and Summer got comfortable while

Michael and their firstborn talked about architecture and craft beer. She was really only half listening when Cooper said, "So what do you say, Mom? Will you and Dad come out to LA and spend Thanksgiving with me this year?

Chapter 50

All the excuses for why they couldn't go were swirling around in her head, but that's all they were, excuses. When they lived in Ohio, both Michael's mom and her mom had hosted a Thanksgiving dinner, so Summer never had a chance to start traditions for her family. But once they'd moved to New Smyrna Beach, Summer had taken over, and whether extended family and friends were there or not, the four Alcotts always spent the day together.

Riley had already said he was going to spend the holiday with Olivia's family in New York, so why not? At least the three of them would be together. Summer looked at Michael, knowing he thought she would say no, and smiled. "We'd love to come, Cooper," she told him, and she meant it.

After hanging up with Cooper, Michael said, "Thanks Summer. I can tell how much it means to Cooper that you agreed to go. He doesn't say anything, but I can tell he's a little envious of your relationship with Riley."

Summer started to argue, but decided it wasn't worth a debate. She and Riley did have a special bond, but only because from the moment he was born, Cooper had been Michael's shadow. She looked away from her husband, wondering how he could be so smart, and yet so clueless. Did he pay attention to anyone's feelings except Cooper's?

"We'd better call Riley," she said instead, "or halftime will be over."

***

The call to Riley went well, and Summer shared their plans of spending Thanksgiving on the west coast with Cooper. "Wow!" Riley chuckled. "You mean none of your famous dumplings or date pudding? How will you all survive?"

Michael was laughing along with his son, but Summer was serious when she answered, "I just thought I'd make them at Cooper's."

"Mom," Riley said, "Cooper's a grown man, and since he invited you to Los Angeles, you need to let him be in charge of the plans."

Summer smiled and said softly, "You're pretty wise, you know that, Riley Alcott?"

"That's because I had a great teacher."

She looked at Michael and could almost read the words he was thinking. *See, that's what I mean about you and Riley.* Summer turned away, keeping her face as stoic as possible, wondering if maybe it wasn't Michael who was envious of her relationship with their youngest son.

They ended the conversation and Summer hung up. *We're going to L.A. for Thanksgiving,* she thought with a little bit of excitement, and then it hit her full force. *We're going to Los Angeles; the Los Angeles where Jake lives.*

Michael went back to his ballgame without another word about Thanksgiving, and Summer went back to the deck to read. But she couldn't. Her heart was pounding, and her hands were shaking at the thought that maybe while she was in California, she and Jake could find a time to meet. She hadn't communicated with him since their sexy conversation the night before, and she wasn't sure she wanted to be the one to initiate one today.

Unable to calm her thoughts down, she went to the kitchen for a Diet Coke and grabbed a beer for Michael. He accepted it with a smile and a thank you and turned back to the television. Summer watched for a minute trying to figure out what was going on, but when Michael yelled, "What the hell was that?" she decided she didn't really want to know. Instead, she grabbed her phone and pulled up Facebook, looking at the posts from Riley and Jake. Riley's had lots of pictures of him with Olivia, thankfully Jake's were all about his blog.

Unfortunately, Tampa Bay lost the football game, so Michael was a little sullen when Summer went in to ask if he was ready to order the pizza. "You know it's just a game, Michael," she said massaging the tension from his neck, "and it's not like you really know those players."

He looked at her as if she'd just dropped in from another planet. "Just a game," he said. "You're cute Summer, I'll give you that, but you know nothing about sports."

"And proud of it," she laughed, but her thoughts were still back on "You're cute." Not exactly the sentiments she was looking for from her husband, but she'd take it.

They ordered from The Seafood Shack, which surprisingly had delicious brick fired pizza. The Mama Mia was one of their favorites, covered with fresh bell peppers, onion, mushrooms, marinated artichoke hearts, pepperoni, and salami, plus two kinds of cheese. It was a pizza lover's dream. While Michael went to pick up their dinner, Summer put glasses in the freezer to chill and sliced oranges for the rims. Nothing went better with pizza than a cold Blue Moon, and even if it wasn't on tap, it was pretty darn good.

"So, what do you really think of spending Thanksgiving at Cooper's?" Michael asked, gooey cheese running down his chin. "I've got to admit I never thought you'd go for it."

"What are you saying? That I'm a hard ass when it comes to traditions?"

Michael almost choked on his beer. "I would never use those words to describe you, Summer, but we all know that you like things a certain way and having your family with you at holidays is one of those."

"I guess I can be controlling about some things, but if it bothered you why didn't you ever say anything?" she asked.

"Because a happy you is what counts and besides, up until now, it's never been a problem. When Riley was in school, he came home for Thanksgiving break and Cooper came here to be with all of us. But now that Riley has his own life, I think Cooper wants to share some of his with his parents." The look Michael gave her made her think that he knew something that she didn't, but when he took another slice of pizza and changed the subject, she knew the Thanksgiving conversation was over. At least for now.

"So, what's your week like?" Michael asked as they cleaned up after their pizza feast. "Have any new clients on the horizon?"

"Nope," she told him, "just finishing up with my new author. Her book is amazing, and I hope we get to meet some day. She's about my age and I think we could be good friends if she lived closer."

"It's the age of e-communication, Summer," he told her, as if she wasn't internet proficient. "You and your author can text or email until the time works out for you to meet in person."

Michael was smiling like he'd just come up with a brilliant plan, and Summer had to turn away to keep her face from showing her feelings. *I know all about e-communications,* she thought, *boy do I know about them!* But out loud she said, "Great idea, Michael."

Chapter 51

The night before they had made love, or had sex, Summer wasn't really sure how to define it. It was nice, and it got the job done for both of them, but it wasn't the hot sweaty passion she craved. The words Bree had used about sex as a purely physical release kept coming back to her, and Summer wondered if that was the problem in her marriage as well. But hadn't they had mind blowing sex only a few days ago? She and Michael weren't Bree and Dan, and she wasn't having an affair, just some racy e-communications with a very handsome younger man.

Now it was Monday morning and with it came their normal weekday ritual. While Michael got ready for the day, Summer made coffee and fixed him a bagel slathered with cream cheese. He took her offerings, gave her a perfunctory kiss, patted her butt, and headed off to work. The only thing different this morning was that Summer had given him a new flavor of cream cheese on his everything bagel. *Big whoop*, she thought.

After warming her mug of coffee Summer went to her rocker for the other part of her morning ritual, her devotions. Once again, she saw the book from Bree laying on the table, and once again she passed it by. Instead, she read the uplifting magazines that her mother had ordered for her, prayed, and thanked the Lord once more for her life. When her mug was empty, she took it to the dishwasher and went upstairs to get ready for the day.

Showered and dressed in jeans and a lightweight hoodie, Summer headed into her morning. Not seeing any emails that needed immediate attention, she threw a load of laundry in the washer and sat down to call Bree to tell her about their Thanksgiving plans.

"Good morning, Bree Ann," Summer teased when her friend answered the phone. "Boy, do I have news to share with my BFF."

"You read the book and you've said goodbye to Jake Ross?" Bree asked hopefully.

Summer sighed, mentally kicking herself for ever telling Bree about Jake. "No, Bree," she answered. "I called to tell you that Michael and I are going to California to spend Thanksgiving with Cooper. Doesn't that sound like fun?"

"But you always have Thanksgiving at your house and then decorate your tree with the boys." Bree answered, not at all with the enthusiasm Summer was hoping for.

"Well, we're doing something different this year. I told you before that Riley isn't coming home so why not go to L.A. and be with Cooper. He asked, and we accepted." Summer knew she sounded a little defiant, but Bree had always been the adventurous one; why wasn't she more excited?

"It's just that you told me Jake lives in L.A. and I wonder if your euphoria has something to do with him." Summer didn't say a word and neither did Bree.

"We're going to Los Angeles to be with our son, Bree, and I wanted to share the good news with my friend. Obviously, this was a mistake. I need to go to work, I'll talk with you later."

Summer hung up the phone caught somewhere between being furious and wanting to scream. Of course, Bree was right, Jake did live in L.A., and yes, she had even thought about asking him to meet her somewhere, but that was just a pipedream, wasn't it? *Well, wasn't it?* She and Michael were going to California to be with their son, end of story.

Summer changed the laundry loads and checked her email again. This time she was pleasantly surprised to have something from her new client, Dena Daniels, with a question about her website. She sat down immediately to respond.

Dear Dena,

161

Before we get into business, I have to tell you that your book is so good! *One Last Love* has everything I look for in a romance and I predict a best seller. I only have about six chapters left but I'm not going to read them until I have the time to sit down and savor every minute. I'm on pins and needles though, wondering what Violet is going to do.

Now about your question. Yes, you can add pictures to your Website gallery through WordPress whenever you have one to share. It's a very easy process, and if you'd like, we can have a phone meeting. I can walk you through it. I know you don't feel comfortable with technology, but I'm always here to help.

Please send me a couple of dates and times that are convenient for you, and I'll give you a call. Again, I loved your book and can't wait for the next one! There will be a next one, right?

Best,
Summer
Summer Alcott
Four Seasons of Summer

407.756.3510

Within minutes there was an answer from Dena, and by the end of the conversation they were already fast friends.

Chapter 52

"I looked at some flights to California today," Michael told her at dinner. "Since we're going all that way, why don't we take a few extra days and see some sights?

"It sounds great," Summer replied, "but can you and Cooper be away from work that long?"

"It's not a problem for me, but we can work around Cooper's schedule. I'm sure he's seen all the tourist attractions anyway, so we can do our thing during the day and be with him in the evenings, or whenever he's available. I'm kind of excited about this trip," he told her.

After dinner Michael said he had some work to do for the Hospital Foundation Board, giving Summer a great time to finish her book. Since it had been raining off and on all day, she decided to take it up to bed and get comfortable.

With her Tervis Tumbler filled with ice water in one hand, Summer shoved her cell in the pocket of her jeans and picked up the book. After sharing her plans with her husband, she climbed the stairs in anticipation of finally finding out the ending to her book. She was just about to slip on her nightshirt when the ping from Messenger sounded announcing a message from Jake.

Jake: Hello, my gorgeous Summer, how was your day? I hope you're not sore at me for not being able to contact you earlier. One of my old friends from my food critic days was in town, and I've been with him all day investigating restaurants.

I've thought about you a lot though, in fact, I think about you all the time.

Summer didn't know how to respond. Other than to tell him she understood about his friend, what else should she say? I think about you all the time, too? Because it was the truth. Even when she was trying to convince Bree that her feelings for Jake were just friendly, she knew it wasn't true. Finally, she decided to go out on a limb and confess.

Summer: Of course, I'm not sore at you, but that is an odd choice of words! We both have jobs and a life, and things pop up, so please don't feel badly about it at all. And just FYI, I think about you all the time, too.

Jake: Speaking of things popping up, I feel another shower coming on.

Summer: You're incorrigible, you know that, right?

Jake: Maybe, but I'm also encourageable.

Summer: Is that even a real word?

Jake: Try me.

Summer: We're coming to Los Angeles for Thanksgiving.

When he didn't respond Summer started to panic, thinking she had read things wrong.

Summer: I didn't mean to insinuate anything there, Jake, and I'm sorry if I made you think I had expectations of seeing you while we're there.

Jake: Quit jumping to conclusions Summer, of course I want to see you.

They continued to message back and forth until Summer heard Michael on the stairs and told Jake she needed to go. As quickly as possible she threw on her night shirt and hopped into bed.

"How was the book?" Michael asked. "Did it have the ending you expected?"

"I haven't made it to the end, but I'm sure I'll love it when I do." Summer smiled sweetly. Remembering to brush her teeth, she climbed back out of bed and walked by her husband, seeing the confused look on his face.

"Go ahead and buy the tickets to California tomorrow," she said smearing toothpaste on her toothbrush. "The closer to Thanksgiving it gets the harder good flights will be to get."

Chapter 53

After that night, Summer and Jake messaged every day. He poured on the charm, and the feeling of being desired that she longed for filled her soul. They teased, they flirted, they even had some serious conversations, but Summer was hooked, and for the first time in all the years she'd known Michael, she began to picture her life without him.

One morning as she sat in her rocker, she looked around the home she loved so much and began to see it for what it was: a house. *I could be happy somewhere else*, she thought, and then glanced at the picture of her family on the mantle. It had been taken when the boys were seven and eighteen, and she loved how young and innocent they both looked. But they were adults now, and if she left, they'd understand.

Summer closed her eyes, daydreaming of what a life with Jake would be like. She quickly snapped to when she realized he had never said anything about the future, only that he wanted to get to know her better.

Picking up her phone, Summer sent him a message that she hoped would clear things up for her, and for a while, it did.

Summer: I need to be courted.

Then she waited, for what seemed like hours but was just a few minutes for him to reply.

Jake: I would love to court you, my beautiful Summer.

And so, it began. The next morning when she got up, Summer had a message on her phone that Jake had sent the night before. He told her again how beautiful she was, how he loved the stylish way that she dressed, and how proud he would be to have her on his arm. He signed off with heart and flowers and the words, *Sleep Well.*

Her heart fluttering, and with a smile on her face, she responded, telling him how much his words meant to her. From that day on, no matter how much they had talked throughout the day, Jake always sent her a romantic message before he went to bed, and she responded each morning when she got up.

But Leda was still in the picture, and Summer couldn't stand it. One day, the hurt and discomfort over knowing Jake was still sleeping with Leda, even while he was romancing her, was more than she could live with, and she knew she had to tell him.

Summer: I know I have no right to say this Jake, but I can't go on with our relationship while I know you're sharing a bed with Leda. Please understand.

Jake: You're a difficult woman, Summer! But Leda leaves in the morning for New York and if things go the way I hope they do, and I can't promise they will, you're the only woman I want sharing my bed.

Summer dropped her phone; she was so happy! There it was. The declaration she had been hoping for. Jake was falling in love with her and now all she needed to do was figure out her life. But of course, first, she had one more question.

Summer: Does Leda understand that when she leaves, you won't be seeing her anymore?

Jake: She knows that I'm not ready for the commitment she wants, but I may see her if I have to travel to New York.

Summer was seeing red and was beginning to feel like a fool.

Summer: I see. So, is Leda your backup plan, or am I? Because you can't have it both ways.

Jake: You suspicious woman. Leda's been good to me, Summer, and I like her, I told you that. Do you expect me to totally end my friendship with her?

Summer: I don't know what I expect, Jake, this whole thing is new to me, and I'm not good at sharing.

Jake: Let's wait and see what happens, okay? I've already been through so much pain and hurt, and I just don't want to be hurt again. And to be honest, I don't want to hurt anyone either.

Summer: Me either

That was their last message that day and Summer was a wreck. Her hope was that once she and Jake could sit down face to face it would give their relationship clarity, but what if it didn't? What if after seeing her in person their age difference stood out to him, or what if once they talked, they found out they didn't like each other after all? These were the questions that Summer couldn't get out of her mind, and they ended up haunting her day.

Chapter 54

After tossing and turning all night Summer woke up to the following message.

Jake: Buenos Noches Mi Amor. I'll see you in my dreams.

It took a full ten minutes for her to stop sobbing and calm down. *He loves me!* She thought. *It says so right there.* Summer had only taken the required amount of foreign language in high school, but even with her limited Spanish, she knew what those words meant. Good Night My Love, it couldn't be any plainer than that, and her reply was short and sweet.

Summer: Buenos Dias Ques tengas un buen dia guapo.

It was several hours before Jake responded with the following words.

Jake: You think I'm handsome? You made my day!

Summer owed Dena Daniels a long overdue phone call, so she sent the author an email to see if she was available for the promised WordPress tutorial. While she waited to see if Dena would respond she looked through her emails, getting rid of the junk and flagging any that she wanted to circle back to.

There was a message from Alex Bailey with an added need to his website, but it was an easy fix that she could work on after her talk with Dena. The only other interesting email was from an author friend of Dena's who wondered if Summer would be willing to build her a website as well. Pleased that Dena was happy enough with her work to recommend her to others, Summer scrolled back to the top to see if she had a response from her yet, and sure enough, she did.

Summer,
I'm available any time today. Call me when it's convenient for you.
Dena

Summer was a big believer in *there's no time like the present*, so she picked up the phone and called Dena Daniels. "Hi Dena," she said into the receiver, "this is Summer Alcott with Four Seasons of Summer. Tell me how I can help you with your website."

It didn't take Summer long to get Dena up to speed on everything she needed to know about WordPress, and once again, Summer assured her that she was only an email away if she needed help. After the work part of the conversation was over, Summer asked if Dena had a minute to talk about her book.

"Absolutely!" she laughed. "I always love talking about my work. Especially since being an author was never on my horizon, yet the book is doing so well."

"I just can't believe that you were a teacher for thirty years, with no desire to write, and yet you wrote such a powerful and believable book," Summer told her. "Did you know someone like Violet in your life, or is she totally make believe?"

When Dena didn't answer right away Summer wasn't sure if they had lost the connection or if she'd struck a nerve. "Dena, can you hear me?" she questioned, and when she heard a small sigh on the other end, Summer knew the problem wasn't with the connection.

"I've never told this to another soul, Summer, but for some reason I feel a true kinship with you," Dena began. "Because the thing is, the story is written around a real person's experiences with love and heartache, and that person is me. Violet's story is mine."

This time it was Summer who was at a loss of words. Dena seemed to understand because she gave her new friend some thinking room before speaking. "I looked you up on Google before asking you to design my website, Summer," Dena began, "you are a beautiful woman with a husband who looks like a movie star, so the two sons you mention are probably handsome young men. I imagine it's hard for you to think about what it was like being married to a sex addict and then having an affair with a man who turned out to be abusive and controlling, but it was my life, Summer, and I made a lot of mistakes. By the time I met Joe, I was a completely different woman than I was when I met husband number one, but all that hurt was still with me. Have you finished the book yet?"

"No," Summer told her, but she had so many questions. "But Dena, please don't think that the pretty pictures you see on the internet truly emulate my life. I have a lot of blessings, I won't deny that, but I've made some mistakes of my own, so don't think that I can't relate. I mean, I can't understand exactly what you went through, but I can understand the pain that being a woman can bring."

They talked for a few more minutes, Dena sharing more of her story and Summer trying to decide how much she should share about Jake, and then Dena's doorbell rang, and they had to say goodbye.

"Please, Summer," Dena said before hanging up, "call me whenever you want to talk."

Chapter 55

Michael came home that night with tickets for their trip to California, as well as with reservations made at The Beverly Wilshire Hotel. "I figured we'd stay with Cooper," she said when she saw the price of the motel. "Isn't that why he invited us, so we could spend time together?"

"Cooper has a nice apartment, but remember it only has one bedroom. Who would sleep on the foldout couch, us or him?" The question made sense, so Summer agreed to a motel but did question if there wasn't a less expensive one they could get.

Michael laughed as he put his arms around her. "Summer, I realize you're frugal, but we don't live in that walk-up apartment anymore, and we can afford this, trust me."

"I know we can afford it," she said wistfully, "I guess all of a sudden I'm wishing Riley could be with us in California."

"Summer, our sons are adults now, with adult lives of their own. Isn't it time you and I started making plans for our future and let the boys make their own?"

Make plans for their future? Summer wasn't even sure what her future was, and the thought of it made her ill. A few days ago, she had told herself that her sons would understand if she left their dad, but now she realized that was wishful thinking. Cooper idolized Michael, even Riley thought his dad was amazing, so there was no way either one of them would understand if she left him for a man thirteen years her junior. And what about their parents and siblings? There had never been a divorce in Michael's family, and her parents thought of Michael as a son.

Summer wasn't sure what the future was going to hold but she did know one thing, someone was going to end up hurt, no matter what she or Jake wanted.

After dinner they called Cooper to tell him they had tickets in hand and arrangements made for their trip west. "Thanksgiving will be here before we know it!" Summer told her son excitedly. "Are we going out to eat or what's the plan?" Mentally she smacked herself because she had agreed that Cooper needed to be in charge, but the mother in her was having a hard time taking a backseat.

"You don't have to worry, Mom," Cooper chuckled, "everything is under control, and I promise you won't starve." Then changing the subject, he added, "Thanks for understanding about staying here, I mean I would have loved it, but I don't think it would have been comfortable for any of us."

Any of us? Summer thought, but when she looked up to see if Michael had noticed it too, he had his head down. "Anyway, I've got to run, poker with the guys tonight, but I can't wait to see you on the twenty-second. I've got a party at my boss's house on Sunday, so we'll talk again when you get here. Just call me once you're settled in your motel, and I'll come to you."

Michael had turned on the TV by the time she said her goodbyes to Cooper, so told him she was going upstairs to try once more to finish her book. "I had a very interesting talk with Dena Daniels," she told him, "and now I'm dying to know how this thing ends."

Michael said he would be up soon, leaving Summer with a head boiling over with thoughts. What did Jake Ross really expect from her, and more importantly, what was she willing to give up for him? How did Dena, aka Violet, resolve her life, and why was Cooper acting so strange? It was all more than she could handle, but the one resolution she was going to have tonight was whether Violet let herself fall in love with Joe, her one last love, or whether she walked away.

An hour later Summer was sobbing, and this time it had nothing to do with her, or her life. *How had Dena made it through so many heartaches?* Most people would have turned to drugs or alcohol to help them cope, but Dena had done neither. At least Violet hadn't done them, and if the book truly was Dena's story, then she hadn't either. Summer wiped her eyes and made mental plans to call Dena the next day. *Any woman who can deal with all the hurt and suffering that she has and still come out on top, will surely understand about my friendship with Jake.* Laying the book aside, she thought of how much she was willing to share and how much advice she was willing to take.

Chapter 56

When the next morning arrived, along with a romantic message from Jake, Summer had decided against telling Dena anything about him. After all, she didn't really know the woman, and the last thing she wanted was for her life to end up in a book. Instead, she decided that after getting Michael off to work and making sure there weren't any website emergencies to contend with, she'd whip up a batch of her famous Double Divine brownies and take them to Nancy Bailey as a welcome to the community gift.

Baking had always been therapeutic for Summer, but it was a joy that came with a double-edged sword. She loved scanning over recipes and changing them up just enough to make them her own, but she loved to eat what she baked, and that was the problem. She knew that her weight phobia was on her, no one had ever fat shamed her, but she liked being slim, and she felt better when she was. Cookies and brownies might be her weakness, but her strength came from being healthy and being able to fasten her pants.

The brownies in the oven, Summer decided that she should at least ask Bree if she wanted to go with her on her visit to Nancy. She had done her best to avoid her best friend for several days, but she knew that was childish and cruel. Bree loved and cared about her; she wasn't just being mean, and it was up to Summer to get things back on track.

The first words out of Summer's mouth when Bree answered the phone were, "I love you Bree, and I don't want any hard feelings between us." *There, she'd done it.*

"I love you, too, Summer, and I promise to keep my feelings to myself about Jake Ross," Bree answered. "Just know that I'm always here."

They made plans for Summer to pick Bree up in the Mustang after lunch, deciding that it was a beautiful day that deserved an outing in a beautiful car. Before starting the brownies, Summer had checked, and Nancy said she would be home and would love a visit.

Dressed in navy-blue ankle-length pants and a red and white striped blouse, Summer felt very nautical. It wasn't until she opened the garage that she realized her outfit was also very well coordinated with her car, but it was too late to go back and change. Laughing at her silliness, she started up her baby and listened like a proud parent to all eight cylinders roaring to life.

The afternoon was a success, and on the way home, Summer and Bree chatted like schoolgirls about how much they liked Nancy and how they needed to plan a dinner for the three couples sometime after Summer and Michael returned from L.A. Summer felt a jolt in her stomach when Bree mentioned L.A. but pushed it down and tried to resume the cheerful conversation with her friend.

"We'll see you at church on Sunday," Summer said, giving Bree a hug, "but we're leaving early on Tuesday for the airport, so this will be our last hurrah until then."

"Today was fun, Summer," Bree said. "I've missed our girl days."

"Me too," Summer replied honestly, "more than you know."

Summer got back into her car and started for home, stopping first at Publix for fresh shrimp for dinner. She had just told the clerk that she needed a pound and a half of the large Royal Reds when a voice came up behind her.

"Well Summer Alcott," the voice dripped like sticky molasses. "Why is it we always meet at the grocery store? I guess that's what a couple housewives like us do, right?" The girlish giggle almost made Summer gag. That and the fact that Lacey Stevens had a full-time housekeeper and cook made her about as much a housewife as the Queen.

"Nice to see you, Lacey," Summer said turning back to take her package of shrimp from the clerk. Looking for a way to escape, she was aware that Lacey was still talking to her.

"Elliott says you make paella almost as good as his mama did," the little hussy purred, "I'd love to get your recipe, so I could surprise him with it."

The "almost" as good as his mama made wasn't lost on Summer, nor was the inuendo that Lacey would be making it. She had just had a fun afternoon with friends, adult friends with their own boobs and butts, and the last thing Summer wanted was to ruin it by sparring with Lacey Stevens. But there was no way in hell she was sharing a recipe with her.

Instead, she pretended like she didn't hear what Lacey was saying to her, and that ending up being the wrong thing to do. Tapping her feet a few times for effect Lacey said as loudly as possible, "I heard about your meltdown at Breakers a couple of weeks ago," she said spitefully. "My mama's going through the change too, and we never know when she's going to come unglued."

Summer's face was as red as the shrimp in her package, but she had no idea what to do or say. She knew she should take the highroad, but somehow, she just couldn't. Instead, she plastered on her sweetest smile and said, "Excuse me Lacey, but I believe you have toilet paper hanging out the back of your skirt." And with that, she turned her cart and headed directly to the Express Lane.

Chapter 57

The Mustang safely in the garage, Summer grudgingly put up the convertible top. "It may be a while before we have another afternoon like this," she spoke to her beloved car. "I promise you an outing again just as soon as possible." She stroked her baby like she would a puppy and thought about her beloved Uncle. *What would you think if I left Michael for another man, Toots?* she wondered. *Would I still be your Sweet Summer Star?* She thought about the nickname Toots had called her all of her life and sighed.

What's wrong with me? Maybe Lacey was right, and all this really was some out-of-control, hormonal, mid-life crises. Whatever it was, she'd know soon enough, because once she and Jake had a face-to-face meeting, she would have to make a decision about her future.

Royal Red shrimp was a favorite of Michael and Summer's, and they both made noises of pleasure as they dipped the succulent shrimp in melted butter. "I can't believe we just found out about these last year," Michael said, wiping butter from his chin. "Who knew there was a shrimp that tastes as good as lobster?" As he grabbed the last piece from his plate, he closed his eyes and savored the delicious flavor.

"Do you have anything important going on in the next few days?" Michael asked, as he took his dishes to the kitchen sink. "I need to spend a couple of hours with Elliott before we leave so he has all the information for the next foundation meeting."

Hearing the name Elliott made Summer squirm, and she knew she needed to tell Michael about her encounter with Lacey earlier that day. "Uh, Michael," she stammered. "I ran into Lacey Stevens today at

Publix, and why does that keep happening? I mean seriously, with all the hours they're open, how can Lacey and I be shopping at the same time?"

Michael looked at his wife, trying to make a little sense out of her story, then spoke. "Could you go back to the beginning, please?" he asked. "I lost something in the translation."

"The thing is she makes me crazy, Michael, and I may have said something I shouldn't have just to shut her up. Anyway, I just thought you should know before you see Elliott, you know, just in case."

Summer crossed her arms defiantly across her chest, waiting for a reprimand, but instead Michael smiled. "I'm sure she deserved anything you said to her."

What the hell? Summer was speechless at Michael's attitude but decided not to rock the boat by saying anything else. Instead, she smiled back, and together they cleared the table and cleaned up the kitchen. There were only a few days until they left for Los Angeles and arguing with her husband was not how Summer wanted to spend them.

The next morning when Summer looked at her phone, there was a wonderfully romantic message from Jake. She was a crier, there was no doubt about that, and the words in the message not only brought tears to her eyes, but they also brought desire to her soul.

Jake: Good Morning my beautiful, Summer. I trust you slept well. I had the most sensual dream about you, truthfully about us, and now more than ever, I can't wait to meet you in person and gaze into those melted caramel eyes of yours.

Can we set a time and place to meet? You haven't even told me how long you'll be here, but I hope long enough that you can come to my home and see the studio where I produce my blogs.

Summer could barely breathe. He'd had a sensual dream about her, and he wanted her to come to his house? What did that mean? Was seeing his studio a ploy to get her into bed, and if it was, did she care? Those thoughts took her to thoughts of making love with him, and even though she knew in her heart they were wrong, she couldn't stop them.

What kind of lover would Jake Ross be? she wondered. Gentle and attentive, or aggressive and enthusiastic? Would her fifty-eight-year-old body be a turn off, or would her womanly hips and still firm breasts, be arousing? She'd been with Michael since she was twenty-three and never been as sexually active as most young women in her generation, but the idea of going to bed with Jake was both thrilling and scary as hell.

Covering her face with her hands, Summer gave her emotions a minute to calm down before replying.

Summer: Good Morning, yourself! I must admit that you write very romantic and intoxicating messages. They feel almost like old-fashioned love letters. I'm not sure a man has ever been as amorous to me as you are. Thank you.

We're staying at the Beverly Wilshire. Is there any place nearby we could meet for coffee on the day after Thanksgiving? I have no idea how busy everything will be, but if you can make it work it's a good starting place. What do you think?

Jake: How about Blue Bottle Coffee at ten o'clock? The concierge will help you get there.

And Summer, I'm just a man doing a mating dance, excited to see my own *Pretty Woman*.

How did you respond to that? She ended up just sending him a Kiss emoji. As soon as it was sent, she realized how suggestive it had been, but there was no going back. She was actually going to meet Jake Ross face to face, even if doing so sent her straight to hell!

Chapter 58

The next few days flew by and before she knew it, she and Michael were on their way to the Orlando International Airport. Summer was filled with nervous energy as she thought about the sexy lingerie packed at the bottom of her suitcase. She'd ordered a pair of lacy panties with a matching bra from La Perla and charged them to her business account. She hoped she'd never be audited, because there was no way she could explain that kind of expense, but her business account was the only one that Michael left for her to manage.

"Are you excited about our trip?" Michael asked her.

"Of course, I am," she smiled at him. "It will be wonderful to see Cooper, but I will miss having Riley with us on Thanksgiving."

Michael took hold of her hand and replied. "I know how much you love having all of us together for holidays, but I'm sure that Riley will have a great time, wherever he is."

Summer nodded but she knew it wasn't Riley she was worried about. Michael was right, Riley was adaptable, and even as close as he was to her, he wasn't having any problem stepping out on his own. But how would *she* do without having both of her boys with her on Thanksgiving, and without all of their family traditions, would it even feel like a holiday?

Switching gears, Michael asked her if there was anything special she wanted to do while they were in LA. "Well," she said cautiously, "my client Jake Ross has asked if I could meet him on Friday, and I told him it would be okay. You don't mind, do you?"

"The only clients I've ever known you to meet with are the local ones. What's different about this guy?"

Summer was grateful for the traffic around them that was keeping Michael from looking her way. *What was different about Jake Ross*, she thought, *besides the fact that I can't get him out of my mind? Oh, and that I fantasize about him, and wonder what he's like in bed?*

"Nothing's different about him, Michael," she finally answered, trying to keep her voice calm and her words coherent. "I just mentioned that we were coming to Los Angeles for Thanksgiving, and he suggested that it would be nice to meet face to face. But of course, if you don't want me to, I won't go." *Try to stop me,* she thought, but kept her expression as stoic as possible.

"If you want to meet him then by all means you should," he told her. "It seemed strange is all. He's the guy that Cooper talked about, right?"

"Jake is very well-known around the world, but since he lives in L.A., I'm sure there's more gossip about him there than anyplace else. Anyway, he seems like a very nice man, and I feel honored that he asked me to design his website and that he wants to meet me." Summer sat back, trying not to look or sound like a child trying to get her own way, and thankfully with the busy traffic, Michael wasn't paying great attention.

"I'm really proud of your success, Summer," he said, "and by all means, you should go and meet Jake Ross in person. My only hope is you don't get stars in your eyes and want to leave New Smyrna Beach for the bright lights of California."

He gave a little laugh and Summer slumped down in her seat. If only he knew! Deciding that she had to quit talking about Jake and their meeting, she asked Michael if Cooper was working on any particular projects. Their oldest son was an architect like his dad, and the two of them could talk designs and building plans for what seemed like hours on end.

Once Michael started talking about his favorite subject, Summer knew she was safe to sit back and daydream about Jake and wonder if there was a future in store for them.

***

Finally on the plane, Summer forgot about Jake and concentrated on not ending up in the ocean. She didn't love flying and was more than happy to have Michael beside her, holding her hand when there was turbulence in the air. She and Michael had flown together several times during their thirty-five-year marriage, and it was comforting for her to know that he understood her fears.

That didn't mean, of course, that in his own excitement he didn't occasionally forget and try to coax her to look down at the topography below them, but Summer never budged. She closed her eyes, held tightly to his hand, and prayed until the plane reached cruising altitude. Once the sign came on saying they could remove their seatbelts, she relaxed, but the seatbelt stayed firmly clasped.

"It's kind of amazing that we had breakfast in Florida, and we'll have dinner in California, isn't it?" Michael asked. "And we might have had lunch somewhere in between if I hadn't found a direct flight."

Summer was thankful they'd only have one take-off and landing, especially since a stop-over would have meant an airport lunch. At six foot three, Michael was able to eat anything and everything, and he was just as lean as he had been at twenty-five. But there was no way she could eat three meals a day without major exercise, and that was one thing she didn't plan to do on this trip. She had lost a little over five pounds in anticipation of her meeting with Jake, and she intended to keep it off, even with a holiday meal looming over her head.

By the time the plane descended for their landing at LAX, Summer was a bundle of nerves. Up until this moment, her friendship with Jake Ross had been a fantasy, but now it was almost a reality. Could she do it? Was she meeting him with the idea of having a brief affair, or was she meeting him because she hoped he wanted her in his life? And what about Michael and their boys? It was all more than she could cope with, and for the first time since she'd opened that first email from him, she wished Jake Ross had never crossed her path.

While they waited for their luggage, Michael held her hand, gently rubbing his thumb over hers. It was as if he sensed that she was nervous and was trying to calm her. The one really nice thing about a long-term relationship, Summer decided, is that your partner can pick up on your moods. True, Michael hadn't quite picked up on her need for more attention and romance, but he was trying hard to help her relax now, and that meant a lot.

While Summer stepped into the ladies' room to freshen up, Michael called a cab, and as soon as their luggage had come off of the conveyor, the driver was there to greet them. He loaded their bags into the trunk, had a brief conversation with Michael, and they were on their way. Summer felt a rush of excitement as she realized they were really in California, and an adventure awaited her.

When the driver pulled up to the hotel, Summer's mouth dropped. "Oh Michael," she squealed. "It's gorgeous, and so big! I guess I should have done some research when you showed me the reservations."

The taxi driver chuckled, "I thought every woman knew about this hotel," he said. "Ever since that movie, it's been on my wife's bucket list, that's for sure. But she's gonna have to keep on wishing 'cause this is way out of my price range."

Michael handed the man two one-hundred-dollar bills and told him to keep the change. Summer wasn't sure whose eyes got bigger, the cab driver's or hers. Two hundred dollars for a cab ride? Her small-town girl background couldn't fathom it, but when she saw Michael pat the man on the back, she realized her husband was just trying to get the taxi driver's wife one step closer to the top of that wish list.

Chapter 59

While Michael checked into the hotel, Summer's eyes wandered around the lobby. She was certain that Michael had chosen it for its architectural structure, but she was going to love it for its grandeur. Everything was so opulent that she became mesmerized by the lavish beauty around her and didn't hear Michael when he called her name.

"Summer," he said again, "are you ready to go to our room?" Without waiting for a reply, Michael took her elbow and directed her towards the elevator.

"I hope you'll be okay with what I've chosen," Michael told her as the bellman opened the door for them.

Room? Summer thought, as they entered. *Crap on a cracker this wasn't a room it was a suite!* And a big suite, too. There was a living room and a bedroom with a huge, canopied bed, and the biggest bathroom Summer had ever seen in her life.

"Michael," she stammered, trying to come up with the right words, "I appreciate all this, I really do, but this is way too much. It has to be costing a fortune. Can't we downsize?"

Michael handed the bellman a wad of cash and then swaggered towards her, looking much like the twenty-five-year-old man who had approached her at a book reading event and swept her off her feet. "Yes," he said, cupping her chin and lifting her face so her eyes met his. "We could downsize, but we aren't going to. Remember the big client I had a few weeks ago? Well, the firm got the job, and I'm leading the design team. It came with a good bonus, and you've seemed so down lately. I thought, what better way to put it to use than to take you away an exciting weekend and try to give you the honeymoon we never had?"

Michael used his thumb to wipe away the tears that were rolling down her cheeks, while Summer got her emotions under control. "But we did have a honeymoon, Michael, and I loved it, didn't you?" She asked, totally bypassing the comment about her recent moods.

"Of course, I did, because I was there with you, but it wasn't the honeymoon you deserved, or the one I wanted to give you." Summer could see the color rising on her husband's handsome face, and knew he was thinking about their four-month courtship, and hurried trip down the alter when they found out she was pregnant.

Summer took a deep breath and asked him the question that had been on her mind for over thirty-five years. "Did you really want to marry me back then?" she asked him, "or were you just trying to do the right thing?"

Michael looked stricken and she wished she could take the question back, but it was too late. "I wanted to marry you the moment I first saw you," he said with a smile. "You were the most beautiful girl I'd ever seen, and you were shy and reserved, not pushy or loud like so many other girls at Ohio State. When you agreed to have coffee with me, I saw you in my future, I just didn't expect that future to start quite the way it did."

Summer nodded, because it hadn't been what she wanted either. But the attraction between them had been so strong that they both got carried away one night and made love, even though Summer wasn't on birth control and Michael didn't have a condom. Afterwards, they'd talked about it, and both agreed that it wouldn't happen again, but it was too late. Cooper was already planted deep within her womb.

Summer became as still as possible, and then continued asking the questions she had agonized over for long. "If you wanted a future with me, why were you so sullen those first few months of our marriage? All this time I've felt like you thought I tricked you into marrying me."

"Oh Summer," he said pulling her close, "I know I acted like a horse's ass sometimes, but it was because I felt like I'd failed you. You didn't have much experience, and I knew that, so I should never have let things get out of hand the night that Cooper was conceived. I wanted you to see me as your *Knight in Shining Armor*, but instead of a castle, I gave you a two-room walk-up."

They held each other for a few minutes, neither one talking, the sound of their breath the only thing breaking the silence. It was the most intimate conversation they had ever shared, but before Summer could tell Michael how much it had meant to her, she heard the ping she had looked forward to the last few months, along with the message, "are you there yet?"

Summer pulled away, not at all sure how to handle the situation, leaving her confused looking husband standing alone. Before he had a chance to say anything, there was a knock at the door and when Summer looked out the peephole, there stood Cooper. Opening the door and pulling her oldest son into her arms, Summer sobbed, letting all the emotions of the last few weeks come pouring out.

"Mom, are you okay?" Cooper asked as he gently pulled away from his mother. "I expected you to be happy to see me, but this is quite a welcome."

Summer looked up and saw the love in her son's eyes and smiled at him. "I guess I'm just a little overwhelmed," she answered truthfully.

Michael reached out to shake his son's hand, but instead put his arms around him and hugged him. "It's so good to see you, Coop," he said. "How is everything?"

For just a second Summer thought she saw some kind of silent message exchange between the two men, but she shook it off as another crazy reaction to an extraordinary day. Putting her arm around her son, she gave him a quick tour of their accommodations.

"Isn't this the most magnificent hotel you've ever seen?" she asked Cooper, her eyes still damp with tears. "I just can't imagine spending all this money on such a fancy place when we came here to be with you."

"But do you like it, Mom?" Cooper asked.

"Like it? I love it!" Summer exclaimed, "but still...."

"Your mother is having a hard time accepting that she's worthy of all this, and a whole lot more," Michael teased, "so I'm hoping that means she won't expect a trip down Rodeo Drive."

Summer sighed, feeling such contentment at being here with Michael and Cooper. The only thing that would have made it better was for Riley to be here with them, and thinking of Riley reminded her that she'd promised to call him once they were checked in. It was when she reached for her phone to call her son that Summer saw and remembered the message that Jake had sent, and her heart stood still. Looking from Michael to Cooper to the message on the phone, she realized she was in over her head and had no idea how to keep from drowning. Thankfully, for the second time in less than an hour, there was a knock at the door, and once again thoughts of Jake Ross were put aside.

"Summer," Michael said as he opened the door partway, "there's a delivery here for you."

Her feet were glued to the floor. Surely Jake wouldn't have sent something to the room he knew she was sharing with her husband. She hadn't mentioned Michael much, but Jake knew she was married, and they were coming to L.A. to be with their son for Thanksgiving. He wouldn't have done something so bold, would he?

Again, Michael called her name. "Summer, come on," he said getting a little agitated, "they need your signature or something."

Willing her feet to move, Summer inched to the door, wondering if this delivery was going to be the end of her family and life as they all knew it. But when she finally got there and looked up to the person standing in the doorway, all the sobbing that she had put a stop to came back.

"Surprise!" Was all she heard, as she felt strong arms wrapping around her. "Happy Thanksgiving, Mom," Riley told her, and the waterworks she had worked so hard to stop were back.

Once the tears finally subsided, Summer started asking the questions that were flying around in her head.

"Will one of you please tell me what's going on?" she said, trying to get her breathing under control. "Obviously you were all in this together, but which one of you is the ringleader?"

"I'm not sure ringleader is the right title," Michael laughed, "but I'll take the credit. It really all started when Cooper invited us to spend Thanksgiving with him, and it just snowballed from there."

"I still don't understand," Summer pouted. "You said you were spending Thanksgiving in New York with Olivia's family, Ri, was that just a red herring?"

When Riley wanted to tease his mom he called her Summer, and this was one of those times. "A red herring?" he asked. "You've been reading too many old detective novels, Summer," he said, taking her hand. "But the answer is no, I really was going to New York until I heard about the plans the architects were working on. And yes, pun intended."

"But what about Olivia and her family? I don't want to get in the way or cause the two of you any problems."

"Mom," Riley said gently, "you haven't gotten in the way of anything. We just decided to slow things down for now. It's not a big deal."

Summer looked at Cooper, expecting him to make some off-color remark, but surprisingly he held his tongue. "I feel terrible," she said, hanging her head in her hands. "If something I said caused you to break up with her, I'll never forgive myself."

"Mom, your thoughts mean a lot to me, I think you know that. You're a smart woman and I respect you, but if this was the right time for Olivia and me, nothing you could have said would have mattered. And we haven't broken up, we're just on hiatus for now. She's still the one, Mom; we just both have some maturing to do before we make a commitment."

"I hate to get in the way of the Riley show," Cooper chuckled, "but we have dinner reservations and traffic is usually bad this time of day."

"Couldn't we just eat at the hotel?" Summer asked. "I'm sure they have wonderful restaurants, and we wouldn't have to go back out."

Expecting to hear what a great idea it was, she was not prepared for the emphatic "No," that came from each man. "Well okay then," she said with a smile. "Give me five minutes and we can be on our way."

Chapter 60

Summer grabbed her purse and headed into the ornate bathroom. The first thing she saw was a huge garden tub big enough for two, plus an enormous shower with double showerheads. Her thoughts turned to all the wicked things she and Michael could do together in this bathroom, and then her heart skipped a beat when she remembered Jakes message.

Locking the door for good measure, she pulled out the boudoir chair from under the vanity and sat down. Her hands were a little shaky as she looked again at Jake's message before replying.

Summer: Yes, I'm here, safe and sound. My youngest son surprised me and he's here in California, too, and apparently, we have dinner reservations someplace that requires going out of the hotel. Anyway, I've got to go, but I'll stay in touch.

She reread the message before hitting send, and she knew it seemed a little cold, but what could she do? It wasn't just Michael in the other room but their sons, and the thought of hurting them was almost more than she could bear.

Hitting the arrow to send the message, Summer slipped the phone in her pocket and hastily ran her fingers through her thick chestnut hair. She added a little bronzer to her cheeks, and a swipe of Josie Maran Lip Sting Plumping Butter in Embrace It to her already generous lips, and she was ready to go. Stepping out of the bathroom door, she adjusted her smile and said, "I'm starving, let's go eat."

Cooper had already called down and had his car brought around, and the valet was there waiting to help Summer into the backseat. Normally

Michael would take the position of shotgun, but surprisingly he joined her in back and motioned for Riley to sit up front with his brother.

"So, what do you think of our surprise?" Michael asked as he took his wife's hand. "I've got to tell you, you're not an easy person to keep things from, Mrs. Alcott. Several times I thought you had figured it out."

Summer looked at his beautiful face and couldn't remember the last time she had seen Michael so excited. He was like a kid in a candy store, and it did nothing to calm the nerves that were starting to overtake her.

On Friday she would be having coffee with Jake Ross, the man she'd been flirting with and thinking nonstop of having sex with, and today her husband gave her the words she'd longed to hear since their wedding day. How she had ended up in this mess she wasn't sure, but the one thing she did know was that tonight she was having dinner with her family for the first time in months, and she wasn't about to let anything spoil it.

The remainder of the ride, Michael held her hand but engaged in conversation with his sons. They talked work and sports for the thirty-minute drive to the restaurant, giving Summer time to try to put her feelings in order. When they pulled up in front of a very colorful building, and Michael came around to help her out of the car, she realized she was no closer to having an answer than she was before they left.

There was no hiding from herself; she had come on this trip with the intention of possibility breaking her wedding vows. Jake had given her back the spark that was missing from her life, and she still wanted to explore it. That being said, she couldn't wait to get her husband into the king-sized canopy bed back at the hotel.

When did I become so sex-crazed? she thought, climbing out of the car. Then realizing that Cooper was talking to her, she put all thoughts of Michael and Jake out of her mind and focused on her son.

Chapter 61

"So, Mom," Cooper said, doing a panorama with his hand, "this is Caliente, the best Mexican restaurant in town."

The building was actually an old house, painted in vibrant splashes of color, but to say it looked like any kind of a restaurant, let alone the best Mexican restaurant in town, seemed a far stretch to Summer. She didn't remember Cooper even being that fond of Mexican food, so she was really confused as to why he had brought them there.

Michael opened the old front door to the house before she could question Cooper about his choice, so she walked with her boys up the winding brick sidewalk and let Cooper help her up the steps. *I don't need help*, she thought to herself, but felt pride at what a courteous man her oldest son had become.

"I really hope you like it, Mom," Cooper said with something bordering on apprehension in his eyes. "This is one of my favorite places in the world."

Before she could even say a word, a very polite host smiled at Cooper and led them to a lovely table near the back of the room. It was adorned with a white linen tablecloth and a vase of dahlias, as colorful and eclectic as the restaurant itself. The man seated Summer without speaking a word, but she swore she saw him give Cooper a knowing nod.

Something didn't add up, and just as she was about to ask what was going on, a striking young woman appeared at the table. Her eyes were the vibrant color of green that Summer associated with tourmaline, and they popped against the contrast of her deep mahogany skin. Her hair was a seemingly endless array of braids wrapped on her head like a crown, leaving Summer to wonder about its actual length. Thinking this must be their server, Summer realized that she was really very hungry, and she couldn't wait to hear what delicacies awaited them. Thankfully, Cooper interrupted her train of thought before she opened her mouth and put her foot in it.

Standing up beside the beautiful woman, Cooper cleared his throat and said, "Mom, this is Cali Reyes, the owner of Caliente."

Michael stood and shook her hand, while Riley sat with a smile on his face, watching the whole thing unfold around him. Summer was all set to tell the young woman what a lovely restaurant it was when Cooper spoke up and dropped a bomb.

"And, well… she's also my girlfriend," he added, clearly not sure how his mother was going to react at the news that the love of his life wasn't the waspy type of girl he'd dated in the past. But occasionally mothers surprise you, and this was one of those times. Summer got out of her chair and put her arms around the obviously nervous Cali Reyes.

"It's such a pleasure to meet you," she said with a smile and a hug. Then turning towards her son, Summer squeezed his hand and whispered in his ear, "She's lovely, Cooper."

The rest of the evening went well, and all thoughts of Jake Ross were out of Summer's mind. She found out that Riley had known about Cali for several weeks and that it had been his idea to get his parents to L.A. to meet her. That of course had meant bringing Michael in on the plan, so while he hadn't met Cooper's new girl, he was aware of what was going on.

After a huge meal that started with shrimp ceviche, followed by Pollo Rojo with yellow rice, and big bowls of creamy guacamole on the side, Summer almost didn't have room for the decadent Crème Caramel that Cali brought out at the end. But after one bite she was hooked.

"Cali," she said honestly, "I understand why my son says this is the best Mexican restaurant in the city, but as far as I'm concerned, it's the best Mexican restaurant in the world."

The young woman blushed, gave Summer a huge smile, and softly answered, "Thank you."

Michael, Summer, and Riley headed towards their waiting car while Cooper stayed back to say goodbye to Cali. Summer turned around to tell Cali once more what a wonderful evening it had been, just in time to see Cooper take her in his arms and kiss her so passionately, that Summer felt it from where she stood. *They're in love,* she thought, as she tumbled into the backseat, and that's exactly the feeling I'm longing for.

Chapter 62

The ride home from the restaurant was a game of twenty question as Summer tried to learn everything that she could about Cooper's relationship with Cali, and why he hadn't told them about her before. At thirty-four, he appeared to be going down the same path as her Uncle Toots, and while she had adored her uncle, she knew how lonely his life had been.

"Tell me everything, Cooper," Summer besieged her son. "How long have you and Cali been dating; where did you meet; where is she from? I want to know it all."

Michael took his wife's hand and did his best to stop the inquisition. "How about let's back pedal a little and let Cooper tell us what he wants us to know," he suggested. Summer shot him a look that he understood perfectly well, so he lifted his hands in concession.

"I met Cali at the restaurant," Cooper said hesitantly. "My boss, Mr. Sturgis, took me there for lunch one day because it was close to a project he wanted me to work on. The service was terrible, the food was cold by the time it arrived at our table, and Mr. Sturgis was fuming. He demanded to see the manager but what he got was Cali." When Cooper caught her eye in the rearview mirror, Summer realized she'd never seen the intensity there that she did at that moment.

"And...?" she encouraged him to keep going.

"Cali apologized to Mr. Sturgis, saying he was right to be upset and not only was there no charge for the lunch, but she also invited him back the next week for lunch on the house. The funny thing is, Mom, I've witnessed grown men cringe when Mr. Sturgis starts one of his rants, but

Cali let him go on and on about how bad her restaurant was without once losing her cool. I'd never seen anything like it."

At this point Riley chimed in. "Evidently the gorgeous Miss Reyes made an impression on my big brother because he called me that night for a lesson in love." Riley turned in the seat and winked at his mother, which totally pissed off his brother.

"No, I didn't, you jerk," Cooper spouted back at him, "I just wanted your opinion."

Summer could see how tightly Cooper was gripping the steering wheel and all of a sudden, she burst out laughing. "It feels so good for us to all be together," she said, wiping happy tears from her eyes. "I can't tell you how much I've missed you guys."

That lightened the mood immensely, and when they pulled up at the hotel, Cooper said he was taking his jerky little brother out for some L.A. nightlife, but they'd be back the next morning to pick up their parents for sightseeing and lunch.

"But you didn't tell me how the story ended," Summer exclaimed. "You can't just leave things like this!"

Again, Riley took control. "I told him what to do, he took my advice, and he got the girl, end of story."

Cooper shook his head and smiled. "I hate to admit but he's right. The kid's got moves. But what he suggested was I go back to Caliente on my own and apologize to Cali, which I did. Turns out a few of the male workers had been harassing a new young hostess, and Cali wouldn't put up with it. She fired the guys, knowing it was time for the lunch rush, but she refused to allow that kind of behavior in her restaurant. It was such a Summer Alcott type of move that I couldn't help but be in awe. And the rest, as they say, is history."

Michael helped his wife out of the back seat and both of her sons met her on the curb.

"It's really important to me that you like Cali," Cooper told her, his hazel eyes looking straight into hers.

Summer had always known that Cooper was his father's son but having him want her approval sent her maternal feelings soaring. "I liked her very much, Cooper, and I hope we'll get to spend some more time with her before we go home."

"She's actually coming for Thanksgiving," he answered, waiting for his mother's reply.

"I'll love that," she smiled and touched her son's cheek, "I'll have another female to keep me company while you guys watch football."

"About that," Cooper continued nervously, "you'll have two females to keep you company on Thursday because Cali's bringing along Lola, her three-year-old daughter."

"Well, that cat's out of the bag, Coop," Riley chuckled as he slapped his brother on the back. "Maybe we need to go inside and do the full monty."

***

The foursome walked into the magnificent hotel without saying a word, each of them deep in their own thoughts. Michael unlocked the door to the suite and ushered his family inside, motioning to the seats in the living area. After a moment of uncomfortable silence, Summer started.

"Cooper," she said slowly, "you're an adult, and I hope you know I respect decisions, but obviously you felt that I wouldn't accept Cali, or you would have told me about her before, am I right?"

All three of the Alcott men squirmed in their seats, none of them comfortable with the conversation or the hurt they could hear in her voice. Finally, Cooper knew he had to step up to the plate.

"Mom," he said guardedly, "you're right, I wasn't sure how you would feel about me dating someone with a mixed heritage, particularly one who has a child." At this point he was getting worked up and added, "And while we're sharing secrets, I need you to know that Cali was never married to Lola's father. She's a single mom who works her ass off to take care of her daughter and run a business. Her dad was in the navy and met and married her mother while he was stationed at Camp Lemonnier in Djibouti City, Africa, but Cali was born right here in

California, and I love her, Mom. I love her more than I ever thought was possible."

Summer got up from her seat and wrapped her arms around her son. "I'm so sorry you didn't feel you could share this with me before. Did you really think I wouldn't understand and support you? Honey, it's the person Cali is that matters, not the color of her skin or whether or not she has a child. All your dad and I have ever wanted for you was to find the person in life who makes you feel whole, and I can tell from the look in your eyes and the words coming from your heart that Cali does that. So, answer me this, am I going to be a grandma?"

Cooper hugged his mother as tightly as possible without breaking her in two. He reached into his jacket pocket and pulled out a small black velvet box and gently opened the lid.

"I wanted to have your blessing first, so Sunday night I'm going to propose to Cali, and if she accepts, then I guess the answer to your question is, yes, you're going to be a grandma, and Lola is going to get one heck of a cool grandmother."

Michael and Riley joined Summer and Cooper for hugs and handshakes and tears, and together they decided to go downstairs to the bar for a bottle of celebratory champagne.

By the time the celebration was over, Cooper and Riley declared it was too late to go out and said they were going back to Cooper's apartment instead. Michael took his wife's hand and led her towards their suite, and into what he hoped was their second honeymoon.

"What a day," he said closing the door. "Things did not go exactly as I thought they would," he chuckled.

"And just what were you expecting, Michael?" she replied, and he could hear the questions in her tone.

"Summer," he said, walking her way, "you were right when you said Cooper's an adult. Let him take care of his love life, and we can take care of ours." He reached out to touch her, but Summer pulled back.

"It has been a big day," she answered, trying to hold back a yawn. "We got up at the crack of dawn and have been on a whirlwind ever since. It's almost one o'clock a.m. at home and I'm exhausted, aren't you?"

"I guess I am," he told her, "but I promised you a honeymoon. Are you turning me down?"

He looked so uncertain that Summer couldn't help but smile. "I'm not turning you down as much as I'm trying to renegotiate. I do remember on our original honeymoon that you would hold me at night when we went to bed, and I could really use being held again tonight."

That was enough to soften the mood and this time, when Michael reached out for her, Summer let him pull her in to his warm, strong arms. It wasn't a prelude to romance; just two people, who knew each other very well, giving and receiving the comfort that they both needed at that moment.

Chapter 63

Gently untangling herself from Michael's arms, Summer looked over at her still sleeping husband and couldn't help but reach out to push a lock of dark hair from his forehead. The blackout curtains were keeping the light out, so she reached for her phone to see what time it was, and it hit her; she hadn't heard back from Jake, and she hadn't thought about him either.

As quietly as possible, she fumbled through the darkened suite until she found the enormous bathroom. Pulling the door behind her, she turned on the light expecting a slew of messages, but there was only one from Riley, saying they would be by to pick them up at ten.

The time on her phone read eight thirty-seven so quickly she typed in a message to Jake.

Summer: Good morning, are you up? Sorry I couldn't get back with you last night, but things got crazy. Cooper's in love! I realize that doesn't mean much to you, but anyway I just wanted to say Hi, and we're sightseeing with the boys today so I probably won't be available. Anyway, have a good day and if you message, I'll reply as soon as I can. S

She hit the send arrow as quickly as possible, peed, and turned on the shower. Not knowing if Jake would return her message while she showered, Summer turned her phone off and slipped it into a pocket of her makeup bag. The last thing she needed was for Michael to walk in just as a notification from Messenger pinged.

The water was steamy and hot, just as she liked it, when Summer dropped her robe and stepped in. The bathroom was well stocked with Salvatore Ferragamo bath products for both men and women, and

Summer almost moaned at the delicious fragrance of the bath gel. She was in her own world enjoying the lavish beginning to her morning, when the door opened, and Michael tried to step in.

"Hey!" she yelped. "What are you doing?"

"I'm trying to create a little honeymoon, but you seem determined to thwart my plans," he chuckled, moving towards her. "Why didn't you wake me up?"

Thankful that she was covered from her neck to her toes with foamy bubbles, she pushed him back through the shower door. "I just got up myself," she fibbed, "and there's a text from Riley that they're picking us up at ten. There's not enough time for honeymoon," she said turning his euphemism for sex around on him, "but I'd love a cup of coffee. Can you arrange that, please?"

As soon as the bathroom door closed, Summer let out a deep breath, trying to release the anxiety that had been building up. Everything about the last twenty-four hours had been out of whack, and for a person who liked to plan her moves, it wasn't sitting well. She knew she should be thankful that Michael was trying to be sweet and romantic, it was all she had thought about for months, but now her head was filled with the events of the night before. Cooper was in love, Riley and Olivia were taking a break, and oh yes, she had a date with Jake Ross in two days. "It's just a shitshow," she said out loud, and then quickly rinsed off so Michael could have his turn.

Michael was lying in bed when she walked out of the bathroom, and she had to admit, he looked good. His dark hair was rumpled, and he'd donned a pair of jeans to accept the coffee cart from the room service waiter, but his chest was bare. *It just isn't fair*, she thought, *that men don't have to deal with cellulite and stretch marks, like women do. Maybe if they had the babies, it would be different*, she giggled, causing Michael to look her way.

Going to the coffee cart he poured her a steaming mug and said, "I knew you wouldn't want much breakfast, but there's juice and cranberry scones if you're interested. I'm going to shower."

Realizing that she had hurt his feelings before in the bathroom, Summer accepted the coffee with a smile, and thanked him. "I really appreciate all this, Michael," she told him honestly, "and maybe we should make this an early night since tomorrow's Thanksgiving."

She watched his face for a sign that he had understood her innuendo. When his gray eyes met hers and he said, "I'd like that," Summer breathed a sigh of relief.

Chapter 64

Summer was slipping into her shoes when the knock on the door of the suite caught her attention. Peeking around the corner, while hobbling on one foot, the sight she saw made her heart skip a beat. Michael and Riley, her husband and twenty-three-year-old son, were hugging like long lost friends, and it took her breath away. The first thought that came to her was, from here, they looked like mirror images. The second was, how could I ever think about breaking my family apart?

The two men separated and Summer entered the room, shoes on and ready to go. "Good morning, Riley," she greeted her son with a hug. "How was spending last night with Cooper?"

Summer was aware that her sons were very different people, with very different personalities, so she was pleased when Riley answered, "It was good. My big brother spent most of the night having phone sex with Cali, leaving me all alone on the couch within earshot. I've got to say," he laughed, "it made for a very uncomfortable night, in more ways than one."

Summer opened her mouth but shut it before saying anything that would put a damper on the day. Her sons were grownups, and intellectually she knew they were sexually active, but they were her children for heaven sakes. And phone sex? That was more than a mother needed to know.

Riley gave his mom another squeeze, realizing he had made her uncomfortable, and told his parents that Cooper was waiting downstairs in a No Parking Zone, so they needed to be going. Thankful to have the conversation off of her sons' love lives, Summer smiled and let him lead them out of the suite.

The California morning was lovely with bright blue skies and sunshine, but the air was just cool enough that Summer was thankful for her linen pants and jean jacket. Cooper had taken a few days off work to spend time with his parents and told them that today was going to be an adventure.

After finding a long-term parking garage, the foursome hopped on a double-decker tour bus, for what Cooper said would be a cheesy tourist trip through Los Angles and Southern California. Summer was glad she had put her hair in a ponytail when Riley insisted they had to sit on the open-air top deck, even though both he and his dad had trouble getting their long lanky frames up the winding staircase.

Cooper was right, the trip was a cheesy tourist trap, and Summer loved every minute of it. Taking pictures to send to Bree, Michael's hand on her thigh, with their sons a row ahead of them, acting more like teenagers than grown men, was exactly the day she needed. The driver shared points of interest along the way, but when they arrived in China Town, the Alcott family decided to get off for lunch and some sightseeing on their own.

"This has been so much fun, Cooper," Summer said. "This is exactly what I've needed." Her smile was contagious and all three of the men laughed and agreed that it had been fun.

"But now I'm starving," Riley told them, "all Cooper had for breakfast was Fruit Loops, and I'm more of an eggs and bacon kind of guy. Come to think of it, why do you have kids' cereal, Cooper? Eating sugary stuff in the morning now that mom isn't around to police your eating habits?"

Cooper growled; Summer lifted her eyebrows in confusion and Michael laughed. "I think maybe Coop has had other overnight guests at his apartment, and he was just being a good host, right son?"

It took Summer a minute to understand what her husband was hinting at, and she chimed in. "Her mother owns a restaurant, Cooper. Surely you can provide a more nutritious breakfast for a little girl than Fruit Loops?"

Cooper threw his hands up in frustration just as Riley saved the day. "Come on," he said. "Here's a Dim Sum restaurant I read about online last night when I couldn't sleep. Some food blogger was saying how good it was."

The words food blogger put her in a tailspin, and for the first time all day, Summer thought about Jake. With all the noise and excitement, she hadn't checked her phone once, and now she was scared to death to check. Letting Riley lead them into the restaurant, she immediately spied the sign for the ladies' room, and excused herself while her family was seated. In a locked stall she finally calmed down enough to look for messages, but there weren't any. Not a single one.

***

By the time she returned to the table, Summer's family had ordered drinks and were looking at menus. Michael stood up to let her into the booth and she did her best to return the smile of contentment he gave her.

"Are you okay?" he asked softly, as she slid in beside him.

"Why wouldn't I be?" Summer snapped, and then wished she could take it back. Her feelings were once again all over the place but ruining the day for her family was not an option.

She took a deep breath, followed by a large sip of iced tea the sever sat in front of her and willed her heart to slow down. *Why hadn't she heard from Jake? Had something happened to him, or was he mad because of her message the night before?* These thoughts were swirling like a cyclone through her brain when she realized that Cooper was talking to her.

"Mom," her son said, "I have dinner all planned for tomorrow, all the way down to the pumpkin pie, but I told Cali about your delicious date pudding, and well, I was wondering if it would be too much trouble for you to make one? Only if you want to, of course."

"Of course, I'll make date pudding for tomorrow," she answered her son, "but that means I'll need to find a grocery store. Where do you even shop in the city?"

"There're markets all over town and if you give me a list, Riley and I will stop after we drop you and dad off at the hotel tonight. That is if you trust me to get the right kind of cinnamon?" Cooper asked with a grin, referring to the year Summer had sent him to the store to get Vietnamese cinnamon, and he had brought home regular run-of-the-mill cinnamon.

"Very funny," she replied, "but I'll bet while we're in Chinatown we can find some really good spices. I can even take some home to Bree."

Her worries about Jake buried once more, Summer feasted on Chinese delicacies with her family while they talked about their plans for the afternoon.

"The food guy was right," Riley said after finishing off the last of the Baozi. "This restaurant is incredible."

"Do you remember what the food guy's name was, Ri?" Summer asked, trying to sound nonchalant.

"Jake something, I think," he answered. "His blog was called *Pushing the Plate Aside.*"

"Isn't he your new client, Mom?" Cooper asked her.

Before she could say a word, Michael answered for her. "Not only did she design his new website, but he's a former world-class food critic, and he's invited your mom for an in-person meeting on Friday."

"Wow, Mom, that's awesome," Riley said with pride. "My mom, designer to the stars!"

Cooper was pensive as he added, "Don't forget what I told you, Mom. I know some guys who used to be friends with Jake Ross, and they say losing his wife really changed him."

Using her trick of counting to ten before answering, Summer tried to come up with just the right answer, but finally settled on the truth. Or at least as much as she was willing to share. "He invited me for coffee to thank me for getting his website done so quickly. No big deal. Now, can we please go find a spice shop?"

That question was enough to satisfy the men in her life but did nothing to satisfy the torment she was experiencing. One minute she was thinking, *what in the hell have I gotten myself into,* and the next, *Jake, where are you and what's going on?*

Chapter 65

Cinnamon crisis averted, the family strolled through Chinatown, stopping for a few souvenirs before finding their way back to a pick-up location for the bus. This time Riley plopped down next to his mother on the upper deck, leaving Michael and Cooper to share adjoining seats behind them.

"Are you alright, Mom?" Riley asked when the noise from the bus was enough to keep others from hearing. "You seem a little down."

Summer thought she had been putting up a good front with her family and was taken back by her son's words. Was he that intuitive, or did Michael and Cooper only see the happy side that she tried to show them? But hadn't Michael just asked at lunch if she was okay? Maybe she wasn't hiding her feelings well at all.

"There's nothing for you to worry about, Riley," Summer said using her best comforting mother voice. "There's just been so much happen since we got here that I'm having a hard time keeping up. I'm fine, really." All that was true; it wasn't a total lie, but what truly weighed her down was Jake Ross, or the absence of him anyway.

Traffic started to get congested, the tour guide continued to talk, and Summer gave Riley's arm a squeeze, watching him closely as he slouched down in his seat. *I can't do this anymore,* she thought. *I can't take a chance of hurting my family over feelings I think I have for someone who's basically a stranger. I just can't.*

By the time they arrived back at the parking garage, the Alcott quartet was exhausted. Summer had hoped they could go to dinner together, maybe even include Cali and Lola, but Cooper told her

Wednesday evenings were Cali and Lola's special time together, and that they'd be with them most of Thursday.

"What happens to Wednesday evenings if you and Cali get married?" Summer asked. "Will you be included in the plans, or will it still be a girls' night?"

Cooper shook his head, "I don't know, Mom, and I'm not sure that it matters. Cali's away from Lola so much while she runs Caliente, I can't begrudge them a night for just the two of them."

Summer wasn't sure she had ever been prouder of her oldest son. "I'm not sure where this new grown-up version of Cooper Alcott came from," she told him sincerely, "but I like it. When you're willing to put someone else's feelings over your own it shows maturity and love. Cali Reyes is a lucky woman."

She couldn't remember the last time she had seen tears in Cooper's eyes, but when he looked at her, she could see how hard he was trying to hold them back. "Thanks Mom," he said, wrapping his arms around her. "You'll never know how much that means to me."

Michael took her hand and led her into the backseat, while Riley sat upfront with his brother. "Are you going to take me out clubbing tonight," Riley teased, "or am I going to have to listen to you and Cali getting it on over the phone again?"

"Riley!" came in stereo from the backseat and Cooper snarled, not happy that his little brother had heard and shared his private conversation from the night before.

"Lighten up," Riley snickered. "Keep in mind that I'm the odd man out in this little weekend love fest, and I need some stimulation. Take me out for a night in the big city so I won't have to think about Olivia and what she might be doing."

"And what do you think she might be doing?" Summer asked him.

"I'm not sure I want to know," Riley answered soberly, "so let's get drunk and act like bad boys for a change. What do you say, Coop?"

After a promise to their parents that they would Uber to the clubs and Uber home, Cooper and Riley dropped them off in front of the Beverly Wilshire hotel and headed back to Cooper's apartment.

Michael put his arm around his wife and led her to their beautiful suite. It had been a fun day with their sons and once again she was thinking how blessed she was. But now they both eyed the massive king-sized bed with the same thoughts in mind.

Summer laid her jacket and purse on a chair, kicked off her shoes and slid her pants down her long legs. Pulling back the silky linens of the freshly made bed, she smiled in anticipation. The sheets felt cool against her skin as she watched her husband strip down to his boxer briefs. Once Michael was settled in the bed, she closed her eyes and said, "Don't let me sleep too long."

Chapter 66

All she could think about was a chugging a glass of water, but when she reached for the Tervis Tumbler that was usually on her nightstand it wasn't there. The room was black and inky, and for a moment she couldn't remember where she was, but slowly patting the bed beside her and finding her still sleeping husband, Summer let out a small sigh of relief, recalling the day with their sons.

The salty, spicy lunch felt like it was sitting on her tongue, and she needed water now! As her eyes adjusted to the dark Summer maneuvered herself from the bedroom into the living area, only knocking into one table. Standing as still as possible to make sure she hadn't awakened Michael, she finally found the chair with her purse and moved towards the bathroom.

The bright light overhead was almost blinding as she grabbed a glass and immersed it in the ice bucket. Not even caring that the melted ice had an unusual taste, she drank three glasses of the fluid before her thirst was quenched. Finally able to feel her lips again, she opened her purse to check the time on her phone, and there it was. The elusive message she'd been waiting for all day.

Her hands unsteady, Summer opened it, not certain what she hoped the message would say. For hours she'd been concerned that he was blowing her off, and after she finally decided she needed to end their friendship, he sends a message. *How like a man,* she thought.

Jake: Sorry I didn't get back with you, but I haven't felt well and just needed to take it easy. Also wanted to check to see if we're still on for

Friday? I'm sure you have lots of family catching up to do. Just let me know one way or another.

"What the heck?" She said out loud before remembering Michael was close by. *Was Jake trying to get out of their date on Friday? Surely that one message when they first arrived wouldn't have changed him so quickly.* Her thoughts were going everywhere when she finally typed back.

Summer: I'm sorry you haven't been feeling well, are you coming down with something? I hope we're still on for Friday because I'm really looking forward to meeting you in person. Of course, if you're ill and don't feel up to, it I'll totally understand. The ball is in your court, I guess.

She hit send, and waited for a response, which surprisingly came right away.

Jake: I'll be fine and I'll be there on Friday. Enjoy your Thanksgiving with your family, see you Friday morning.

No heart shaped emojis, no telling her she was beautiful or gorgeous, just I'll see you on Friday morning. Something wasn't right but to be honest, she wasn't even sure if she cared anymore or not.

***

The phone safely back inside her purse, Summer walked into the bedroom, trying to decide whether to wake Michael or not. It was almost seven thirty, way past their normal dinner time, but tomorrow would be a big day of eating, so maybe they could skip dinner. When she entered the room, her husband was awake, his dove gray eyes looking so deeply at her she felt as if he was looking right into her soul.

"Hey," she said shyly, as if they hadn't been waking up together for thirty-five years. "How was your nap?"

"Just what I needed," he answered with a yawn. "How about you? Did you get some sleep?"

"I did, and now I'm thinking about something to eat. Are you up to going downstairs for a sandwich and a beer?"

Michael stretched all six feet three of his lean body and nodded. "Actually, I'm starving. Give me five minutes to get ready and you're on."

Summer used the time while Michael was in the bathroom to text their sons and quickly shed the rest of her sightseeing clothes. She slipped a cream-and-coral, cotton print dress over her head. It wasn't fancy, but it hugged her curves, and she'd fallen in love with it as soon as she'd tried it on. Pared with some chunky bracelets and high heeled sandals, she felt that she was dressed appropriately for a casual dinner, even in a swanky hotel.

Turning around to grab her purse, Summer saw Michael standing behind her with the same look in his eyes as before, and she wasn't sure that was a good thing. "You're looking at me funny, Michael," she blurted out. "Do I have broccoli in my teeth or something?"

He moved towards her like a cat stalking its prey but stopped when he was just a few inches away. "You take my breath away, Summer," he said, reaching out to move a chestnut curl away from her face. "I probably don't tell you that enough, but you've gone from the beautiful girl I met in a bookstore to the stunning woman I share my life with."

Wait, what? Did those words just come out of Michael Alcott's mouth? Before another thought entered her head or she could try to respond, the mouth that had just paid her the most amazing compliment of her life was on hers, with a kiss so raw she thought her knees would buckle.

"Michael," she stammered when he let her up for air, but he wasn't in the mood to talk.

"Come on, woman," he chuckled, pulling her towards the door, "I need food now so I can ravish you later."

All Summer could think is, *who is this man and what has he done with my husband?*

The restaurant was fairly empty for the night before Thanksgiving, which let Summer and Michael be seated right away. They both looked over menus and decided that as late as it was, and with Cooper's promise of a traditional Thanksgiving feast, sharing was the thing to do.

The server brought their drinks, tall frosty mugs of their favorite Blue Moon beer, and took their order. They were only halfway through the beer when plates with half a Ruben sandwich and big scoops of creamy coleslaw were set before them.

"Oh yum," Summer almost purred. "I'm so hungry." She took a big bite of the toasted marble rye, piled high with corned beef, Swiss cheese, sauerkraut, and gooey dressing, and made a sound that caused Michael to look her way.

"I like it when you make that sound, Summer," he teased her, "but I'm not sure I've ever heard it outside of a bedroom."

Summer felt her face get hot, but she wasn't about to let him have the last word. "Really?" she questioned saucily. "Because I remember making this sound in the backseat of your car and on the couch of our first house." But as soon as the words were out of her mouth, she wanted to take them back. Because yes, there had been some occasions in their marriage where they'd been inventive with the lovemaking, but they seemed like a lifetime ago, and that was the problem. She wanted them back.

Michael gave her a nod, but after her comment, they concentrated on eating and talking about safe subjects like their sons and what Cooper would really serve them for Thanksgiving dinner. Summer wanted to kick herself for opening her mouth and putting her foot in it, but she didn't know how to get the moment back.

When the server brought the check, he shared that the piano bar was still open, and that tonight, in honor of Thanksgiving, the martini special was pumpkin spice.

"What do you say, Mr. Alcott," Summer said in a low, sultry voice. "You want to buy your wife a martini?"

The martinis turned out to be much better than either of them expected, so after the first, they each decided to have one more. The music was lovely, and they were feeling mellow and relaxed when Michael whispered in her ear, "I'm ready to get you upstairs and see if I can help you make that sound again. What do you say?"

She said yes.

Chapter 67

Summer hadn't felt this aroused since the morning in the bathroom a few months earlier. Michael kept his arm around her all the way back to their room, and she thought he was going to kiss her in the elevator. But that move was too cliché for Michael Alcott. Instead, he gave her a sexy look and a wink, and Summer knew that Anastasia Steele had nothing on her.

They were barely in the door of their hotel suite when the seduction began, and oh what a seduction it was. Michael turned the lights down with the dimmer switch, making the room look soft and inviting. He unbuttoned his shirt, letting Summer get a look at his still hard abs and then sauntered in her direction. With one move he had her backed against the wall with her dress up around her waist.

At this moment she wished she had on the pair of sexy lace panties she had purchased with Jake Ross in mind, but instead she was in her everyday cheeky ones. *At least they're black,* she reasoned, but having Jake pop into her thoughts put a damper on her mood, and she struggled to keep up with her husband's advances.

"Michael," she said, trying to push them both back into the room, but he was having none of it. Before she knew what hit her, Michael had slipped his hand in her panties and was doing amazing things to her soft sensitive parts.

Later, as they lay in bed, Summer was in a state of satiated sexual stupor. She wanted to ask him what had come over him, and why now of all times, but she knew she couldn't. Michael had given her the night of earth-shattering passion she'd been longing for, and she'd loved every minute of it. Was he really trying to create a honeymoon vibe, or could it be he'd been listening when she told him she needed more attention?

After having a tall mug of beer and two pumpkin spice martinis, not to mention two earthshattering orgasms, Summer could barely keep her eyes open. Her head was nestled on her husband's chest, his long fingers massaging her back, and despite her good intentions, she fell asleep and into a deep dream.

In the dream she and Michael walked on the beach by their home, holding hands as they watched the surf and talked about their day. From a distance she saw a man jogging in their direction and as he approached, she realized it was Jake Ross. In a moment of shear panic she tried to pull Michael back in the direction they had come from, but he kept walking forward, taking Summer along with him.

When the man was upon them, he ran straight through their clasped hands, knocking Michael off guard so that he let go of Summer before he toppled into the sand. When she looked up, both men were reaching for her, trying to pull her in their direction, and Summer froze. *Was this going to be her life?*

Her heart was pounding as her eyes popped open and she realized where she was. Michael had fallen asleep, his arm still draped over her shoulders and her head still on his chest, oblivious to the terror welling up inside his wife.

Summer knew she was in deep and had to make a decision. She and Michael had a history together, not to mention two sons whom they both adored, so why was Jake Ross still messing with her mind? Settling deeper into Michael's embrace where it was warm and safe, she kept her eyes open, afraid of sleep and the dreams it might bring.

Chapter 68

At some point she must have fallen asleep because when she opened her eyes, Michael was sitting on the bed, freshly shaven, a glass of cold orange juice in his hand. "Happy Thanksgiving," he said, handing her the drink.

She downed the entire glass before answering. "Happy Thanksgiving to you, and thanks, I really needed that. What time is it anyway?"

"Around eight, but if you're going to make date pudding this morning, I think we need to leave here before ten. Cooper's going to pick up Cali and Lola, so I told him we'd take a taxi to his apartment. You good with that?"

Summer nodded and threw back the covers, forgetting that she was totally naked. Blushing she tried to grab the sheet, but Michael got to it first and was playing tug of war with her.

"You know we've been married for thirty-five years, why do you keep trying to hide your body from me?" he questioned teasingly. "You didn't mind me seeing it last night."

"I was preoccupied last night and forgot about my self-image issues," she answered, "so be a good husband and give me back the sheet. And a cup of coffee would be nice, too." Michael relinquished the said sheet without another word and went in search of coffee.

Two cups of rich, black coffee later, Summer was finally able to face the world. Michael had left her alone since the sheet incident earlier, which had given her some time to sort through her thoughts. The dream had spooked her, there was no denying that, but in the light of day, with the alcohol stupor lifting from her brain, she decided that the combination of strong liquor and Michael's unaccustomed sexual advances had just confused her, but she was fine. Really, she was fine.

After a hot shower and slathering her body with the decadent smelling products in the hotel bathroom, Summer Alcott was feeling like herself again. She pulled her long chestnut curls into a topknot of her head to keep them out of her face while making the date pudding. Black cotton cropped pants and a black and white silk stripped blouse were casual enough for a family day with her guys, but dressy enough to show her future daughter-in-law that she had some fashion sense.

Daughter-in-law! All of sudden it hit her that she was going to spend the day with Cali and her daughter Lola and have to keep Cooper's proposal a secret. As much as she loved that Cooper had wanted her blessing, it now seemed like a huge confidence to keep, and she was almost sorry she had hounded her son into his confession.

Too many secrets she thought in frustration. Grabbing her jacket to join Michael in the living room, she caught him on the phone with the cab company and decided to use that moment to send Bree a text. Of course, the moment she put in her passcode the first thing she saw was the white square with the blue circle inside, and she had a message.

Her eyes focused on her husband so she would know if he ended his call, she clicked on the app and read the only two words. Happy Thanksgiving. With shaky hands she typed in Happy Thanksgiving to You, and then quickly put her phone in her purse. She could text Bree later.

"The cab will be here in ten minutes," Michael told her. "How about we explore the hotel a little before we leave?"

Everything about the Beverly Wilshire hotel was beautiful, grand was the word that came to Summer's mind. She knew that Michael was drawn to the magnificent architecture, but she loved it because it reminded her of a castle, and what girl didn't want to feel like a princess?

They were just about to take some pictures of the outside décor when their carriage, or cab to be more precise, pulled up out front. Michael helped Summer into the back seat and off to their first Thanksgiving at the home of their son.

"To be honest, I'm a little nervous," she said. "We've only been to Cooper's apartment once and it was definitely a bachelor pad. Do you think he's bought a table? He was eating off TV trays the last time we were here."

"Summer," Michael said, smiling at his wife, "everything will be fine. Cooper's grown up a lot since we were here last, and I don't think he would have invited us to visit if he wasn't prepared. Just relax, okay?"

"Do you think Cali's going to be cooking? I hate to think of her going to all that trouble for us when I could have easily done it."

Michael gave her the look he used to give the boys when they were pushing things too far, which caused her to cross her arms over her chest and pout. "You're cute when you do that," he teased her, and that caused her to laugh.

Riley was there to let them in, and Michael had been right, she had nothing to worry about. Cooper's apartment was tastefully decorated, and yes, there was a contemporary style table and six chairs in the dinning alcove. Summer looked everything over with both pride and regret. Michael Cooper Alcott had definitely become an adult, but how had she missed it?

"I need to get started on the date pudding. Do you think Cooper will mind?" she asked Riley.

"Nope, we left everything from your shopping list on the counter, and Coop even drug out a pan and all that other junk you use in the kitchen," Riley teased her. "And if you notice, I think he even put out Grandma Cooper's old blue mixing bowl."

Summer gently examined the bowl, remembering how much she had loved mixing cookie dough with her mom in that bowl. She'd given it to Cooper when he had gotten his first apartment, but over the years that memory had faded. Now here she was, cooking in her son's home, while he picked up the girl of his dreams and her daughter. Talk about a reason to be thankful.

"We're back," Cooper announced from the hallway, and with a little trepidation Summer went out to meet them. Lola Reyes was a miniature version of her mother, but instead of braids she had long, beautiful curls. With the same mossy green eyes, and burnished mahogany skin, it was all Summer could do to keep from engulfing the little girl in her arms. But she didn't have to worry about being cautious because Lola jumped into her arms and asked, "Are you going to be my best friend?"

Trying to hold back her emotions, Summer nodded.

"What do I call you?" Lola asked, her big eyes staring right at Summer. No one had given that question any thought, so Summer had to think fast. She didn't feel it was fair to suggest grandma at this point, so she pulled a name from her past, one that she loved more than her own.

"Well, when I was a young girl, I had an Uncle Toots and he said I was his sweet Summer star, so he called me Star. It's a special name that only he used, but I'd love it if you would, too. What do you think?"

Lola thought for a second and smiled, "I always wanted my very own star," she giggled, letting Summer know she agreed.

After shooing Cali out of the kitchen, Summer took Lola and plopped her up on the counter. All thoughts of what they were eating for Thanksgiving dinner left her mind as she talked with the pintsized beauty. "When Cooper was a little boy, he used to sit on the counter with me when I baked," Summer explained. "Do you help your mommy in the kitchen?"

"Mommy doesn't cook much at home," Lola told her, "but sometimes I get to go with her to Cadienty, and she lets me watch."

Summer smiled at the little girl's pronunciation of Caliente and thought about how hard it must be to be trying to raise a child on your own and keep a business running. Despite how much Michael had worked throughout their marriage, he was always involved in the raising of their boys, and for that she had been grateful.

The date pudding had just gone into the oven when Summer heard a knock on the door. Wondering if Cooper had invited someone else for dinner, she stepped out of the kitchen just in time to see him take two large bags from someone's hands. When he turned around and saw the perplexed look on his mother's face he smiled. "Grubhub, Mom," he smiled. "It's the next best thing to home cooking."

Chapter 69

The rest of the day flew by, and for Summer, it was one of the best Thanksgivings she had ever spent. Her new best friend Lola stuck to her side like glue, and when Cali tried to encourage her daughter to give her Star some space, neither the little girl nor her new friend would hear of it.

"I've been waiting years for a little girl to play with," Summer told Cali. "Don't try to stop my joy now." She saw the nod that Michael gave her, letting her know that he understood her comment, and it was like salve on a wound. *He understands that I'm thinking about our daughters*, she thought, and that made her very happy.

After dinner, calls were made to both Summer's and Michael's parents at their prospective Thanksgiving celebrations. Summer's family was with her Aunt Esther in Columbus and Michael's was at their cottage at Indian Lake where she and Michael had honeymooned. They knew how fortunate they were to still have their parents and were thankful that all four were healthy and active.

While the men watched football, Lola went down for a nap, but only rested after assurances that her new best friend would be there when she awakened. It was the perfect opportunity for Summer and Cali to get to know each other, so with wine in hand, they sat down at the little ice cream table in the kitchen and got comfortable.

"I can't tell you how much your kindness to Lola and me means," Cali started the conversation. "I know Cooper's been worried about what you would think, and to be honest, so have I."

Summer looked into the eyes of the woman her son loved and reached for her hand. "I'm sorry that either one of you felt a moment of unease over how Cooper's dad and I would react, but it's all behind us now. I'd love to know more about your life, and Lola's of course, that is if you want to tell me."

Cali took a sip of wine and pulled her phone from her pocket. Flipping through pictures she showed one to Summer of a beautiful woman who looked very much like an older version of Cali, and a robust man with red hair and green eyes. "My dad had planned on the navy being his being career," she began, "but when he met my mother while he was stationed in Africa, everything changed. Dad says it was love at first sight for him, but Mom says it took her a little longer."

Summer looked at the lovely young woman beside her and smiled, hoping it would encourage her to go on.

"Anyway," Cali continued, "my dad's family was less than enthusiastic about his choice and said that he needed some time to think things through before doing something that might ruin the rest of his life. The implication was clear, so dad did what he knew was right. He married my mom and brought her back to the States as his wife."

"So, they ended up accepting her, right?" Summer asked, but Cali shook her head.

"They wouldn't even meet her," Cali answered, and Summer could see the pain on her face. "When dad's time was up, he decided not to reenlist, and he and Mom settled here in Los Angeles. I was born two years later and for the most part had a great childhood."

Summer could feel the *but* coming, so she stayed quiet. "Over the years," Cali continued, "Mom became more and more homesick, and without any family here, they made the decision to move back to Africa. I was sixteen at the time and didn't want to go, so they compromised. They would stay in California until I turned eighteen and could legally be on my own, but then they were leaving. I think they thought I would change my mind, and I hoped they would change theirs, but it just didn't happen. They left a few weeks after my eighteenth birthday, and I've only seen them in person a few times since."

"But what about Lola?" Summer questioned, unable to understand how anyone could turn their back on a child.

"I went through a lot of rebellion after my parents left," Cali said honestly. "For a while, I refused to even talk with them. I was a total brat, I know that now, but I can't change what I did. When I found out I was pregnant with Lola, I was attending culinary arts school and knew that I wanted to have my own restaurant someday. My parents tried to get me to come to Africa and let them help me, but I refused."

Both women took big gulps of wine before Cali finished her story. "Lola's father ran off when I told him I was pregnant, but my folks did come back when she was born. They really wanted me to go home with them, but I just couldn't. I found a young mother in my apartment building to watch Lola while I went to school and worked, and in the end, it made me a stronger person. My dad has lung cancer now and can't really travel, so I hope to take Lola to Africa before he passes. And that," she said, "is the story of Calista Arjuna Reyes."

"Calista?" Summer questioned. "Somehow I thought Cali was an abbreviated form of Caliente, and you named the restaurant after yourself."

"Lots of people think that," she laughed, "but nope, I'm Calista. Actually, I named the restaurant Caliente after my dad's hot temper. He's a typical redhead and gets steamed pretty easily, but underneath it all he's a big pussycat. When his parents died, he found out that they had never changed their will, and he was still named as the sole beneficiary. They hadn't been wealthy by any means, but Dad ended up with around $200,000.00. He insisted I take every penny to try to make up for never having my grandparents in my life. I put a bunch into the restaurant and saved the rest for Lola's education. Anyway, I thank my dad every time I walk in Caliente, and he loves knowing where the name came from.

Neither one of them spoke for a moment and then Cali continued, "Your son isn't very good with secrets," she grinned. "I know about the ring. What I need to know before he asks me the question is if you can accept a daughter-in-law who looks like me and comes as a package deal?"

Summer thought her heart would break as she enveloped Cali in her arms. "I would be honored to call you my daughter," she said, the tears running down her cheeks. "And you just try to take my best friend away from me now and you'll have a fight on your hands."

The two women were still hugging and crying and laughing when Michael, Cooper, and Riley entered the kitchen. "Is everything okay?" Cooper questioned, looking from the love of his life to his mother.

"Everything is just perfect," Summer answered, taking his hand, "just perfect."

"Well, while we're all enjoying sunshine and rainbows," Riley grinned, "this would probably be the best time to tell you that I'm going back to Boston in the morning."

"Tomorrow?" Summer asked as she moved from Cali to her youngest son. "But I thought you were staying with us until Saturday."

Riley ran his hands over his face, looking so much like Michael did when he was younger. "I was, Mom," he finally smiled, "but after watching you and Dad, seeing how in love you still are, and now Cooper too, it made me realize how much I miss Olivia. We talked last night, and if I leave for home early tomorrow, we can still have a long weekend together, and we really need that."

Riley had always been his mother's son and the look on his face was almost her undoing. He loved her, of that she had never doubted, but there was a more important woman in her son's life now, and she had to let him go.

"What time are you leaving?" she asked him softly and was rewarded by a pair of strong young arms enveloping her in a hug.

"Thanks Mom," he said, and for just a moment John Riley Alcott was still hers.

***

When Lola woke up from her nap, they had dessert, and everyone raved about the date pudding. Cali asked if Summer would mind sharing the recipe, and of course she said yes. Lola ate the freshly made whipped cream as if it were ice cream and even asked for seconds, making them all laugh.

After dessert, Cooper and Cali challenged Michael and Riley to a game of euchre while Lola *styled* Summer's hair. It was a fun family evening, but all too soon Cali said they needed to be going.

"I have a restaurant to open in the morning," she said with a sigh, "and a little girl high on sugar to try to put to bed. I hate to leave; it's been a wonderful day, but hopefully we'll see each other before you go back to Florida?"

"After everything we ate today, I can't believe I'm thinking of another meal, but how would it be if we came to the restaurant tomorrow for a light early supper?" Michael asked. "Unless you have other plans that is, Summer."

Her face heated as she felt all eyes on hers. *Other plans? What kind of other plans? Like the one where she went back to the studio at Jake Ross's home and spent the afternoon in his bed?* She hadn't given Jake a thought since her Happy Thanksgiving message that morning, and now she felt as if her family was staring into her mind and reading her thoughts. But she said, "It sounds lovely."

Cooper hugged his parents goodbye and reminded his dad that he'd pick him up at nine o'clock the next morning for a tour of his office and to visit the project he was helping to design. Cali hugged them too, but just as she tried to scoop up her daughter, Lola was once again in Summer's embrace.

"This has been the bestest day I've ever had, My Star," she said, the expression on her face so sincere. "When are we going to play again?"

Summer looked over the four adults who were waiting just as anxiously for her answer as Lola was. "Well," she said, laying tiny kisses all over the little girl's face, "if it's okay with your mommy, why don't we take you with us to dinner tomorrow at Caliente?"

Cali nodded, Cooper grinned, and the three were out the door. As she watched them walk down the hall, Summer realized she agreed with Lola. It had been the bestest day ever.

Summer started cleaning up in the kitchen and soon Michael and Riley were beside her, wrapping up leftovers and scraping dirty plates.

"I'm really glad I came," Riley told them. "I'd forgotten how much fun the Alcott family is, well when I'm around anyway," he laughed. "But truthfully, it has been a great weekend and I think it was good for all of us."

Summer looked at her son and then her husband, so alike and yet so different, and for the first time in days she remembered her mantra. *My life is blessed*, she thought, and she meant every word of it.

On the way back to the hotel, she and Michael held hands but were quiet, each deep in their own thoughts. When they arrived at their suite, Michael pulled her close and said, "I hope you're not expecting a replay of last night because I'm pretty sure I have a turkey leg sitting sideways in my stomach," he grimaced.

Just the thought had Summer laughing out loud as she shook her head. "I'm stuffed, too," she answered, "and it's a little early to go to sleep, so why don't you find a game on TV while I go take a long hot bath in that fancy tub?"

Michael kissed the top of her head and turned her towards the bathroom. "That's an offer I can't refuse," he said and grabbed the remote.

Chapter 70

She had hoped the bath would relax her and calm her restless nerves, but it had been a long night in bed with no real sleep. The Thanksgiving feast, combined with the secret life she'd been fantasizing about, had left her with an ache that no fancy bathtub could fix.

Michael was in the bathroom, she could hear the water running, so she knew it was morning despite the blackout curtains. Closing her eyes, Summer thought about the past few months, and more importantly the last few days, and knew that today someone was going to be hurt; she just wasn't sure who it would be.

The coral-and-cream dress that she'd worn with Michael on Wednesday was what she had planned to wear for her meeting with Jake, but somehow it seemed wrong to wear it now. The memory of that night with her husband was still fresh in her heart and she didn't want to tarnish it; she couldn't.

Pulling a black pencil skirt from her suitcase, she paired it with a white silk button down shirt, and the black Louboutin heels she had brought. It was dressier than she needed for a casual coffee date, but it was the last decent outfit she had left. And to be honest, at this point it was probably better to look like a professional executive than a woman who'd been dreaming of a clandestine affair.

She was rummaging around in the bottom of her travel bag for undies when her hand skimmed the lacy gray lingerie she had purchased for the occasion. Pulling her hand back as if she'd been bitten by a snake, Summer heard movement, and when she turned around, there stood Michael, a towel around his waist and his hair still damp with a look of concern on his face. It seemed as though he had something important he needed to say, but instead he just smiled and said, "Good morning."

Summer shoved the sexy lingerie as far down into her luggage as they would go and pulled down the lid. "Morning," she answered, moving away from the suitcase, "Did you sleep okay?"

"Let's put it this way," he chuckled, "the turkey leg affliction went away sometime in the night, but I've slept better, that's for sure. I'm going to need a lot of strong coffee to make it through my day with Cooper."

Summer wanted to put her arms around him and hold him close, but she was afraid to. If she felt Michael's touch, she knew she'd break down, maybe even tell him about the secret she was carrying around, and that was the one thing she couldn't do.

"Do you want me to call down for coffee and juice?" Summer asked, trying to act as if this was a normal morning and not the one where she had planned to betray her husband.

Michael shook his head. "Coop will be here in less than twenty minutes, and I still need to shave and dress. I'm sure he'll know someplace we can stop. How about you? Do you need something to eat or drink before your appointment?"

Appointment? That sounded so business like, and Summer wished more than anything that a business meeting was what she was headed for. "No, I couldn't eat a thing," she answered honestly, "and since I'm meeting Jake Ross at a coffee shop, I'll just get a cup there."

As soon as Michael stepped back into the bathroom, she grabbed her purse and pulled out her phone, but there was no message from Jake. Her fingers hovered over the keys, trying to decide if it was too late to back out, but for some reason she couldn't. Jake Ross was the client she had befriended, then flirted with, and dreamed about, and now she was going to meet him face-to-face and decide for sure which direction their relationship was headed.

Cooper arrived just as Michael was coming out of the bedroom. Looking at the two of them together brought back an onslaught of memories. Cooper's first birthday, Michael coaching his little league games, the day he had told them he wanted to study architecture, even his college graduation. How had she forgotten all those special times?

The three of them talked briefly about the day before, and how great it had been having the entire family together, and then the guys were headed out the door. Cooper was halfway to the elevator when Michael turned back.

"We haven't really talked about your meeting today," he said. "Are you okay with being on your own? Coop would understand if I needed to be with you."

Summer melted at his words. This was the Michael Alcott she had been needing, the one who cared about her life, and saw her as more than just his wife. But right now, she had a mission to complete, and it wasn't one he could be a part of.

"Don't be silly," she told him. "I'm a big girl and I'll be fine. The coffee shop isn't too far away, and I wouldn't take this day away from you and our son for anything. Now go, and I'll see you back here later this afternoon because we have dinner planned with our soon-to-be granddaughter."

Michael pulled her into a hug and said, "Have fun today. I love you."

A slap to her face couldn't have made her feel worse.

Chapter 71

After Michael left, she took a minute to send a text to Bree. Summer needed her best friend in the worst way right now, but there was no way she could share her feelings with her. Instead, she told her about how much fun they were having, their wonderful family Thanksgiving, and that Cooper had a girlfriend. But not one word about Jake Ross. She told Bree she needed to go and would see her in a few days and went into the bathroom to finish getting ready.

When she looked in the mirror, Summer saw a woman who maybe didn't look fifty-eight, but didn't look thirty either, and that's what she'd been longing for. To be young and spontaneous, sexy and desirable, with skin that bounced back when you touched it and a rear end that was still perky and firm. She could flirt with Jake Ross, maybe even let him take her to bed, but it didn't change the facts; she was getting old.

Carefully applying her make-up to go along with her professional attire and pulling her mane of chestnut curls into a low ponytail, Summer dressed for her date with destiny. She knew now that she had to tell Jake the truth, that she loved her husband, and couldn't risk losing her family by continuing anything other than a friendship with him. Her stomach was a mass of knots as she remembered a poem her dad had recited to her when she was twelve and he caught her in a lie.

"Oh, what tangled webs we weave, when first we practice to deceive," he'd told her, and for the first time she realized just how true those words were.

Slipping on her heels Summer wondered for the first time how tall Jake Ross was. The men in her life were all well over six feet, and even with her highest heels on, Michael and her sons were taller than she. Not that it mattered, of course, but she realized it was one of the things she didn't know about the man she'd become infatuated with.

According to the concierge, Blue Bottle Coffee was an easy stroll from the hotel, but it had been a long time since Summer had walked in high heels, and it didn't take long before she was regretting her choice of footwear. Women in business suits and tennis shoes were whizzing by her, and if it wasn't for her dislike of going barefoot, she would have taken off her shoes and carried them.

Watching the crowd around her and thinking about her aching feet helped keep Summer from focusing on her date with Jake, and all too quickly she was standing in front of Blue Bottle Coffee. She stepped away from the entrance to give herself time to get her emotions under control and then slowly opened the door. And there he was, looking right at her, and all she could do was smile.

Summer willed her aching feet to move, and as they did, Jake stood up to greet her. He was of average height, she guessed, and he had the most beautiful blue eyes she had ever seen. He still had the blond surfer dude look that consumed her dreams, and when he shook her hand, a flash of electricity cursed through her body. *I'm in deep shit,* she thought, remembering her decision to end anything other than a friendship with him. She was thankful when instead of a hug, he gestured for her to sit down.

But when he spoke, the deep rich voice she had imagined was replaced by one that was very soft and difficult to hear. The words, "Hi Summer, you're even more beautiful in person," seemed almost as if they caused him pain.

A server came by and sat two mugs of coffee down in front of them. "I went ahead and ordered," Jake said in his whispery voice. "I hope that's okay."

Summer nodded and reached for the mug, thankful to have something to do with her hands. She needed to say something, she knew that she did, but at that moment, her voice seemed to be as lost as his was.

Jake picked up the small blue bottle of cream and offered it to Summer. When she shook her head, he added some to his coffee, gave it a stir and then answered the question that was trying to form in her mind. "My throat was slit during the accident," he said, pulling his collar back just enough that she could see the scar. "The damage was irreparable, but the doctors say I'm lucky to be able to talk at all."

He looked at her with expectation but that only increased her nervousness. She'd never really asked him about his injuries from the accident, and now she wished she could disappear. Not that his voice changed the person she'd come to know, but the fact that she'd only been thinking about herself, and not the man, who as Cooper had told her, was broken.

"Is that why you decided to write a blog instead of going back to being a food critique?" Summer asked, her words finally slipping out.

"It's part of the reason," he admitted. "The other part is I'm not comfortable around crowds of people like I used to be. And to be honest, the industry has changed in the last six years, and I'm not sure there would have been a place for me, even if I'd have wanted to go back."

Summer took a sip of her now tepid coffee, trying to come up with something appropriate to say to him that didn't sound patronizing. Their conversations early on had given him confidence because they were hidden behind a screen; she understood that now. Just as hiding behind electronics had allowed her to give in to her fantasies of having a love affair with a younger man. She was afraid that anything she said now would make Jake feel that she couldn't be with him because of his injuries, but that wasn't it at all. As she fumbled for the words, he spoke them for her.

"Summer," he said, reaching for her hand. "What are we doing here?"

"Um, having coffee?" she answered a little too flippantly.

"That's not what I meant," he said guardedly. "I saw you on Tuesday evening with your family. I was so anxious to see you in person that I was there waiting outside the hotel when I sent you the message asking if you had arrived. When you came out of the hotel, you walked right past me without knowing I was there." He let go of her hand and looked at her expectantly, waiting for a reply. When she didn't say anything, he continued.

"I watched you with three very large men, and all four of you were smiling and happy. The look on your face was one of contentment and joy, and I'm not about to get in the middle of that."

"Jake…" Summer started, willing the tears not to fall.

"It's okay," he assured her, "really. Before I met you, I was so depressed. For five years I watched my beautiful bride linger in that hospital bed, but at least she was alive, and I could touch her and talk to her. When she finally died, I wanted to die with her. For the past year, I've struggled to even get up in the morning, and when I did, it was to an empty house and a day of loneliness. I thought my life was over, and then you came into it. I'll always be grateful to you for pulling me back into the world of the living, but now, it's time we both moved on."

"I don't understand," she said, the tears falling in earnest now. "We're friends, what happens to our friendship?"

"Please don't cry, Summer. You're too beautiful to have tears on your face. As for our friendship, it's still there; it's just going to be different now."

Summer shook her head, not ready to give up. "I don't know what's right anymore, but I know that I haven't felt as alive in years as I have since I met you. Tell me, what am I supposed to do now?"

Jake gave her a gentle smile that lit up his face and her heart. "I did tell you. Go back to your family and your life and leave me to rebuild mine. I appreciate everything you've done, and we'll still be business associates and friends, but that's the most it can ever be. I need someone in my life, a loving companion that I don't have to share with another man, and that's not you; it never was."

Chapter 72

Summer laid on the bed, curled in a ball, her hand wrapped tightly around a sparkly pink wand with a gold star on top, and cried. The walk home from her date with Jake was a blur in her mind, but the last few minutes before she'd walked out the door of the coffee shop kept running bouncing around in her head like a tennis ball.

Jake had stood up and moved beside her, the look on his face gentle and caring. She could feel the mascara running down her cheeks but as hard as she tried the tears would not be controlled. "Goodbye, my gorgeous friend," he'd told her as he pulled her close for a sisterly hug and kiss on the cheek.

And that quickly, her fantasy walked out the door, leaving her alone in a strange coffee shop in a strange city with an aching heart and throbbing feet. How she'd made it back to the hotel in one piece was a mystery, but she had, and now she had nothing to do but wallow in the mess she'd made of her life.

"Summer?" she heard Michael calling her name. "Summer, are you here?"

Her sobbing was so hard that she couldn't even answer, but it didn't take him long to find her. "Summer," he said, "pulling her into his arms. "Are you hurt, please tell me, what's going on? Did something happen in your meeting with Jake Ross?"

The comfort of Michael's strong arms and the warmth of his touch helped her to relax, but the weeping persisted. He continued to hold her and stroke her back, shushing her as you would a crying baby, and finally she was able to take a deep breath and get herself under control.

"Why are you here?" was the question she asked. "You're supposed to be out with Cooper."

"I'm here because Riley's been texting and calling you for over an hour to let you know he made it home safely, and when you didn't respond, he called me. Do you have any idea how worried we've all been?" He pulled her so tightly to his chest that Summer could feel the pounding of his heart, and she thought hers would break when he spoke again.

"I'm losing you. Aren't I?" he questioned, and when she looked at his face, she saw tears in his eyes.

"What? Why would you say that, Michael?" she stammered, scared to death that he had somehow found out about her inappropriate relationship with Jake Ross.

"Because you've been so unhappy, so unlike yourself. The outbursts, the drinking, all signs that you weren't happy with me and our life anymore, and I haven't known what to do."

"Is that what this week was about, Michael?" she asked softly.

He nodded and hung his head. "I know you don't think I listen to you, or I don't pay attention to what you need, and I admit, sometimes I don't. But Summer, you can't spend every day for thirty-five years with someone, especially someone who's your whole world, and not know when that person is miserable. Maybe I went about it the wrong way, but I thought maybe if we could start over, I could make you happy this time."

His gray eyes were filled with so much emotion and pain that she couldn't help but reach up and stroke his face. "I wouldn't go as far to say that I've been miserable, Michael, but I have been struggling. Struggling with getting older, with feeling like you aren't physically attracted to me anymore, and with needing more, but not even knowing what that is. You're not losing me, Michael, but I feel like I've kind of lost myself, and I need to find the way back."

They held on to each other for a few minutes, luxuriating in the familiar touch of a longtime partner. When Summer finally pulled away, she spoke from her heart. "I love you, Michael Alcott, and this week I've realized just how much you and our family mean to me. But I need you

234

to know that I'm not ready to give up the excitement and passion that we had when we were younger, and I'll never quit wanting to know that you still find me sexy and desirable. If I live to be one hundred, I'll still want that."

"You realize that when you're one hundred I'll be one hundred and two," he chuckled, "but I'll do my best to keep up with you."

"The last few days have been wonderful with lots of surprises, and I wouldn't change a thing. Cali and Lola are already part of our family and I love them, but as much as I'm going to miss them, I'm ready to go home. I want to sleep in our bed and walk on the beach holding your hand. I want to see Bree and meet my new friend Dena Daniels, walk down Flagler Street, and have a Blue Moon at Breakers. My life is in New Smyrna Beach with you, and I'm ready to get back to it."

"Thank God," was all he said.

"Now where is our son?" she asked.

"He had a few errands to run, and I told him I'd call him if the afternoon was going to work, but I don't want to leave you."

"Of course, you're going to leave me. This day is important to you and Cooper, and besides, I need a nap. I didn't sleep well last night, and my eyes are itchy and sore. You go spend time with Coop, and let me sleep for a couple of hours, because we have a dinner date with a special young lady.

"So that explains the scepter you were holding on to when I came in?" he laughed.

"I kind of remember seeing it in a shop window on my way home from my business meeting," she told him, refraining from calling her meeting with Jake anything personal. "The star on top called out to me."

"Speaking of your business meeting," Michael said cautiously repeating her words, "I take it something happened in yours to cause you to be so sad?"

Choosing her words carefully, Summer replied. "It wasn't quite what I anticipated when we set it up a few weeks ago, but that's what happens with anticipation, it's often better than the real thing."

She watched Michael's face for any sign that he was going to question her, but he didn't.

"Now tuck me in and go call Cooper. I don't want to scare Miss Lola tonight by looking like a gargoyle."

Michael pulled the covers around her and ran his hand gently over her hair. "I meant what I said earlier, Summer," he said, his voice deep with emotion. "You are my world."

Chapter 73

This time when she slept there were no erotic dreams of making love in the sand or having to choose between Michael and Jake. In fact, there were no dreams at all, just two hours of much needed peaceful sleep. Summer slowly untangled herself from the sheets and blinked her eyes a couple of times to make sure they still worked. When she was finally able to focus, she inched from the bed into the bathroom.

Sleeping in your clothes is never a good idea, and it definitely didn't help the image that Summer saw staring back at her from the mirror. The ponytail she had so artfully created that morning had hair sticking out every which way, like the Scarecrow from *The Wizard of Oz*, and her face was covered with black streaks from mascara and eyeliner that was unfortunately, not waterproof. Her wrinkled silk shirt and nice black skirt could hopefully be salvaged at the drycleaners, but she had her doubts about the rest of her.

Somehow she was able to get her tangled hair out of the band and shoved into one of the complimentary shower caps provided by the hotel. The steam was rising from the two faucet heads as she undressed and dropped her clothes on the floor, and then there was bliss. Pure, unadulterated bliss as the hot water cascaded over her body and soothed her damaged soul.

After gently washing her face and scrubbing her body she sat down on the solid marble bench and let the hot water stream over her weary feet. It was the most relaxed she'd felt all day. As the water started to change from hot to cool, she sighed, knowing it was time to trade the comfort of the shower, for the real world.

By the time Michael returned from his day with their son, Summer was dressed and ready to have one last family dinner before heading home to Florida. She was lounging on the couch, drinking a Diet Coke from the minibar, and watching QVC on the television in the living room when he came in.

"Hey," he said coming up behind her and gently massaging her neck. "How are you feeling?"

How was she feeling? Better than she was earlier, but not back to normal. Summer knew it was going to take more than an afternoon nap and a hot shower for that to happen if it ever could. But to Michael she said, "Much better, thanks; now tell me about your day with Cooper."

Summer could see the excitement on her husband's face as he talked about the oldest son and the project he was working on. It had to be gratifying for your child to follow in your footsteps careerwise and be a success at it, and she smiled watching the animation on Michael's face. When he had told her everything about his day, he became quiet and asked, "What can I do to make you happy again?"

The question was so out of the blue that Summer couldn't quite respond. "Right now, go get ready so we're not late for our dinner with Lola. After that, I'm not sure. I'm not unhappy, Michael, so much as I'm confused."

"Confused about me and our marriage?" he questioned.

"No, confused about me. Now go, and let's hope I left you some hot water."

Michael leaned down and kissed her. She could tell that he was unsure of himself, and it made her feel terrible. Michael Alcott had always been confident, and she didn't want to ever be the reason he lost confidence.

They had arranged to meet Cooper and Lola at Caliente at five, which gave Michael plenty of time to shower and change before a cab picked them up. Summer was determined not to ruin this last dinner with her family by letting them see the turmoil she was dealing with inside, so she put on her best happy face before they walked out the door.

She held the sparkling pink scepter tightly in her hands, excited to give it to Lola, but dreading to say goodbye. Summer wished that Lola was nearby so she could be a real grandmother, like the ones she had growing up, but it just couldn't be. Cali and Cooper had a life in California, and hers was in Florida with Michael.

"I can see the wheels turning in your head, Summer," he told her, gently. "You're not looking forward to saying goodbye to Lola, are you?"

She shook her head. "Or Cooper or Cali," she admitted. "I want to go home, I need to go home, but I'd love it if our family could all live closer together. I never realized until now how difficult it must have been for our parents when we moved to New Smyrna Beach."

"But they made it through, and we will, too. We gave our sons wings to fly, Summer, but we also gave them deep roots. We'll always be a part of each other's lives, but it's going to be different now."

She looked at her husband, the man she had promised to love and cherish until death parted them and smiled. "It's going to be fine; I know that, Michael. I'm still a little fragile is all. Bear with me, okay?"

"As long as it takes," he said, and those were the exact words that she needed to hear.

Chapter 74

Cooper and Lola were sitting on the front porch swing at Caliente when they arrived. As soon as Lola saw them walk up, she rushed into Summer's arms. "My Star!" she shouted joyfully. "I've missed you all day."

Summer thought her heart would melt. She was already agonizing over leaving her new little family and now this. Doing her best not to let Lola see tears in her eyes, she switched subjects and presented Lola with the wand she'd been holding on to so tightly.

"This is a special princess wand," Summer told Lola, watching the expression on the little girl's face. "Whenever you miss me, you just wave the wand, close your eyes, and think of your own special star. I'll always be there, Lola in your thoughts and in your heart, and you'll always be in mine."

"Do you think we could Facebook sometime?" Lola asked. "Mommy and I do it with Nanny Reyes on our girl's day."

Cooper laughed at his mother's look of confusion. "I think she means Facetime, Mom, and yes Miss Lola, we will definitely Facetime with your star and my dad."

"He needs a name, too," Lola declared, pointing in Michael's direction. "How about if I call you Mr. Mike?"

Michael squatted down to her level and gave her the smile that had captured Summer's heart all those years ago. "I think that's a fine name," he said, and picked her up and carried her into Caliente.

The host gave them the same secluded table they had on their first night there, and once again, Summer was charmed by the lovely décor.

When Cali came out to greet them, she announced that her assistant manger was working that night, which meant she could sit for a while.

Since Michael had requested an early light supper, Cali had taken the liberty of preparing something special just for them. Avocado chicken salads on a bed of fresh field greens and plump ripe tomatoes, along with warm cinnamon sugar tortilla chips, was the perfect meal to have after their Thanksgiving feast the day before.

They ate and they laughed, regaling Cali with some of Cooper's antics as a child, even the Mother's Day he'd brought Summer breakfast in bed all on his own. He'd been so excited to bring her the bowl of cereal, not realizing that he'd topped it with salt instead of sugar!

It was such an enjoyable evening that Summer didn't want it to end, but she could see the restaurant was starting to fill up, and she didn't want Cali to lose customers because of them.

"This has all been wonderful, Cali, I can't tell you how much I've loved being here tonight, but we need to get back to the hotel. We have an early flight in the morning and haven't even thought about packing," Summer told the beautiful young woman who had taken her son's heart.

"I understand, but it's meant so much to me, to Lola and me both. Thank you for coming tonight. I feel like we've really gotten to know each other, and I know this isn't goodbye," Cali replied as she got up to receive the hugs coming her way.

"Definitely not goodbye," Summer said with a smile, "definitely not goodbye."

Cooper was saying goodnight to Cali. Michael was trying to hail a cab, and Summer was walking with Lola when the little girl pulled on her hand. "My Star," she started, "can you keep a secret?"

"I'm a great secret keeper," Summer answered. "Do you have one to tell me?"

Lola nodded and motioned for Summer to get closer. When she did Lola whispered, "I think my mommy loves Coop."

Summer looked into the green eyes that were staring at her with such hope and asked her, "Can you keep a secret?"

Lola nodded and Summer got as close as possible and whispered back, "I think Coop loves your mommy, too."

They hugged, and cried, but when Cooper reached out to Lola, she willingly left the comfort of Summer's arms for his.

"I love you My Star," Lola called as she settled against Cooper and waved her sparkly wand. "Don't forget to Facebook me!"

Michael could see his wife's lip start to tremble, so he put his arms around her and pulled her close. "You don't look like any grandmother I've ever known," he told her, "but then you always have been in a class by yourself. Come on Mrs. Alcott, let's get ready to go home."

Chapter 75

When she woke up on Sunday morning, Summer looked the room over thoroughly to make sure she was really home. The clock on the bedside table said it was nine thirty, so she knew there was no chance of making it to church. Instead, she snuggled back under the covers, thankful to be in her own bed with her husband, where she belonged.

After her disastrous meeting with Jake, everything had been such a whirlwind that she hadn't really thought about what would happen now that she was home. Would he still send her his blogposts to read before he posted them? Would there still be the thrill of a message from him coming in? Saying goodbye to her family in California and coming home to New Smyrna Beach had consumed her thoughts since that Friday morning, but now, once again she was thinking of Jake. *I guess the first move will have to be up to him,* she told herself defiantly, and she moved as close to Michael's warmth as possible.

After three days and no word from Jake, Summer started to worry. *They agreed to still be friends so how could he just walk away from her like this? Hadn't she meant anything to him at all?* Her thoughts were all over the place, so finally on Thursday morning, after doing her devotions and taking care of clients, she sent him a message.

Summer: Hey! I thought we were still going to be friends...does that mean no communication?

She waited for the bubbles, but they didn't come. She pulled up his Facebook page, but there was nothing of importance. Intellectually she knew that he was doing the right thing by leaving her alone, but emotionally she was mad, and more importantly she was hurt.

Michael was trying hard to give her the attention she'd told him she needed, and most nights after dinner they took walks on the beach, holding hands and sharing their days. Never once did he bring up her meltdown in California, and never once did she let on that she was anything less than content. She was trying to come to terms with the past few months but letting go of Jake Ross was turning out to be more difficult than she had thought.

Summer continued to design websites, when there was a request, but this close to Christmas business was slow. It was as she was working at the computer one morning that it popped up: an email from Jake.

Hi Summer,

Sorry I missed your message, but I needed to get away and took a trip with a friend to the Dominican Republic. We were pretty far off grid so I didn't have great internet options.

I hope your trip to L.A. was good overall and that you're happy to be home.

I need to unpack and work on tomorrow's post. Take care my dear friend.

Jake

That's it? They'd flirted to the point where all she could think about was him and how he made he feel, and that was all he was giving her? True, they'd called a halt to the romance, but this sounded like a brush off too. Summer's heart was pounding, and her fingers were frozen. She had so much she wanted to say, so much she needed to make him understand, but instead she did nothing. *Let him see how it feels to be ignored.*

She met Bree for lunch and told her all about their trip to California. Bree was ecstatic with the news about Cali and Lola and said she couldn't wait to meet them. But when she tried to bring up the meeting with Jake, Summer cut her off.

"It was a mistake," she told her friend, trying not to give her real feelings away. "You were right, so let's just leave it at that."

Bree caught her up on some Christmas activities coming up at church and told her she'd gone Black Friday shopping with Nancy Bailey but had missed having Summer there, too. It was a typical lunch between friends with one exception. Inside, Summer was crumbling. She knew her infatuation with Jake had been wrong but letting go of him was harder than she had ever thought it would be.

It was a struggle hiding her pain from the people she loved, but Summer knew she didn't have a choice. She'd let herself get too involved because it had been an easy thing to do, and it felt so good. As long as she and Jake were just flirting online it had all seemed so harmless, but she realized now that it had been anything but. The problem was, she missed him.

Summer hugged her friend goodbye and headed home. The air was getting cooler now and she tried to get her thoughts into the Christmas decorating she always loved so much, but all she could think about was Jake.

Maybe reading will get my mind off him, she thought, as she opened her Kindle. But every book she had downloaded was a romance with the cover of a gorgeous man or a young couple in an embrace. Definitely not what she needed.

The book that Bree had given her, *FerVent,* was still on the table beside her chair, so she picked it up and leafed to the first chapter, and the words seemed to leap right off the page at her. As she read, the tears began to fall, and soon she was in an all-out sob.

"What have I done?" she asked out loud. "I have everything I've ever wanted; why do I keep yearning for something I know is wrong?"

By the time Michael came home for dinner, soup was simmering on the stove, and the book had been read cover to cover. Tomorrow was a new day, and she knew exactly what she needed to do.

Chapter 76

Summer was surprisingly calm the next morning after seeing Michael off to work, and she found that for the first time in weeks she had some clarity around her life. She read her devotions, allowing them to bring her strength before picking up her cell phone. She needed someone to talk to who would listen and not judge, and even though Bree was her dearest friend, this was not something she could help with.

She prayed as she scrolled through her contact list, uncertain of what she would say or what the reaction would be. But when Summer heard the, "Hello," on the other end, she breathed a sigh of relief.

"Dena," she said, "this is Summer Alcott. Any chance you have a minute to talk?"

Letting go of Jake was one of the most difficult things she'd ever done. But finally with Dena's help, she found the strength she needed. She called Dena when she had the urge to message him and found that her new friend had secrets of her own to share. Every day, Summer's resolve grew, but it took a specific question before she could get him out of her mind for good. It was a question that Summer had never even asked herself.

"Are you in love with him?" Dena asked pointedly.

Summer thought about it for a moment before answering. "No," she said, "I'm in love with the way he makes me feel."

"And your husband, are you still in love with him?"

"Of course, I love Michael, that hasn't changed."

"What if the situation was reversed, Summer? How would you feel if Michael was having a relationship with a woman online, even if it was never physical?"

For a moment Summer couldn't breathe. She had asked herself the same question early on in her secret life with Jake, but she'd pushed it back into the far corner of her mind.

"I'd be devastated," she answered truthfully.

Dena didn't say another word. She didn't have to. Summer knew what she had to do if she was ever going to move forward, so she thanked her friend for her help and worked on a plan.

A little while later she composed a message to Jake.

Summer: I want you to know how much your friendship has meant to me. It's been one of the best times I've ever experienced, but it's also one of the worst times. I've made mistakes and crossed lines that have caused nothing but pain for both of us, but I want my life back and the only way for that to happen is for us to totally say goodbye.

I owe you a debt of gratitude, Jake, because all of this with you has made me realize what I have and how much I love my family. I pretended that I could live a double life, but I couldn't, and you knew that, didn't you?

Even as I write this my heart is breaking for the loss of our friendship. I'm so sorry for everything and hope that you can forgive me.

I will never forget you, Jake Ross, and I wish you nothing but the best. Maybe you can still work things out with Leda, but if not, there's someone special out there just waiting for you and the love you have to give.

An email has been sent with the name and number of a good web designer if you ever need help, but please don't ask for anything else from me. Goodbye Dear Jake. Please remember me as the girl who reached out in friendship, and not the one who got so caught in her pursuit of romance and her lost youth that she nearly lost sight of what really matters, Summer

As soon as she hit send Summer disabled her Facebook account and deleted his contact information from her phone, and then she turned it off. She didn't really think Jake would try to change her mind, but if he did, she wasn't sure she'd be able to say no to him. Everything she'd told him was the truth. Now, she just had to learn to live her life without the thrill of his messages and the wonderful way that his words made her feel.

Her emotions were raw, but surprisingly she didn't cry, and she didn't call Dena and she didn't call Bree. Instead, she picked up the landline and called someone else. When she heard the familiar voice on the other end, Summer smiled, knowing that she was going to be okay.

"Hey handsome," she said to her husband. "How would you like to have lunch with a married woman?"

And when he laughed, she closed her eyes and thought *my life is blessed.*

***

Jake read the message again. He'd read it every night for the past week, but the words never changed. She'd left him for good and he accepted it; he had no choice.

He was almost forty-six years old, and he'd only felt a special magic with two women in his life. The first one he'd lost to a terrible accident, one he still blamed himself for to this day. And the other? Well, he'd sent her away before he could ruin her life like he had Beth's. He knew that he'd hurt Summer that morning they'd met for coffee, but not nearly as much as he'd hurt himself.

So just like last night, and every night since Summer had told him goodbye, he took a brandy snifter from the bar and poured himself a cognac. He swirled the caramel-colored liquid, thinking how like the color of her eyes it was and lifted it in the air. Before ever taking a drink, he said in a soft, whisper-like voice, "Here's to you my beautiful, Summer," and lifted the glass to his lips.

Note from the Author

CANCER SUCKS!!!

Almost 3 years ago I was diagnosed with a brain tumor that turned out to be a cancerous Astrocytoma. During the biopsy I had a blood vessel rupture that left me with stroke like systems on my right side. Today I am cancer free and am doing therapy three days a week at the Center for Neurological Development in Burkettsville, Ohio. It has been a great struggle, but I thank God every day for the blessings that I have.

I am so grateful for my husband Bob who has provided me both physical and emotional support. He is my rock, and I cannot imagine going through this without him. I love him so much!

To my doctors and many therapists, I am so appreciative for your care, support, and encouragement. Your guidance has helped me make improvements in my recovery process.

I would like to dedicate this book to everyone who has helped me through these challenges – family, friends, fans, doctors, and therapists.

I will NOT give up!!